The Broken One

A Poetic Journey

By

Naomi Bent Moody

All Rights Reserved

For permissions, publishing, or legal inquiries, please contact:
Support@bookwritingleague.com
For contacting the author directly, please email:
naomibentmoody12@gmail.com

Library of Congress Control Number (LCCN):

2025942532

ISBN: 978-1-969319-21-1

Printed and Published
by
Book Writing League

www.bookwritingleague.com

Support@bookwritingleague.com

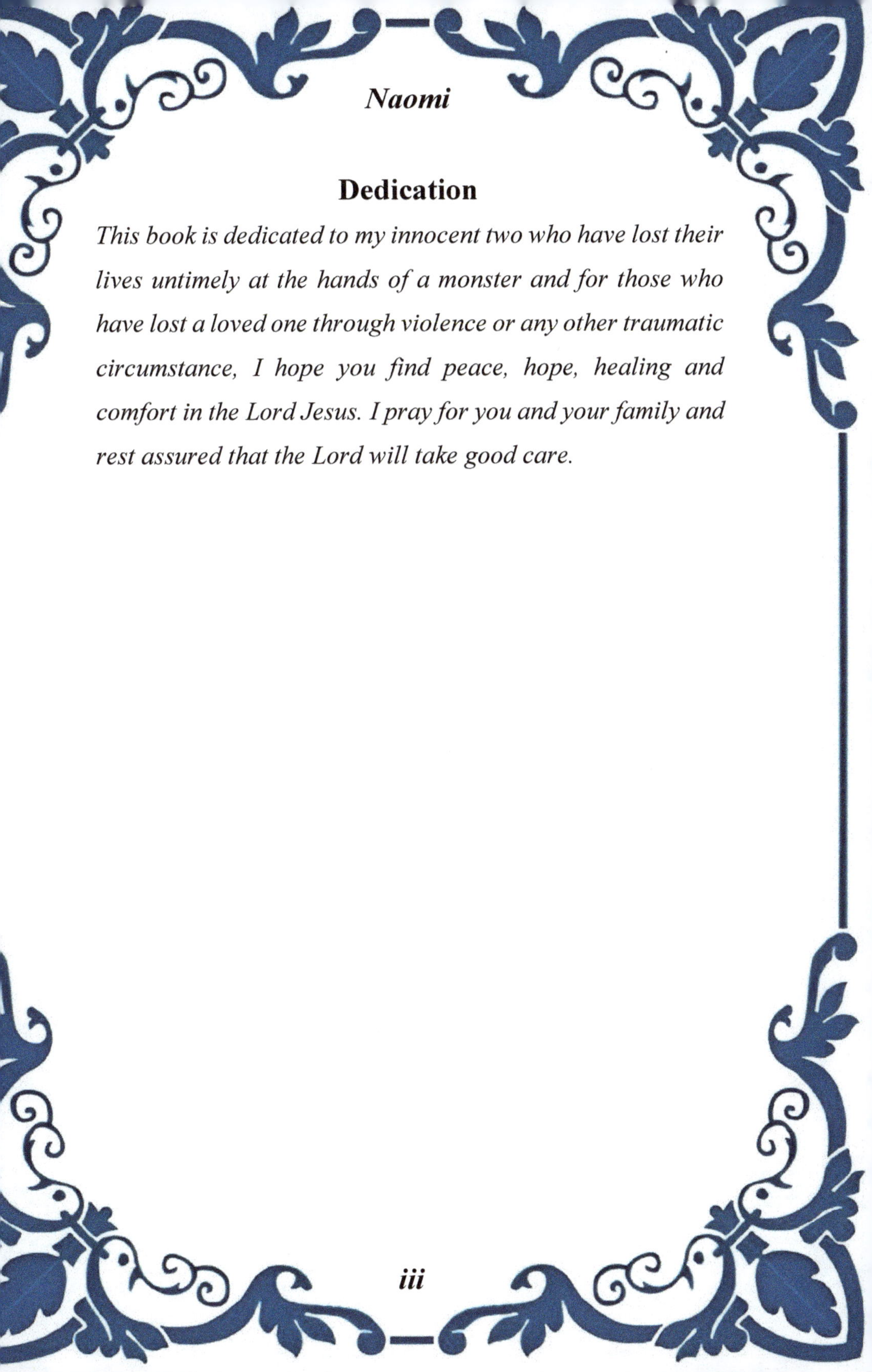

Dedication

This book is dedicated to my innocent two who have lost their lives untimely at the hands of a monster and for those who have lost a loved one through violence or any other traumatic circumstance, I hope you find peace, hope, healing and comfort in the Lord Jesus. I pray for you and your family and rest assured that the Lord will take good care.

Acknowledgment

First and foremost I'd like to give praises to our creator above for giving me the strength and endurance to push through the pain and hurt to write this book, secondly to my husband and children who played a big part in motivating me on days I felt like I could not go on, for their words of encouragement, prayers and late nights spent with me to make sure my dream become a reality.

To Joshua and his team for their hard work and dedication and all the effort and persistence you have shown, I appreciate it.

Thank you!

Naomi Bent Moody

Naomi is a devoted mother, loving wife, and proud grandmother whose poetry is deeply rooted in the textures of real life — beautifully messy, tenderly human, and at times, quietly heartbreaking. Her words flow from a lifetime of experiences: years spent loving with her whole heart, enduring quiet losses, and learning to hold sacred space for the things in life that cannot be fixed.

Shaped by the rhythms of family, the persistence of memory, and the unspoken ache that often lies beneath everyday moments, Naomi writes not to solve life's pain, but to honor it — to give it a name, a voice, and a place to rest on the page…

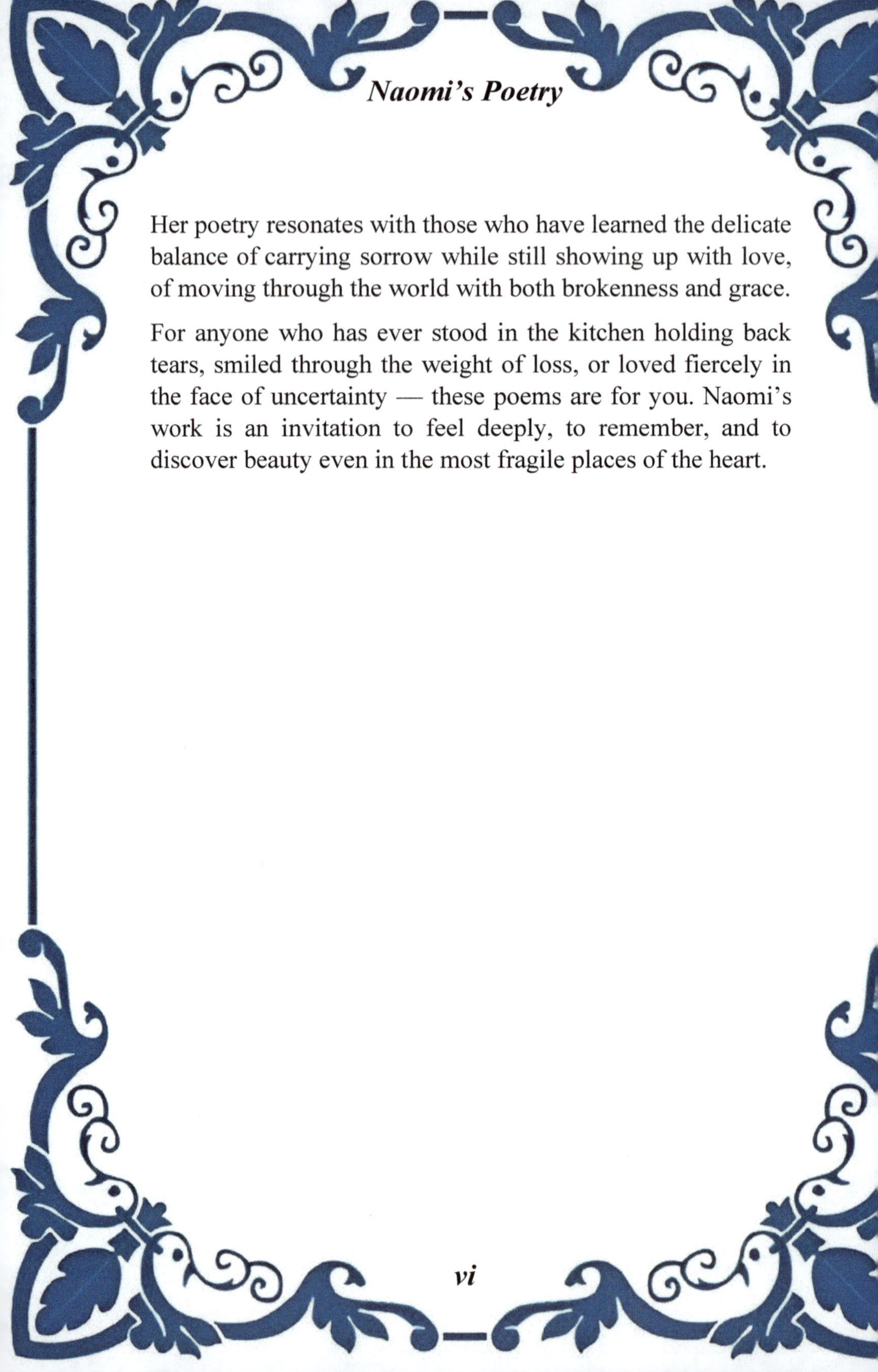

Her poetry resonates with those who have learned the delicate balance of carrying sorrow while still showing up with love, of moving through the world with both brokenness and grace.

For anyone who has ever stood in the kitchen holding back tears, smiled through the weight of loss, or loved fiercely in the face of uncertainty — these poems are for you. Naomi's work is an invitation to feel deeply, to remember, and to discover beauty even in the most fragile places of the heart.

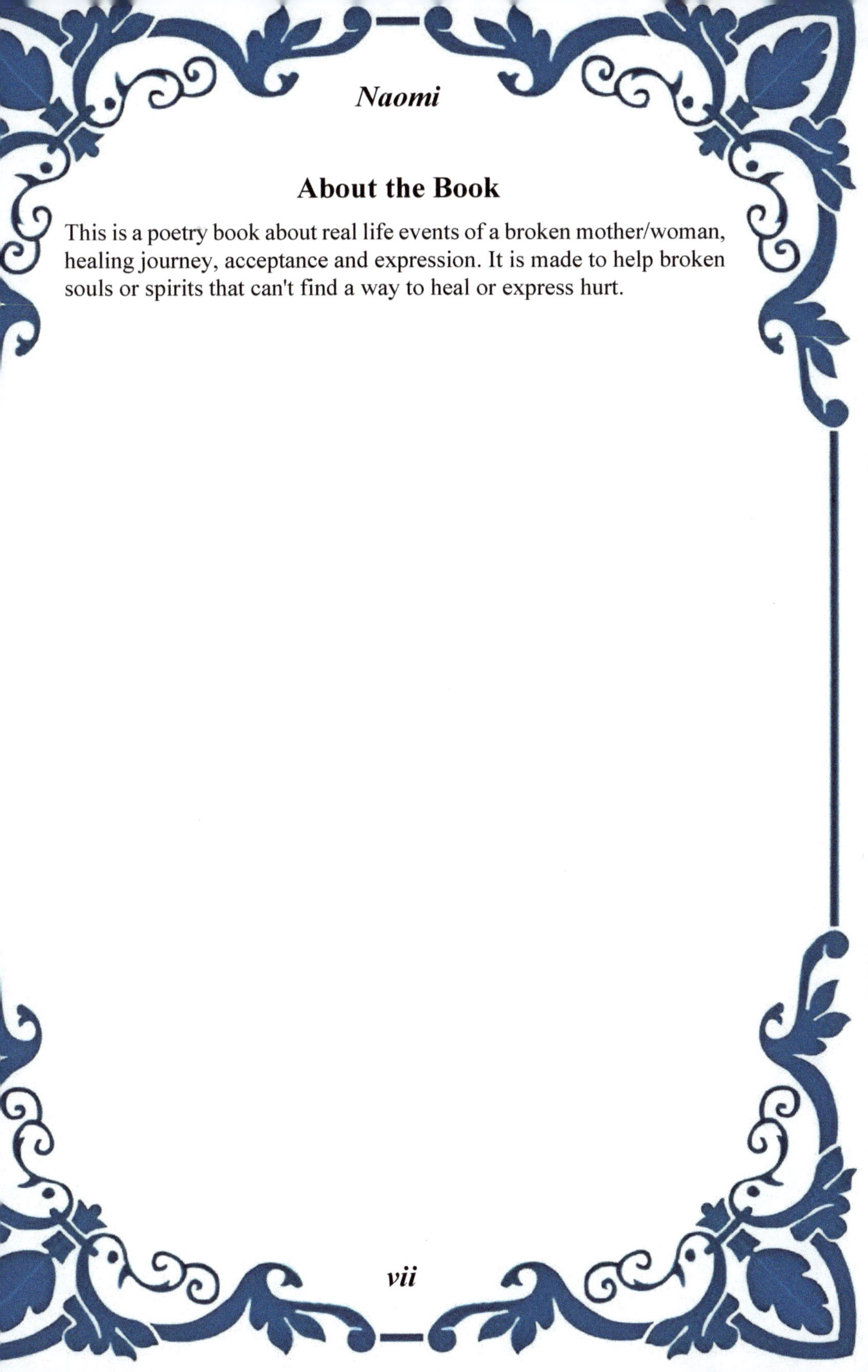

About the Book

This is a poetry book about real life events of a broken mother/woman, healing journey, acceptance and expression. It is made to help broken souls or spirits that can't find a way to heal or express hurt.

Naomi

A PAINFUL MOTHER

Another mother cries another child is gone, another home is broken how long will this last? Mental torture, emotional torture is like a blooming spring, another day has passed the murder is still fresh in my mind what did her child do or did to deserve this kind of torture? Confusion and corruption never showed up their faces they were hiding in desolate places. Sadism plays the killer without provocation "when will this end"? As a mother I felt betrayed, sleepless nights, fasting hours, hopeless moments who could this be? bitten by the demon (murder) she faced it all alone. Men are born from women why do they appear so cold towards us? What if every woman decided not to have a child what would the world do? men you were born to nurture us, protect us, love us and not abuse us. The question is still asked why? why? why? The game is still playing, the ball is still rolling, who will be there to stop the goal from scoring? Abductors, kidnappers take a look at your mothers, your daughters, sons, sisters, aunts, Brothers, uncles and fathers would you like this for yourself? How would you feel to be eating the same meal that you have prepared for another family? you can't be paid enough to carry a load of shame, disgrace, to mentation, guilt, unforgiveness, hate reflection of your gruesome and brutal act it will be playing right back just stop!!

October 14, 2014

Time: 7:30 am.

ANOTHER MOTHER CRIES...
ANOTHER CHILD IS GONE
WHY?

THE KILL

They kill the teacher so she will never teach again,

They kill the nurse so she will never care for a patient,

They kill the architect so she will never design a plan,

They kill the pilot so she will never fly a jet,

They kill the mother so she will never bear a child.

They kill the entrepreneur so she will never start a business.

They kill the cook so she will never taste her own hand.

They kill the farmer so she will never own a farm.

They kill the doctor so she will never save a life.

They kill the pastor so she will never preach a sermon.

Look World!! please let us be protective of each other,

Our youths are our future, let us treat them right!
Just remember I alone cannot grow my child!

(Just remember mi alone cyan grow mi pitney)

It take a village to raise a child.

August 18, 2015,

Time: 7:20 pm.

They kill the mother
so she will never bear a child.
It takes a village to raise a child.

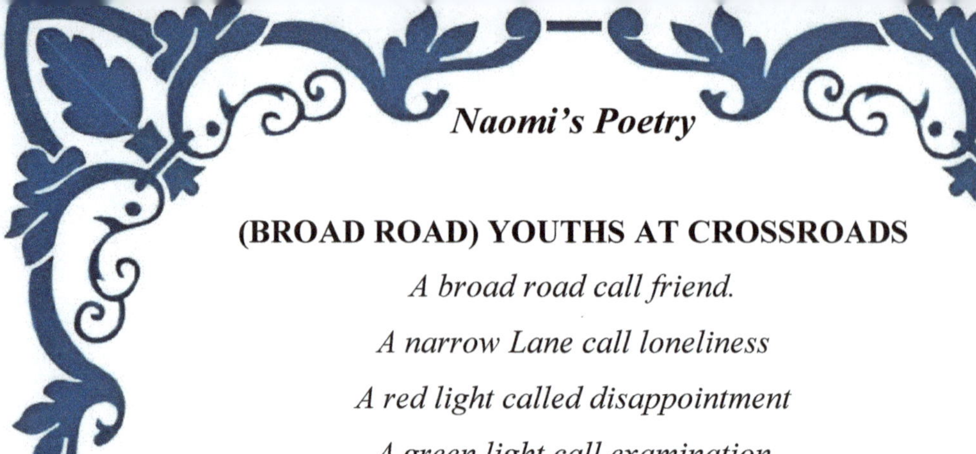

(BROAD ROAD) YOUTHS AT CROSSROADS

A broad road call friend.

A narrow Lane call loneliness

A red light called disappointment

A green light call examination

A hotspot called caution heavy units with weights

A dot call collision

A careless stare call consequence

A skillful hit call survival an empty space that will never be filled

A bright light calls escape A dead end call judgment

check yourself and don't diss yourself you can make it happen! it begins with you!

Date: August 30, 2015,

Time: 1:34 pm.

A broad road call friend...
A narrow lane call loneliness.

"Check yourself and don't diss yourself—
It begins with you."

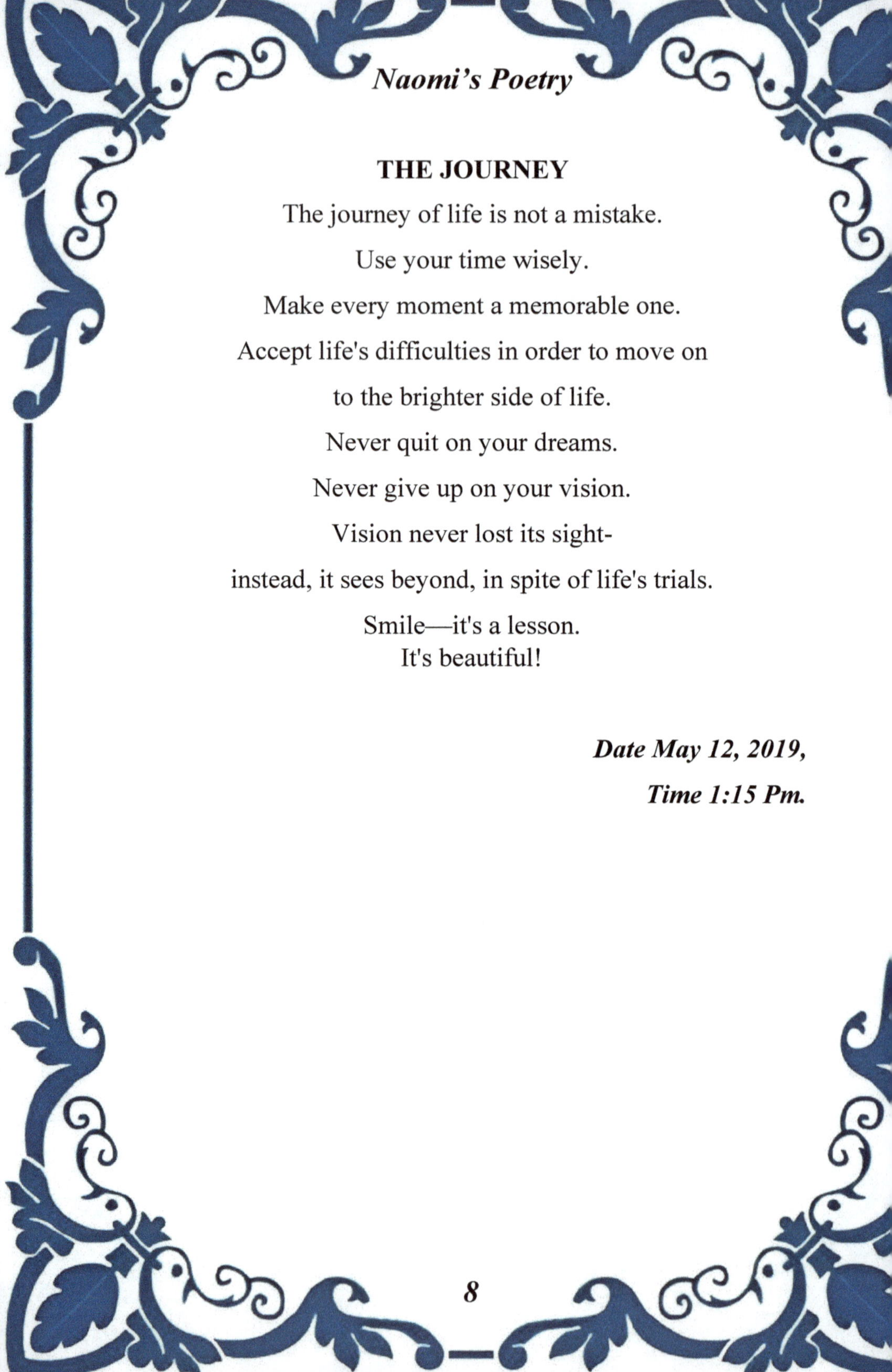

THE JOURNEY

The journey of life is not a mistake.

Use your time wisely.

Make every moment a memorable one.

Accept life's difficulties in order to move on

to the brighter side of life.

Never quit on your dreams.

Never give up on your vision.

Vision never lost its sight-

instead, it sees beyond, in spite of life's trials.

Smile—it's a lesson.
It's beautiful!

Date May 12, 2019,
Time 1:15 Pm.

The journey of life is not a mistake.
NEVER QUIT ON YOUR DREAMS.

TO CHOOSE

To choose is to live.

"But live how?"

To die is to end all the plans of the future,

where the doors of tomorrow will never be open again.

I choose to live—and live right,

right where my mind is stayed in positive activation.

To choose right, sometimes stop lights may enter.

Just remember that they are not permanent,

if you positively and progressively choose to do right!!

Choose today!

August 14, 2019,

Time 1:12 Pm.

To Choose is to Live.
LIFE
CHOOSE TODAY!

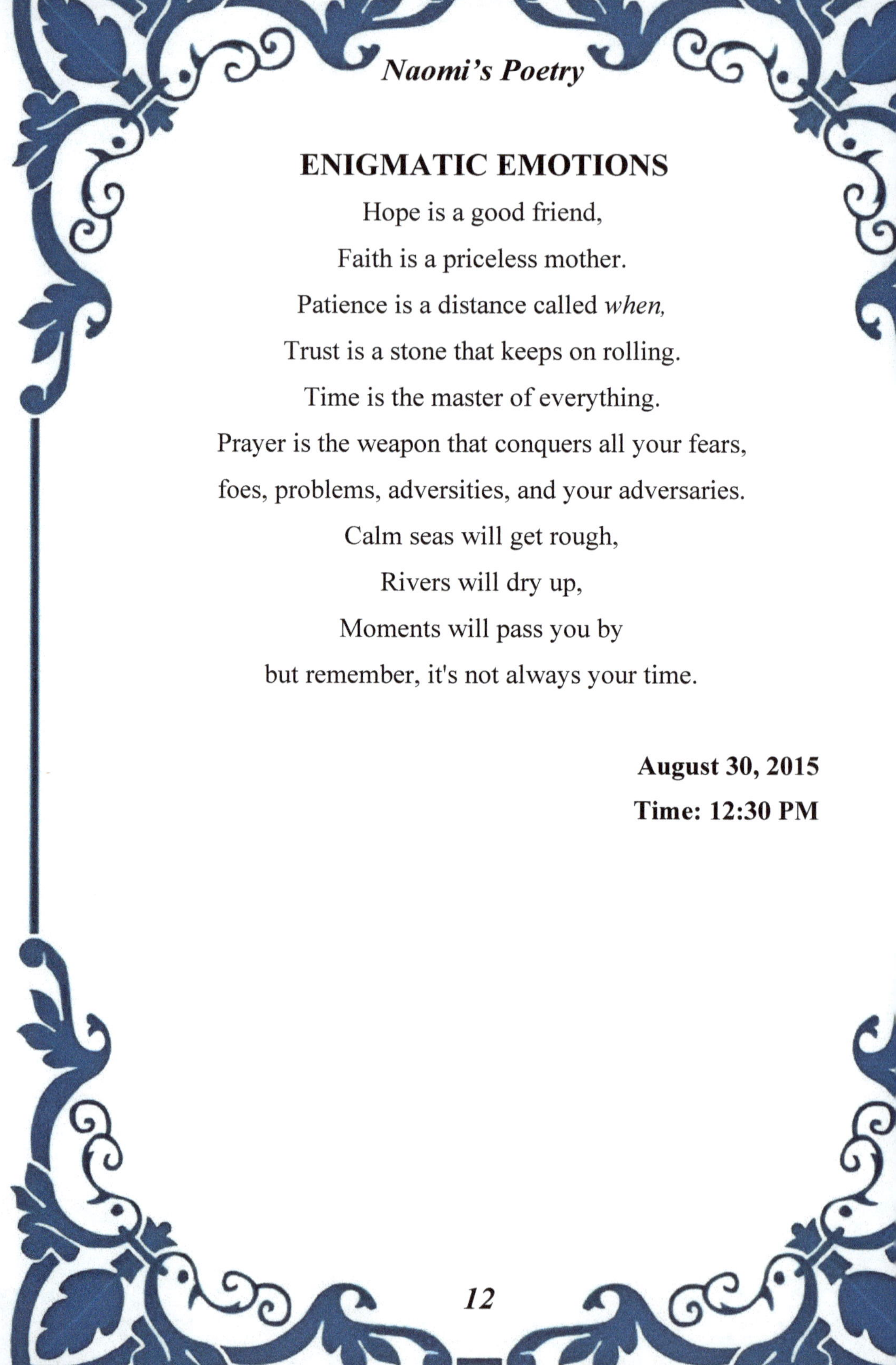

ENIGMATIC EMOTIONS

Hope is a good friend,

Faith is a priceless mother.

Patience is a distance called *when,*

Trust is a stone that keeps on rolling.

Time is the master of everything.

Prayer is the weapon that conquers all your fears,

foes, problems, adversities, and your adversaries.

Calm seas will get rough,

Rivers will dry up,

Moments will pass you by

but remember, it's not always your time.

August 30, 2015
Time: 12:30 PM

But remember,
it's not always your time.

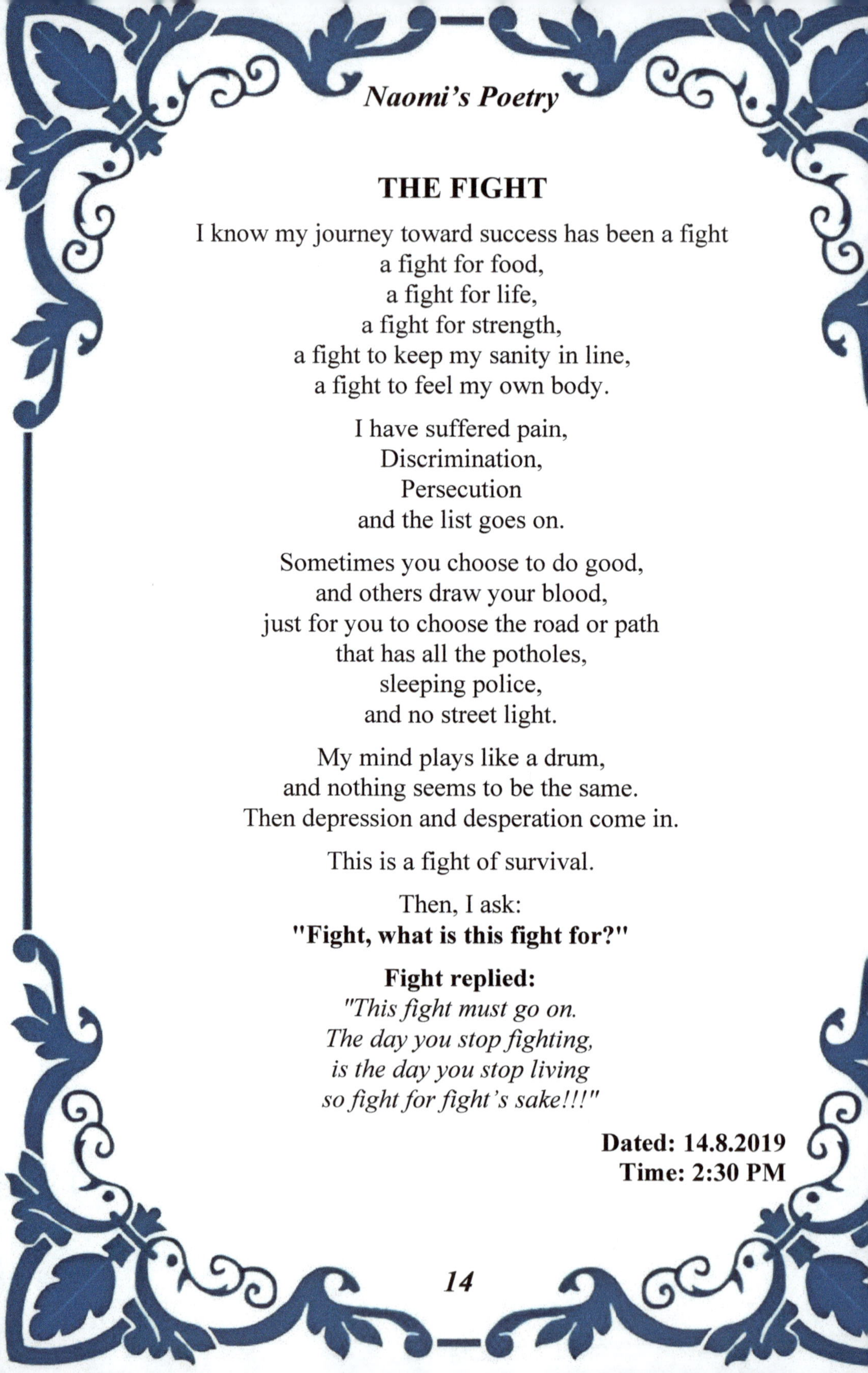

THE FIGHT

I know my journey toward success has been a fight
a fight for food,
a fight for life,
a fight for strength,
a fight to keep my sanity in line,
a fight to feel my own body.

I have suffered pain,
Discrimination,
Persecution
and the list goes on.

Sometimes you choose to do good,
and others draw your blood,
just for you to choose the road or path
that has all the potholes,
sleeping police,
and no street light.

My mind plays like a drum,
and nothing seems to be the same.
Then depression and desperation come in.

This is a fight of survival.

Then, I ask:
"Fight, what is this fight for?"

Fight replied:
*"This fight must go on.
The day you stop fighting,
is the day you stop living
so fight for fight's sake!!!"*

**Dated: 14.8.2019
Time: 2:30 PM**

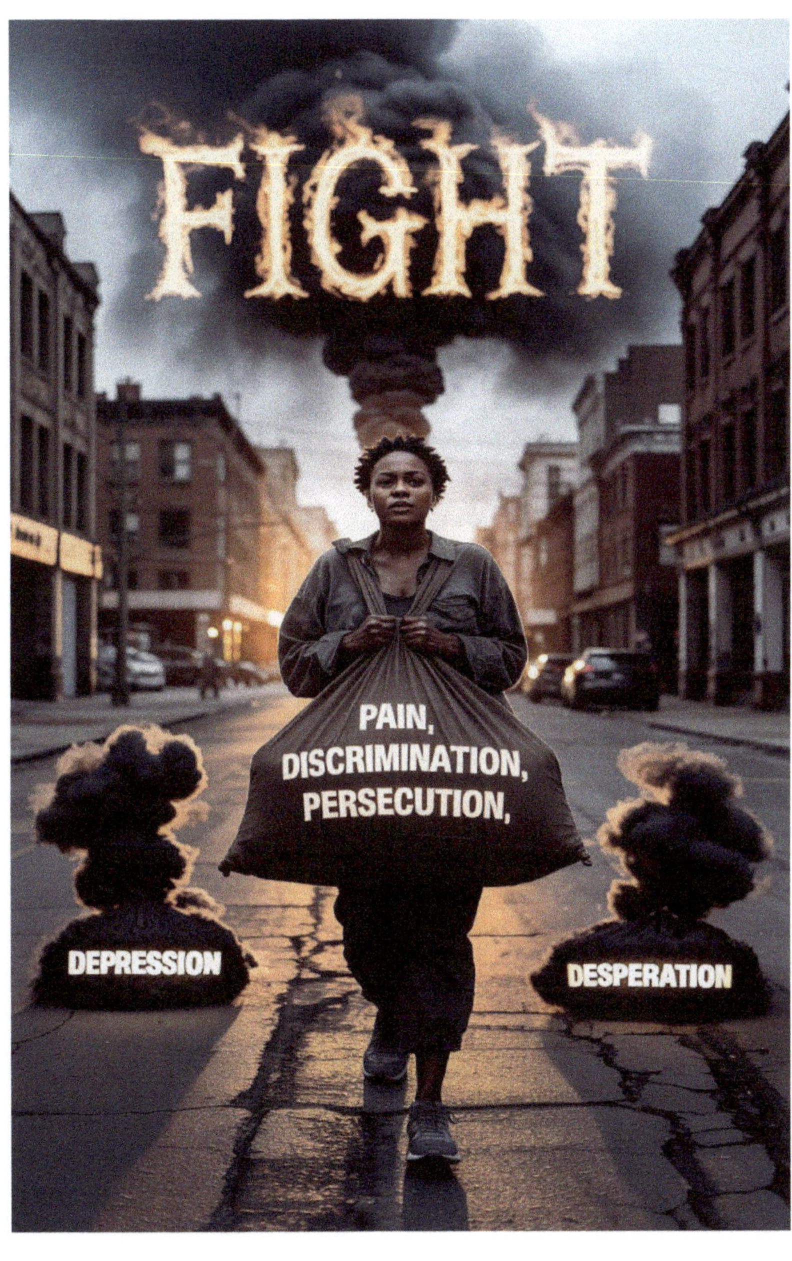
FIGHT
PAIN,
DISCRIMINATION,
PERSECUTION,
DEPRESSION
DESPERATION

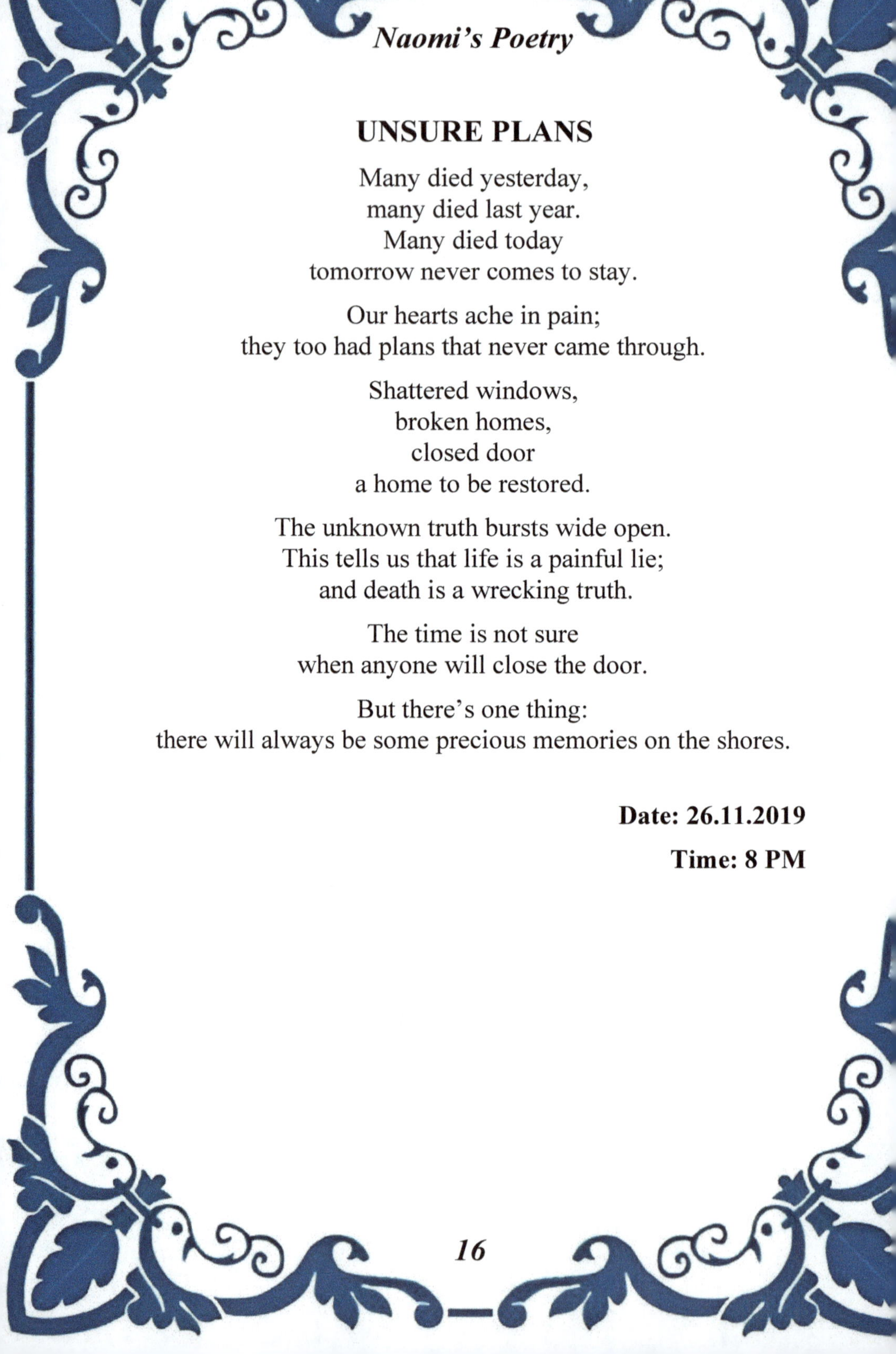

UNSURE PLANS

Many died yesterday,
many died last year.
Many died today
tomorrow never comes to stay.

Our hearts ache in pain;
they too had plans that never came through.

Shattered windows,
broken homes,
closed door
a home to be restored.

The unknown truth bursts wide open.
This tells us that life is a painful lie;
and death is a wrecking truth.

The time is not sure
when anyone will close the door.

But there's one thing:
there will always be some precious memories on the shores.

Date: 26.11.2019

Time: 8 PM

Life is a painful lie
...but memories remain on the shores.

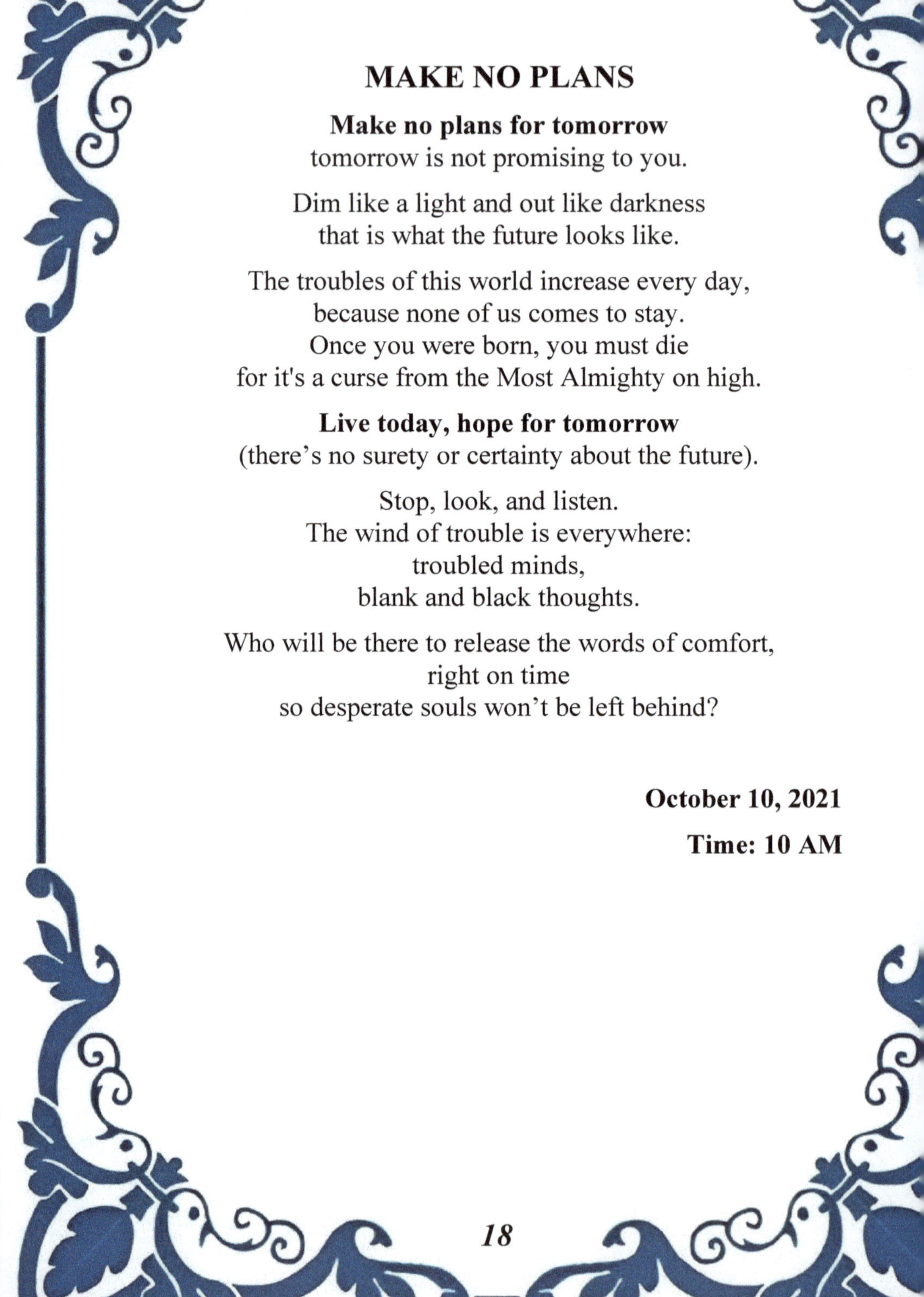

MAKE NO PLANS

Make no plans for tomorrow
tomorrow is not promising to you.

Dim like a light and out like darkness
that is what the future looks like.

The troubles of this world increase every day,
because none of us comes to stay.
Once you were born, you must die
for it's a curse from the Most Almighty on high.

Live today, hope for tomorrow
(there's no surety or certainty about the future).

Stop, look, and listen.
The wind of trouble is everywhere:
troubled minds,
blank and black thoughts.

Who will be there to release the words of comfort,
right on time
so desperate souls won't be left behind?

October 10, 2021

Time: 10 AM

Make no plans for tomorrow —
tomorrow is not promising to you.

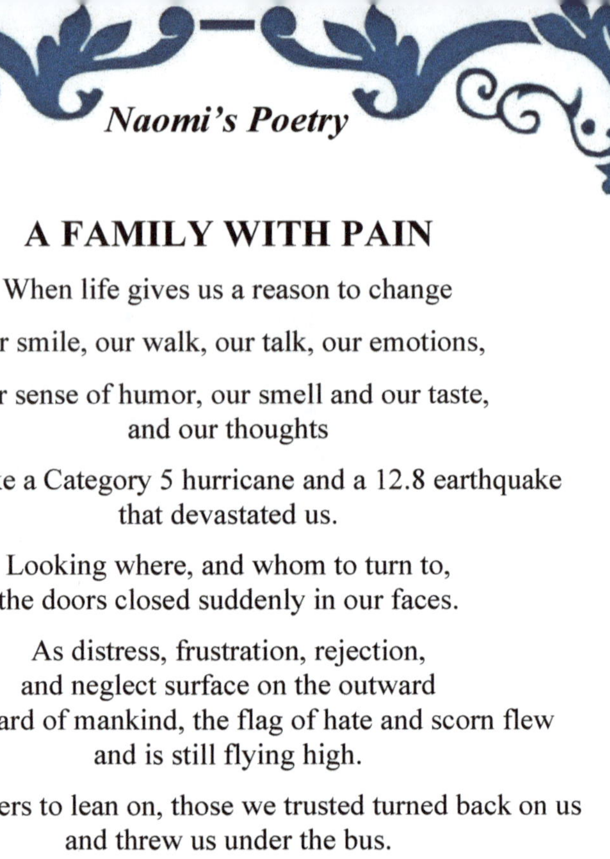

A FAMILY WITH PAIN

When life gives us a reason to change

our smile, our walk, our talk, our emotions,

our sense of humor, our smell and our taste,
and our thoughts

this is like a Category 5 hurricane and a 12.8 earthquake
that devastated us.

Looking where, and whom to turn to,
the doors closed suddenly in our faces.

As distress, frustration, rejection,
and neglect surface on the outward
and inward of mankind, the flag of hate and scorn flew
and is still flying high.

No shoulders to lean on, those we trusted turned back on us
and threw us under the bus.

Bridges, and ocean floor, and the streets that we travelled on
are now so lonely and dark.

The places are cold and empty,
as depression tries to creep into our lives.
Anxiety wants to be our best friend.
Lies stare and stared us into our faces,
thinking better days are over with us.

The world turned its back on us,
pretending not to see.

Yet only a few still have hope in us,
knowing that we will shine again
like a diamond.

For the darkness of this world
will never outshine the light
of God's beautiful creations.

July 8, 2023
PM: 2:01

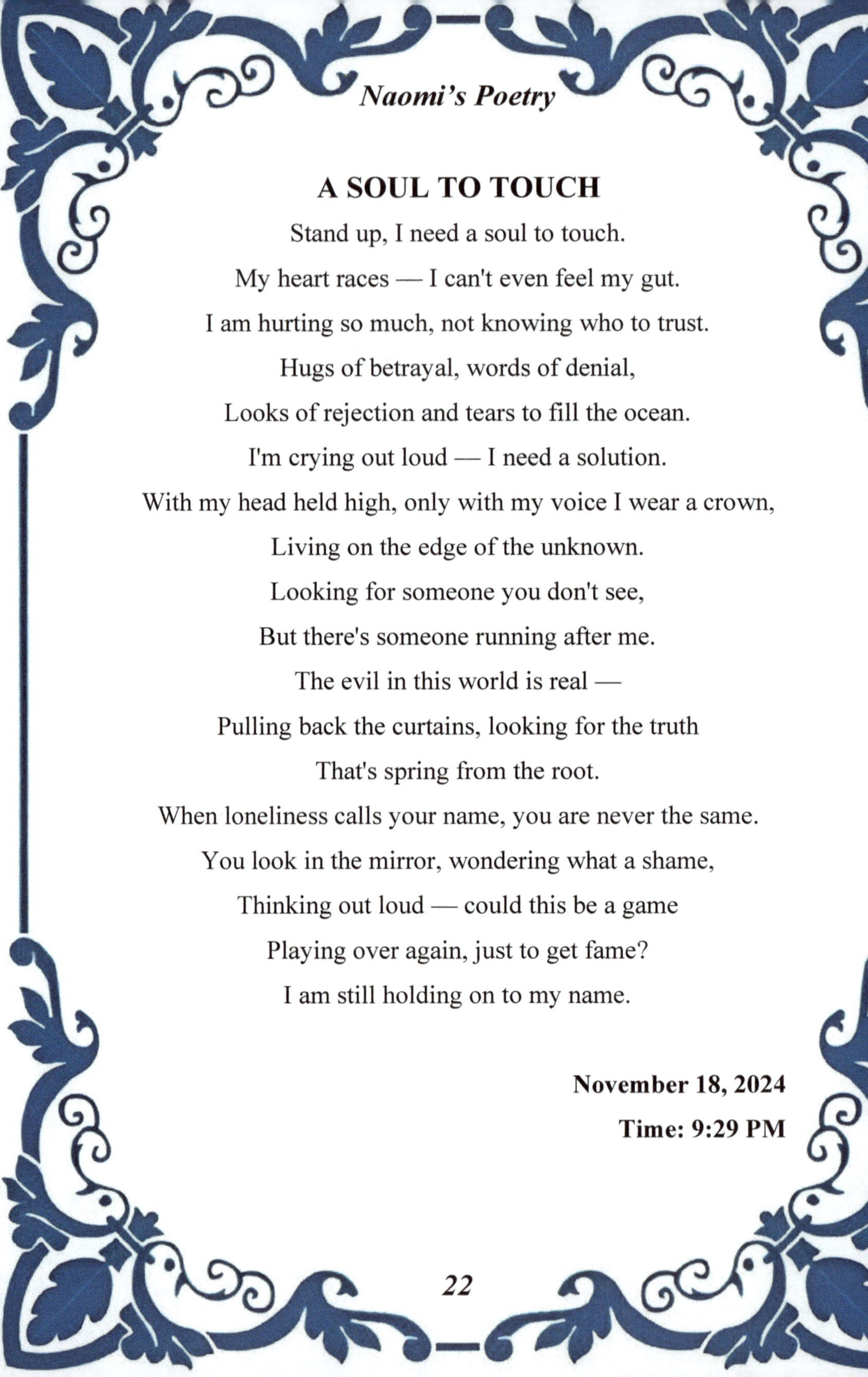

A SOUL TO TOUCH

Stand up, I need a soul to touch.

My heart races — I can't even feel my gut.

I am hurting so much, not knowing who to trust.

Hugs of betrayal, words of denial,

Looks of rejection and tears to fill the ocean.

I'm crying out loud — I need a solution.

With my head held high, only with my voice I wear a crown,

Living on the edge of the unknown.

Looking for someone you don't see,

But there's someone running after me.

The evil in this world is real —

Pulling back the curtains, looking for the truth

That's spring from the root.

When loneliness calls your name, you are never the same.

You look in the mirror, wondering what a shame,

Thinking out loud — could this be a game

Playing over again, just to get fame?

I am still holding on to my name.

November 18, 2024
Time: 9:29 PM

Hugs of betrayal, words of denial...
yet i am still holding on to my name

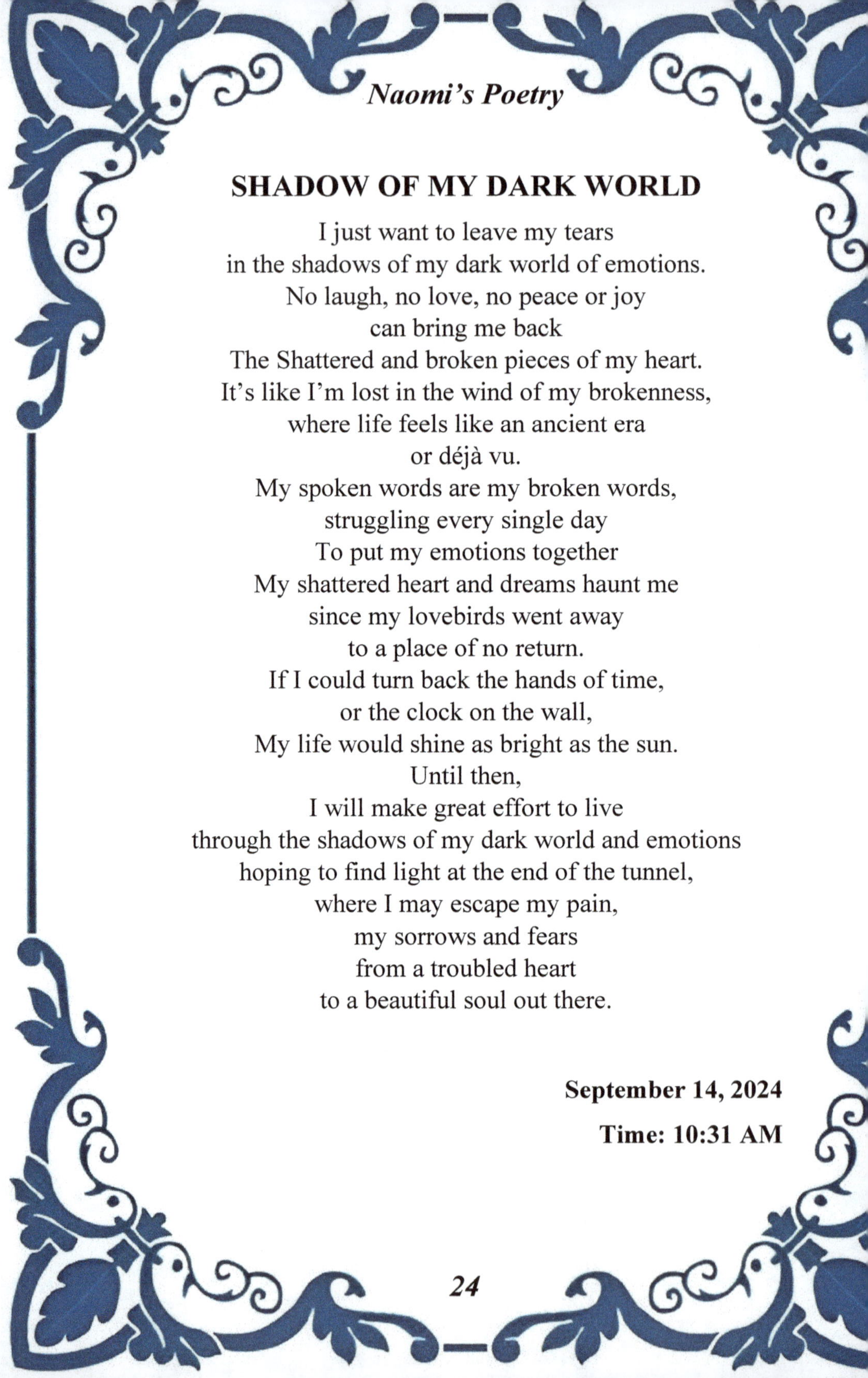

SHADOW OF MY DARK WORLD

I just want to leave my tears
in the shadows of my dark world of emotions.
No laugh, no love, no peace or joy
can bring me back
The Shattered and broken pieces of my heart.
It's like I'm lost in the wind of my brokenness,
where life feels like an ancient era
or déjà vu.
My spoken words are my broken words,
struggling every single day
To put my emotions together
My shattered heart and dreams haunt me
since my lovebirds went away
to a place of no return.
If I could turn back the hands of time,
or the clock on the wall,
My life would shine as bright as the sun.
Until then,
I will make great effort to live
through the shadows of my dark world and emotions
hoping to find light at the end of the tunnel,
where I may escape my pain,
my sorrows and fears
from a troubled heart
to a beautiful soul out there.

September 14, 2024

Time: 10:31 AM

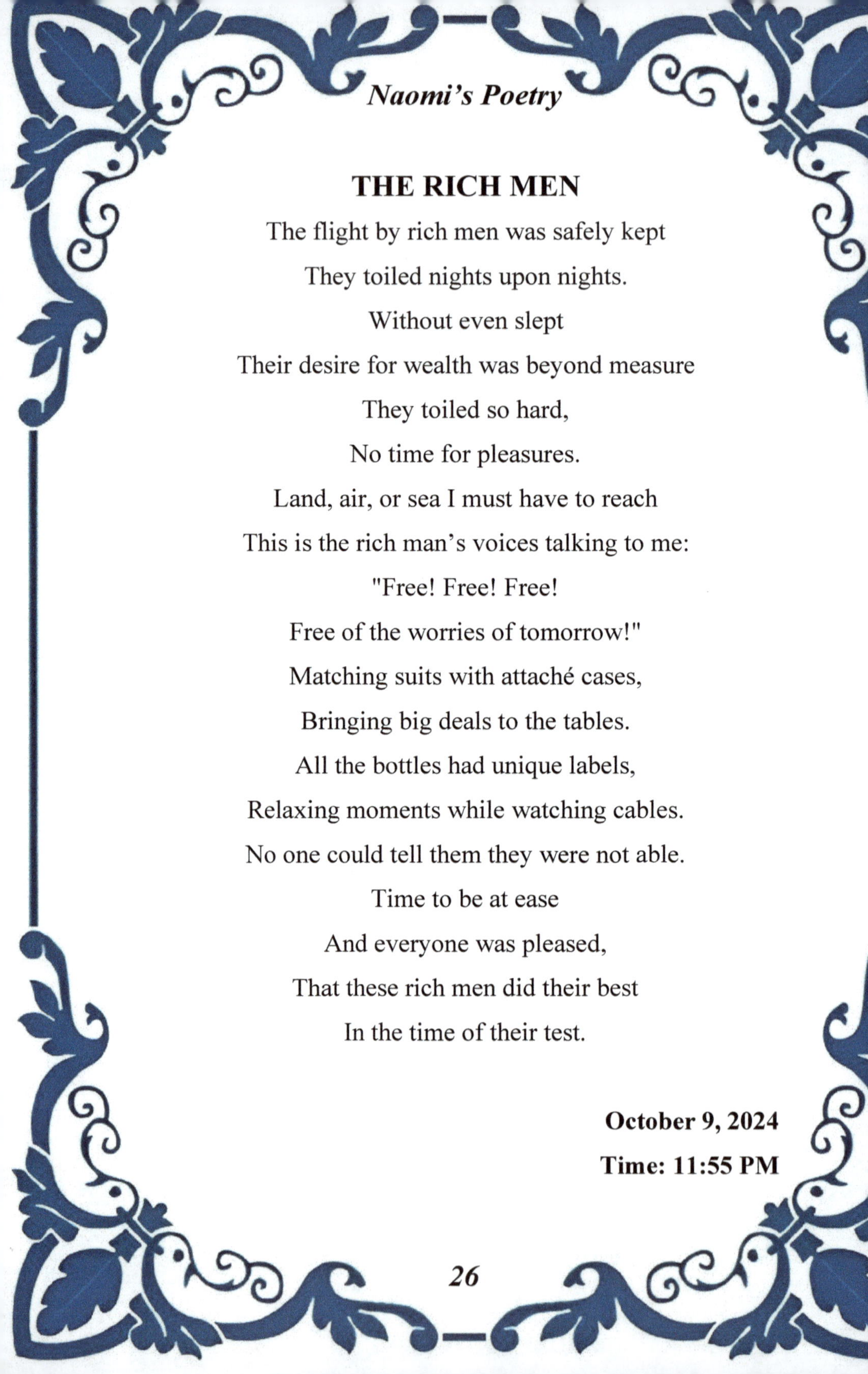

THE RICH MEN

The flight by rich men was safely kept

They toiled nights upon nights.

Without even slept

Their desire for wealth was beyond measure

They toiled so hard,

No time for pleasures.

Land, air, or sea I must have to reach

This is the rich man's voices talking to me:

"Free! Free! Free!

Free of the worries of tomorrow!"

Matching suits with attaché cases,

Bringing big deals to the tables.

All the bottles had unique labels,

Relaxing moments while watching cables.

No one could tell them they were not able.

Time to be at ease

And everyone was pleased,

That these rich men did their best

In the time of their test.

October 9, 2024

Time: 11:55 PM

Free of the Worries
of Tomorrow!

SELF WAR

I am fighting a silent war that no one knows about. A war that I have hope to win someday to come. A mental, emotional, psychological, spiritual, financial, and physical war with myself and life's journey
a war that's waiting for peace, peace in every ally mentioned above.

Note to self:
Remember how far you have come and the bridges that you have crossed in this race of war.

War, this is a note to you:
I need my peace, love, joy, family, sanity, health, wealth, life, and most of all, happiness.

You came from nowhere and attacked me suddenly, trying to endanger my life so I would be hopeless, helpless, cold, selfish, and crazy.

So, you won.

But let me remind you—**War**—of the fighter in me.
I'm a survivor, and I will win.

09/10/2024
9:50 PM - Wednesday

FEAR,
LOSS,
PAIN
PEACE,
JOY,
STRENGTH,
SURVIVOR

THE MIND

There is a lot going lately, and without prayer I will be
crazy.
The pain of hurt, stress, life's test. Only to imagine what
next.
The cry for help seems dark and hopeless. Life is priceless.
This gift is timeless—who can we live to impress?
Running from my past, evading into the present, asking
myself: who promised me the future?
When life isn't at its best,
The only thing I can do is breathe and believe.

Thursday, October 24, 2024

Time: 3 PM

a
thousand
unspoken
thoughts

A CRY FOR HELP

The scream of a shattered heart, a broken home, a wounded
mindset with many stories to be told.
The screams for help and hope seem vain, while I am
suffering me mental and emotional pain.
Trying to live through the agony of my trauma that uprooted
the true version of me, forcing me to be someone else that I
refuse to be.

During my crisis, I face it all alone.
Some persons pretend to be sorry but never gave me the
support for a quick-change.
I beg and plead for help, hoping one day this too may end.

My mind is as big as the world.
I have traveled many places only in my mind.
I have seen many things only in my mind.
I have done many things only in my mind.
I have hidden many things only in my mind.
I have fought many battles only in my mind.
I have heard many things only in my mind.
I can only love those who I have lost—only in my mind.

October 24, 2024

Time: 7:59 PM

help me...

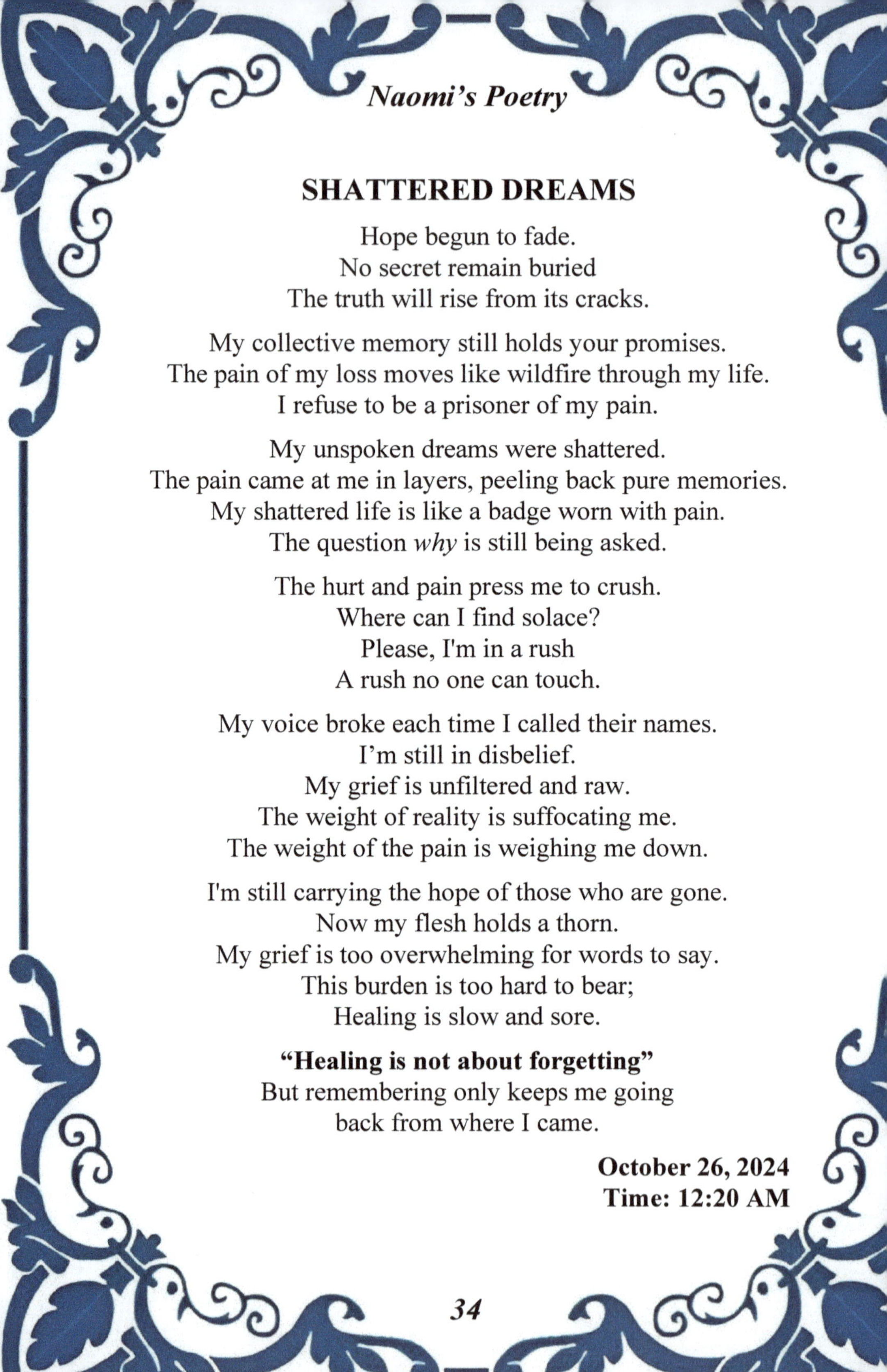

SHATTERED DREAMS

Hope begun to fade.
No secret remain buried
The truth will rise from its cracks.

My collective memory still holds your promises.
The pain of my loss moves like wildfire through my life.
I refuse to be a prisoner of my pain.

My unspoken dreams were shattered.
The pain came at me in layers, peeling back pure memories.
My shattered life is like a badge worn with pain.
The question *why* is still being asked.

The hurt and pain press me to crush.
Where can I find solace?
Please, I'm in a rush
A rush no one can touch.

My voice broke each time I called their names.
I'm still in disbelief.
My grief is unfiltered and raw.
The weight of reality is suffocating me.
The weight of the pain is weighing me down.

I'm still carrying the hope of those who are gone.
Now my flesh holds a thorn.
My grief is too overwhelming for words to say.
This burden is too hard to bear;
Healing is slow and sore.

"Healing is not about forgetting"
But remembering only keeps me going
back from where I came.

October 26, 2024
Time: 12:20 AM

MY UNSPOKEN
DREAMS
WERE
SHATTERED,

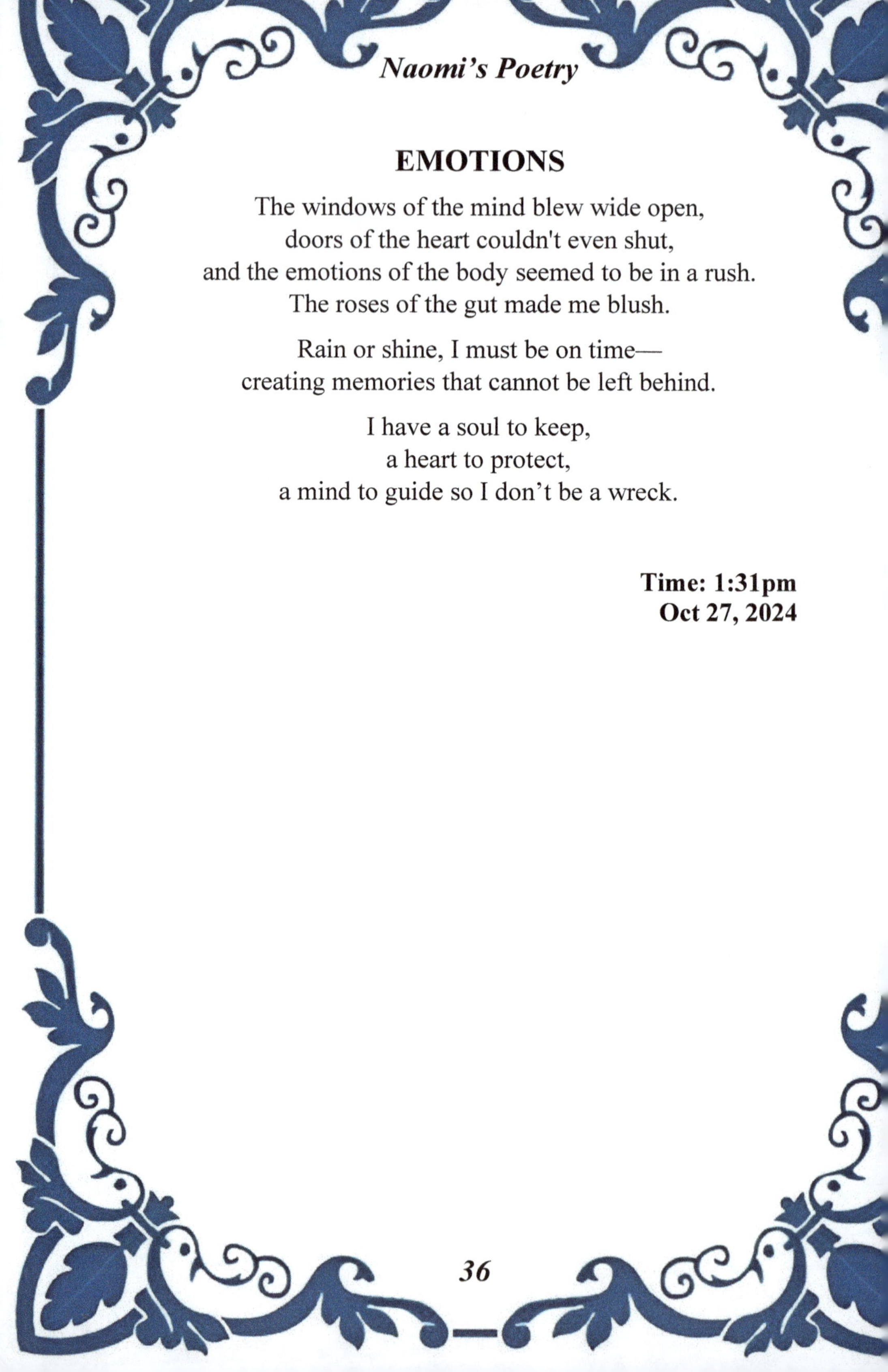

EMOTIONS

The windows of the mind blew wide open,
doors of the heart couldn't even shut,
and the emotions of the body seemed to be in a rush.
The roses of the gut made me blush.

Rain or shine, I must be on time—
creating memories that cannot be left behind.

I have a soul to keep,
a heart to protect,
a mind to guide so I don't be a wreck.

Time: 1:31pm
Oct 27, 2024

SOUL
HEART
MIND

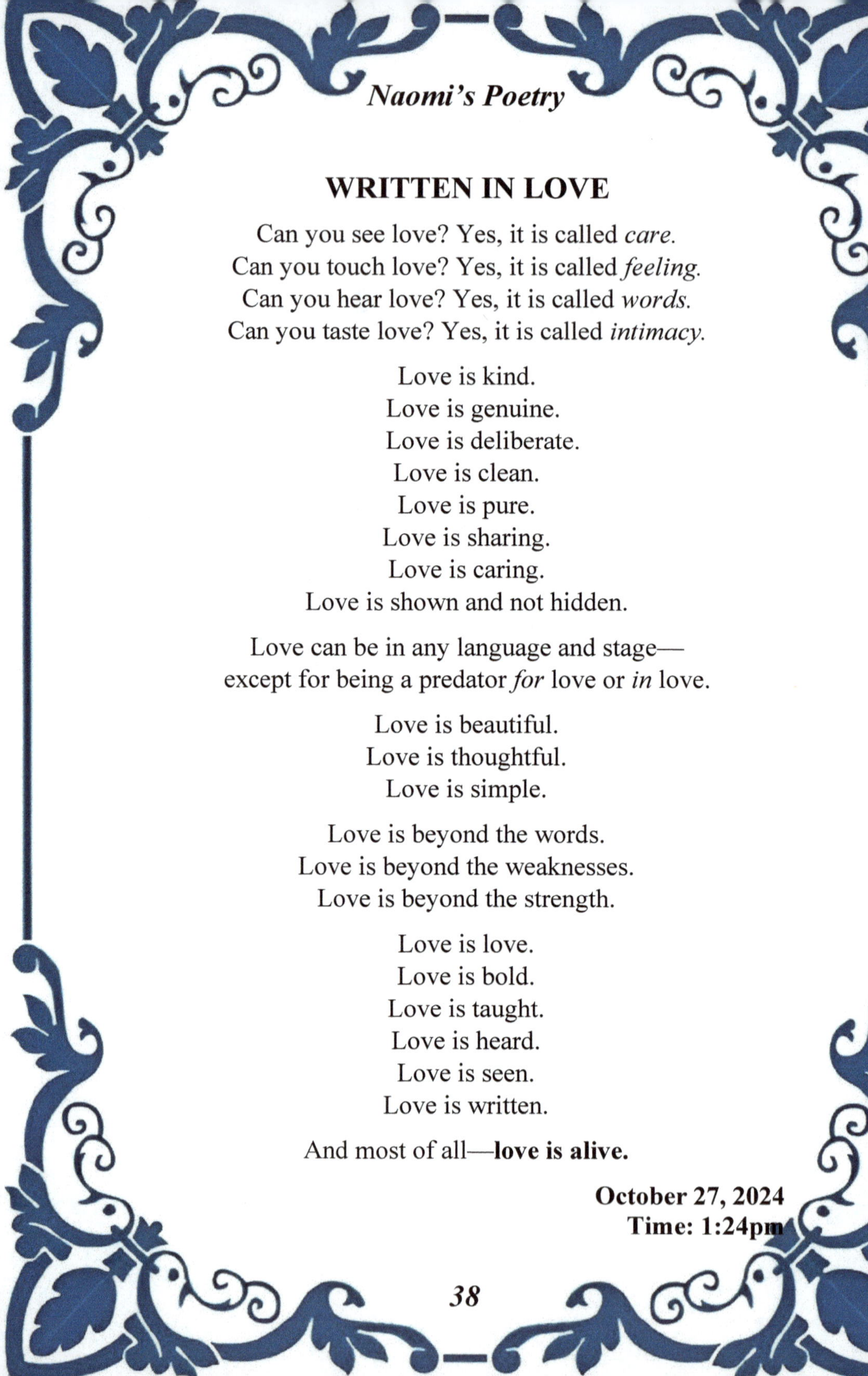

WRITTEN IN LOVE

Can you see love? Yes, it is called *care.*
Can you touch love? Yes, it is called *feeling.*
Can you hear love? Yes, it is called *words.*
Can you taste love? Yes, it is called *intimacy.*

Love is kind.
Love is genuine.
Love is deliberate.
Love is clean.
Love is pure.
Love is sharing.
Love is caring.
Love is shown and not hidden.

Love can be in any language and stage—
except for being a predator *for* love or *in* love.

Love is beautiful.
Love is thoughtful.
Love is simple.

Love is beyond the words.
Love is beyond the weaknesses.
Love is beyond the strength.

Love is love.
Love is bold.
Love is taught.
Love is heard.
Love is seen.
Love is written.

And most of all—**love is alive.**

October 27, 2024
Time: 1:24pm

"We were not created to hurt
other. forgive, love, hug, kiss,
and embrace each other."

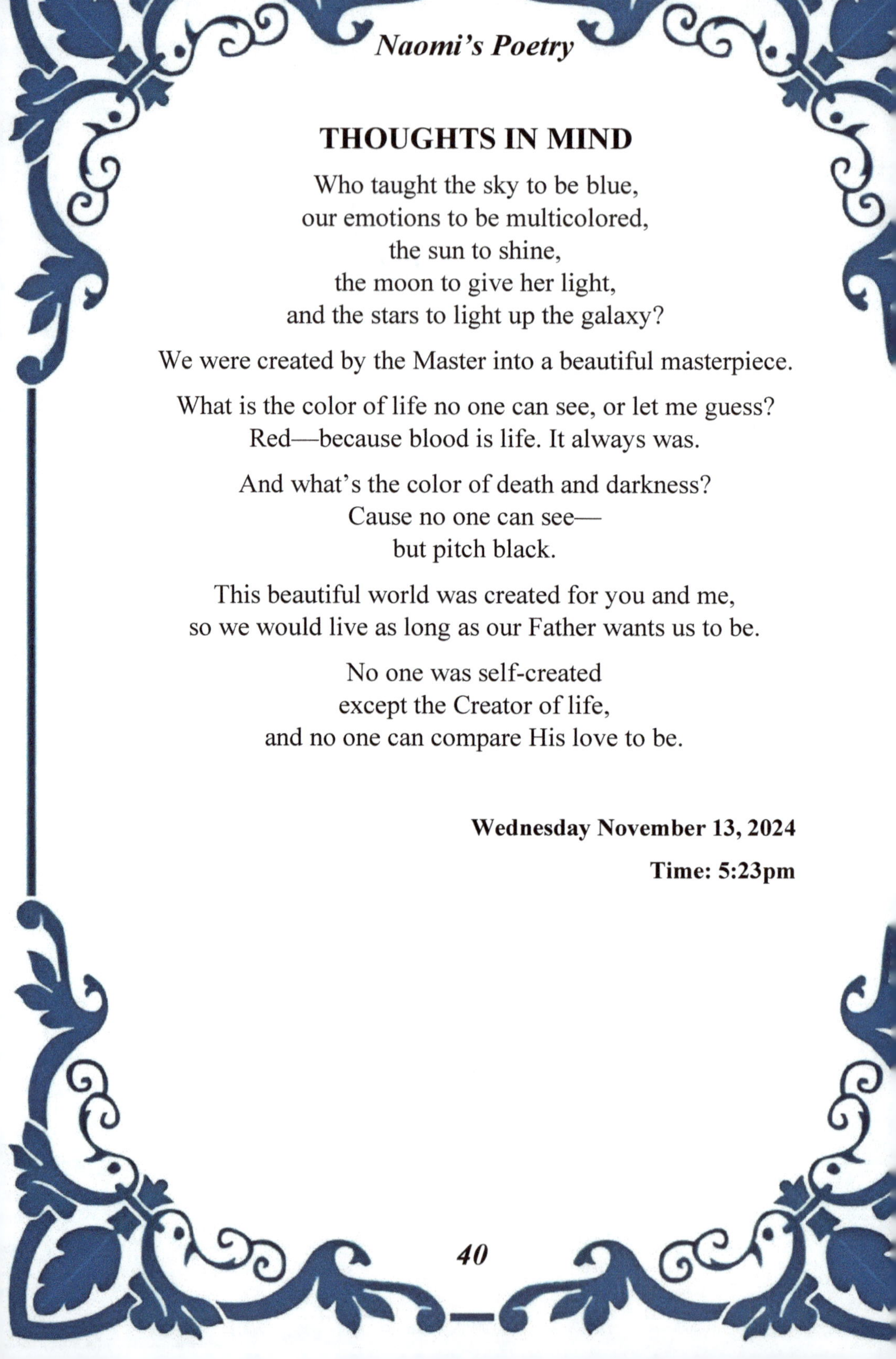

THOUGHTS IN MIND

Who taught the sky to be blue,
our emotions to be multicolored,
the sun to shine,
the moon to give her light,
and the stars to light up the galaxy?

We were created by the Master into a beautiful masterpiece.

What is the color of life no one can see, or let me guess?
Red—because blood is life. It always was.

And what's the color of death and darkness?
Cause no one can see—
but pitch black.

This beautiful world was created for you and me,
so we would live as long as our Father wants us to be.

No one was self-created
except the Creator of life,
and no one can compare His love to be.

Wednesday November 13, 2024

Time: 5:23pm

We were created by the Master
into a beautiful masterpiece

REALTIME

I take a walk on the ocean shores,
listening to the seashell making noisy roar,
feeling so relaxed, forgetting that I was wearing socks,
looking for my footprints now.

I'm in a shock—my prints are not there!

Now I have to turn back,
watching my shadow giving me a map.

Thinking deep, wishing I could sleep,
making memories that I must keep.

The creeks from the woods—
maybe I should walk on till tomorrow
and see all that I could.

Without thinking, I changed my mind,
waiting to see the sun pop up with a shine.

Nov 13, 2024

Time: 5:33pm

watching my shadow giving me a map

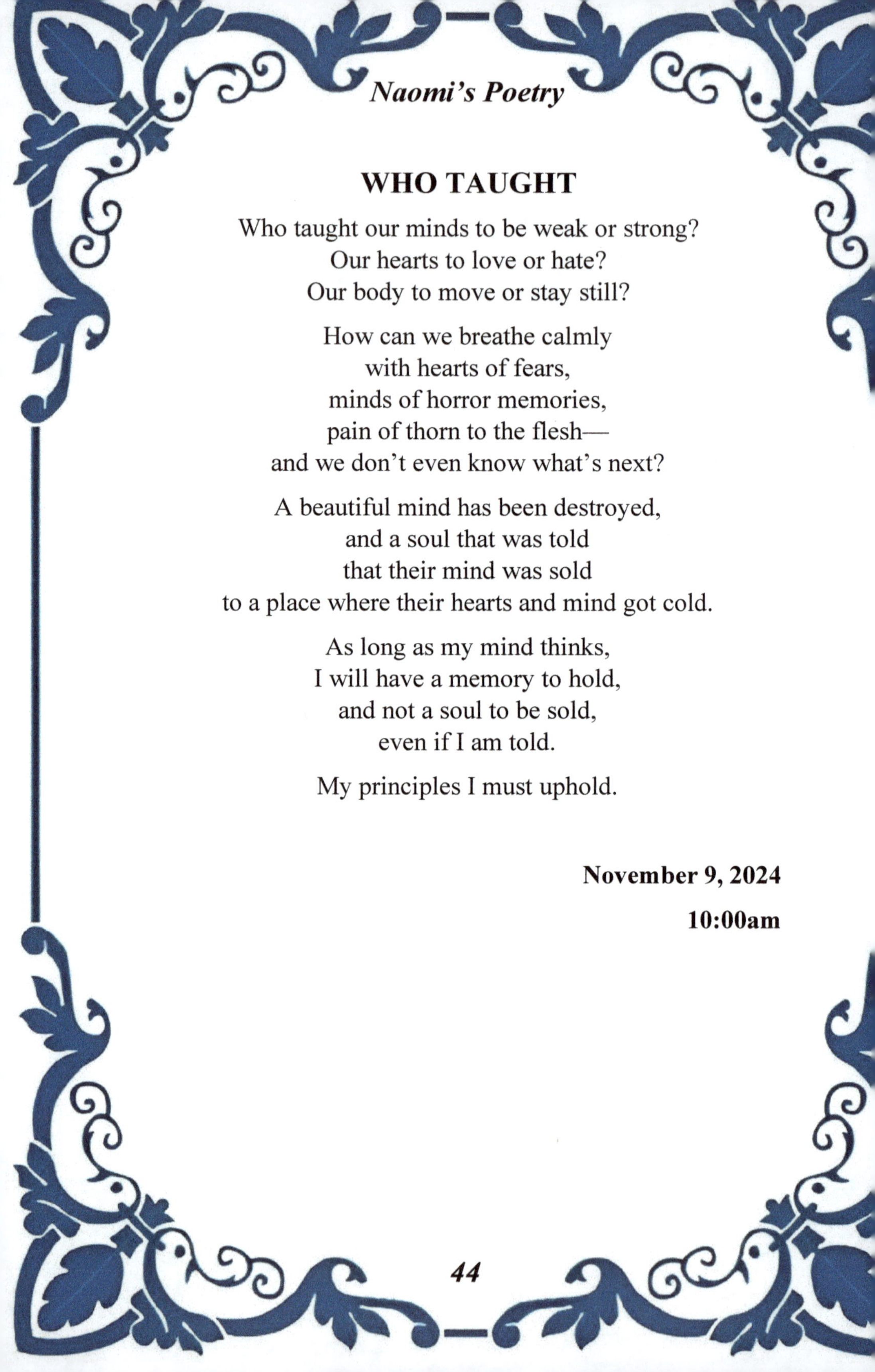

WHO TAUGHT

Who taught our minds to be weak or strong?
Our hearts to love or hate?
Our body to move or stay still?

How can we breathe calmly
with hearts of fears,
minds of horror memories,
pain of thorn to the flesh—
and we don't even know what's next?

A beautiful mind has been destroyed,
and a soul that was told
that their mind was sold
to a place where their hearts and mind got cold.

As long as my mind thinks,
I will have a memory to hold,
and not a soul to be sold,
even if I am told.

My principles I must uphold.

November 9, 2024

10:00am

"WHO TAUGHT OUR MINDS
TO BE WEAK OR STRONG?
OUR HEARTS TO LOVE OR
HATE?"

TOGETHER

I just want to spend time with my family and friends,
the way life is,
even though time has an end.

We are here today—let us not pretend,
because we very well know that time has an end.

The life we dream of,
the journey we walked,
we can't even mention anything about our thoughts.

This world and life owe us nothing.
We ought to tread cautiously in order not to get trapped
trapped in our mind, body, soul, heart, and spirit.

This time we live, let's stay close,
eye to eye as we see each other every day.

If life could speak for itself,
then we would know the difference between good and evil.

We were not created to hurt each other.
Forgive, love, hug, kiss, and embrace each other,
because we are in this together.

November 16, 2024

Time: 6:29 pm

Forgive, love, hug, kiss,
and embrace each other,
echanes because
we are in this
Together

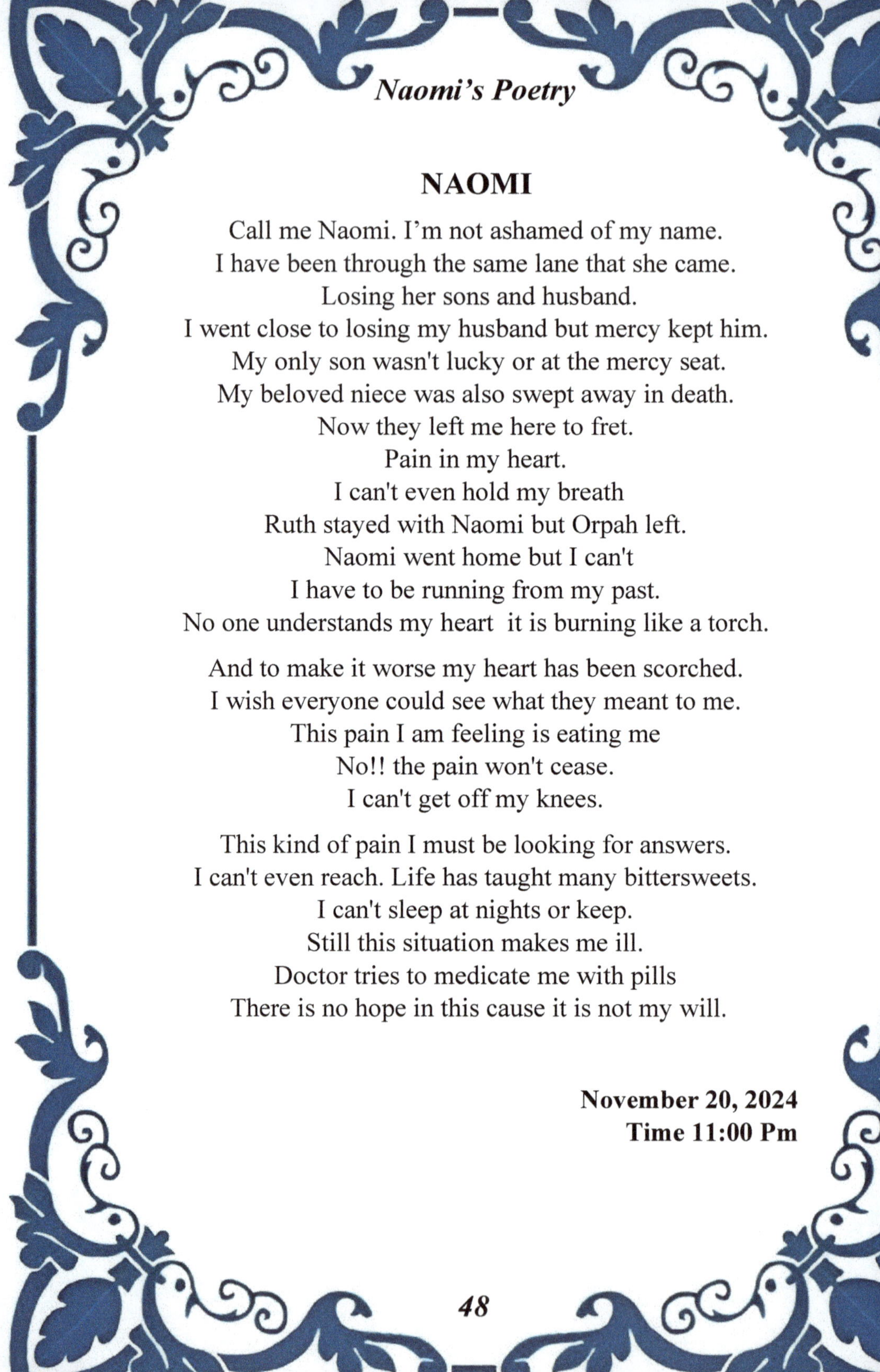

NAOMI

Call me Naomi. I'm not ashamed of my name.
I have been through the same lane that she came.
Losing her sons and husband.
I went close to losing my husband but mercy kept him.
My only son wasn't lucky or at the mercy seat.
My beloved niece was also swept away in death.
Now they left me here to fret.
Pain in my heart.
I can't even hold my breath
Ruth stayed with Naomi but Orpah left.
Naomi went home but I can't
I have to be running from my past.
No one understands my heart it is burning like a torch.

And to make it worse my heart has been scorched.
I wish everyone could see what they meant to me.
This pain I am feeling is eating me
No!! the pain won't cease.
I can't get off my knees.

This kind of pain I must be looking for answers.
I can't even reach. Life has taught many bittersweets.
I can't sleep at nights or keep.
Still this situation makes me ill.
Doctor tries to medicate me with pills
There is no hope in this cause it is not my will.

November 20, 2024
Time 11:00 Pm

Call me
Naomi.
I'm not ashamed
This pain i name
of am feeling
is eating me

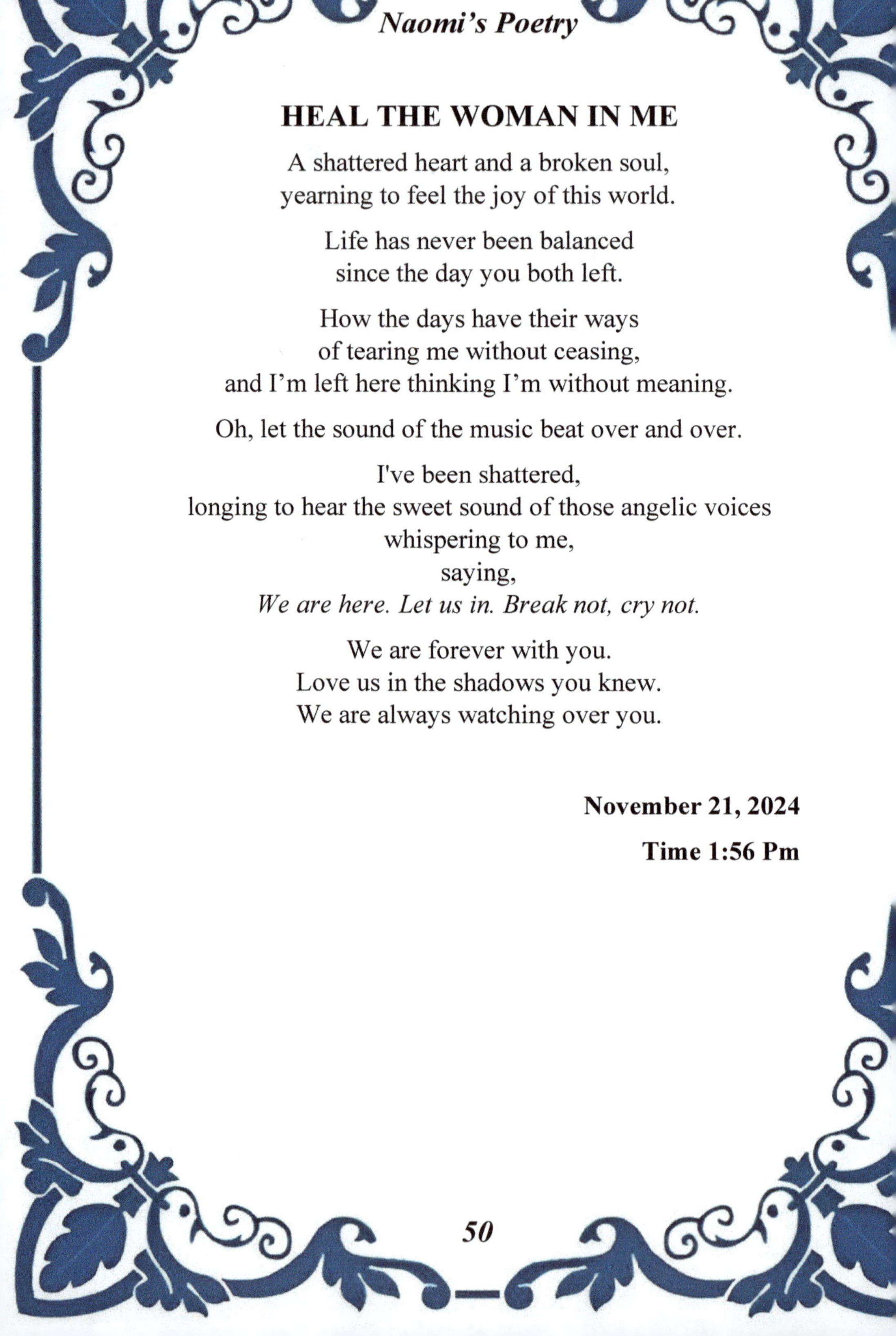

HEAL THE WOMAN IN ME

A shattered heart and a broken soul,
yearning to feel the joy of this world.

Life has never been balanced
since the day you both left.

How the days have their ways
of tearing me without ceasing,
and I'm left here thinking I'm without meaning.

Oh, let the sound of the music beat over and over.

I've been shattered,
longing to hear the sweet sound of those angelic voices
whispering to me,
saying,
We are here. Let us in. Break not, cry not.

We are forever with you.
Love us in the shadows you knew.
We are always watching over you.

November 21, 2024

Time 1:56 Pm

We are here.
Love us in the shadows you knew.

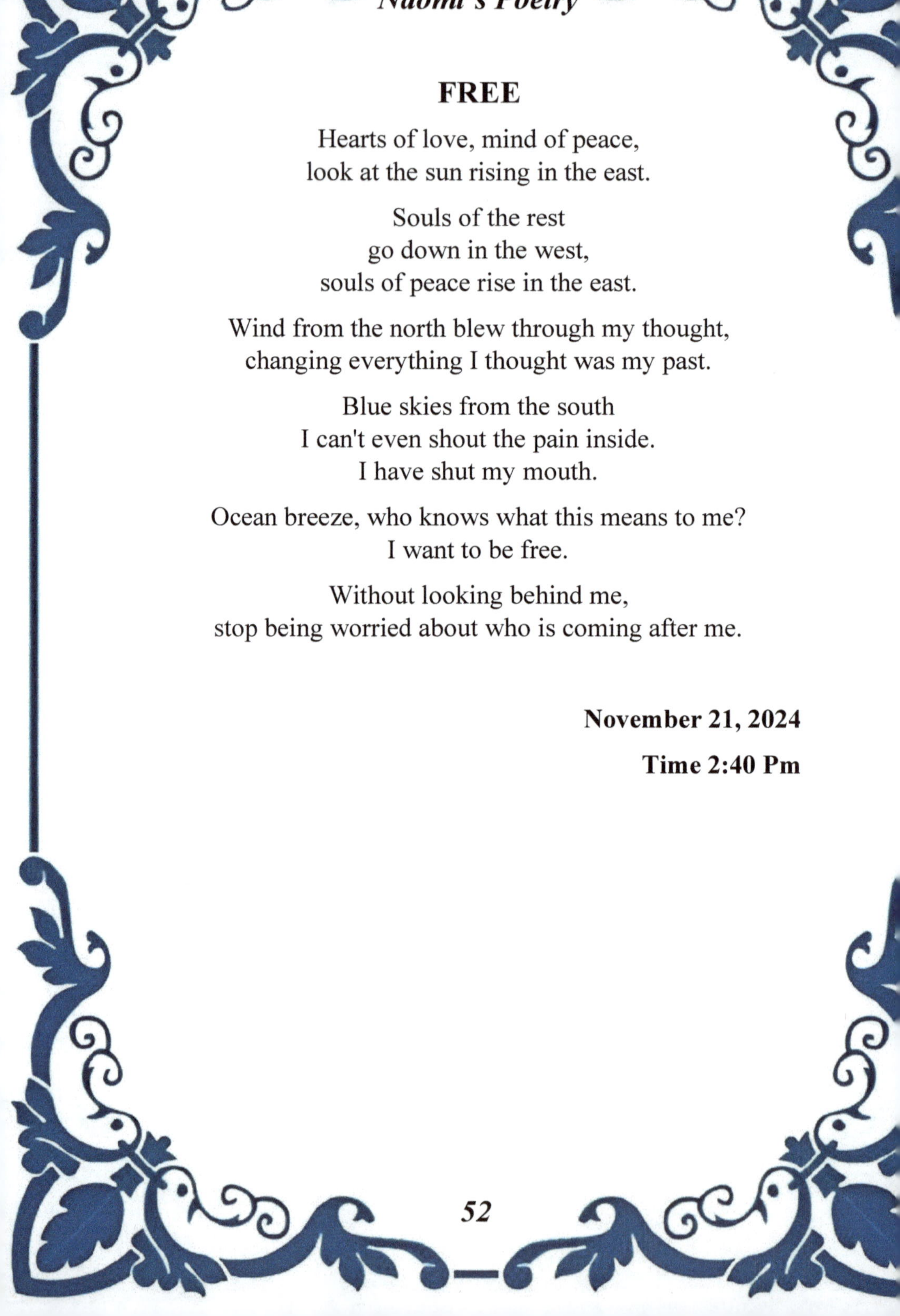

FREE

Hearts of love, mind of peace,
look at the sun rising in the east.

Souls of the rest
go down in the west,
souls of peace rise in the east.

Wind from the north blew through my thought,
changing everything I thought was my past.

Blue skies from the south
I can't even shout the pain inside.
I have shut my mouth.

Ocean breeze, who knows what this means to me?
I want to be free.

Without looking behind me,
stop being worried about who is coming after me.

November 21, 2024

Time 2:40 Pm

I WANT TO BE FREE,
WITHOUT LOOKING BEHIND ME

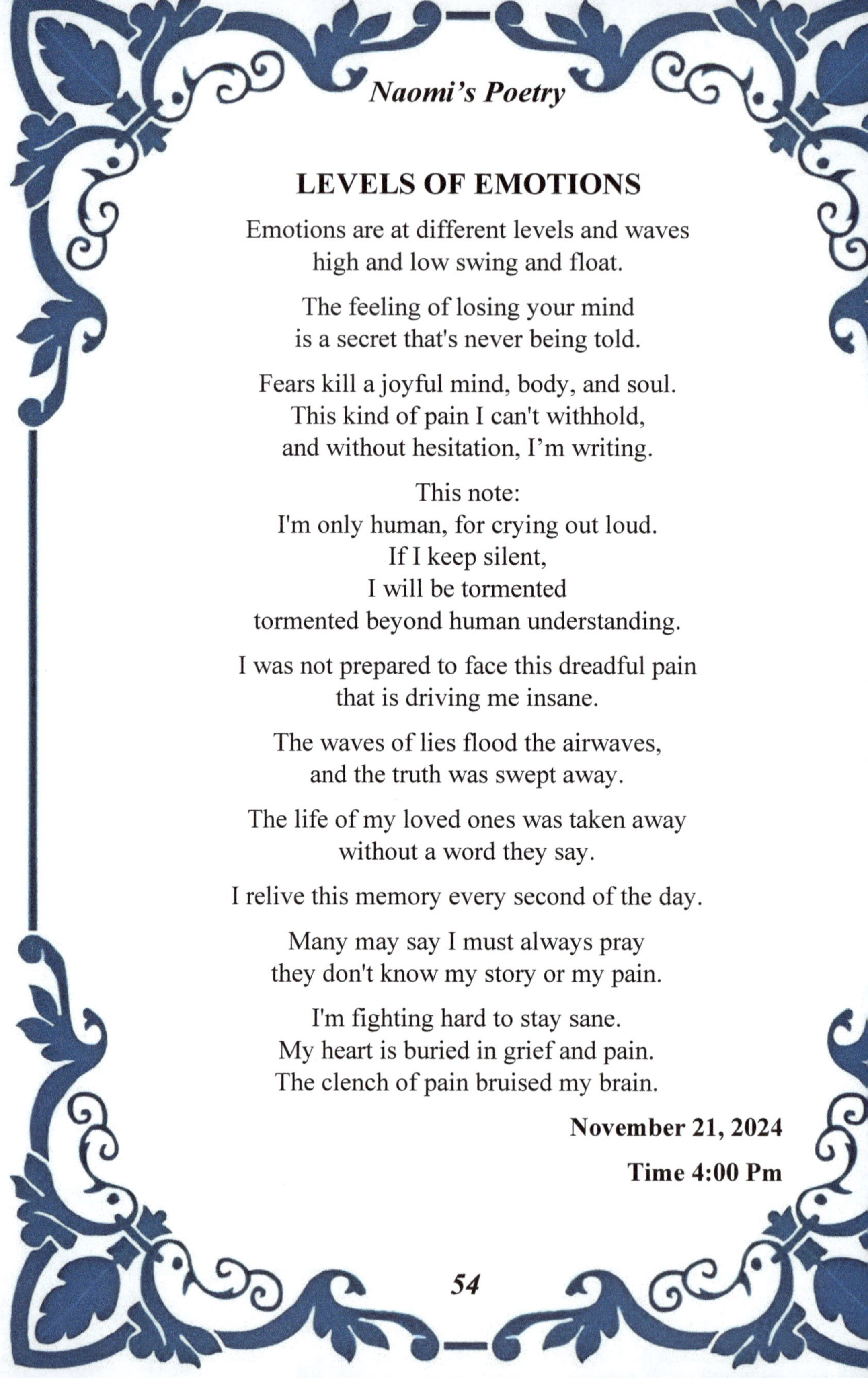

LEVELS OF EMOTIONS

Emotions are at different levels and waves
high and low swing and float.

The feeling of losing your mind
is a secret that's never being told.

Fears kill a joyful mind, body, and soul.
This kind of pain I can't withhold,
and without hesitation, I'm writing.

This note:
I'm only human, for crying out loud.
If I keep silent,
I will be tormented
tormented beyond human understanding.

I was not prepared to face this dreadful pain
that is driving me insane.

The waves of lies flood the airwaves,
and the truth was swept away.

The life of my loved ones was taken away
without a word they say.

I relive this memory every second of the day.

Many may say I must always pray
they don't know my story or my pain.

I'm fighting hard to stay sane.
My heart is buried in grief and pain.
The clench of pain bruised my brain.

November 21, 2024

Time 4:00 Pm

each
is step is
a level of
of emotion
I must climb

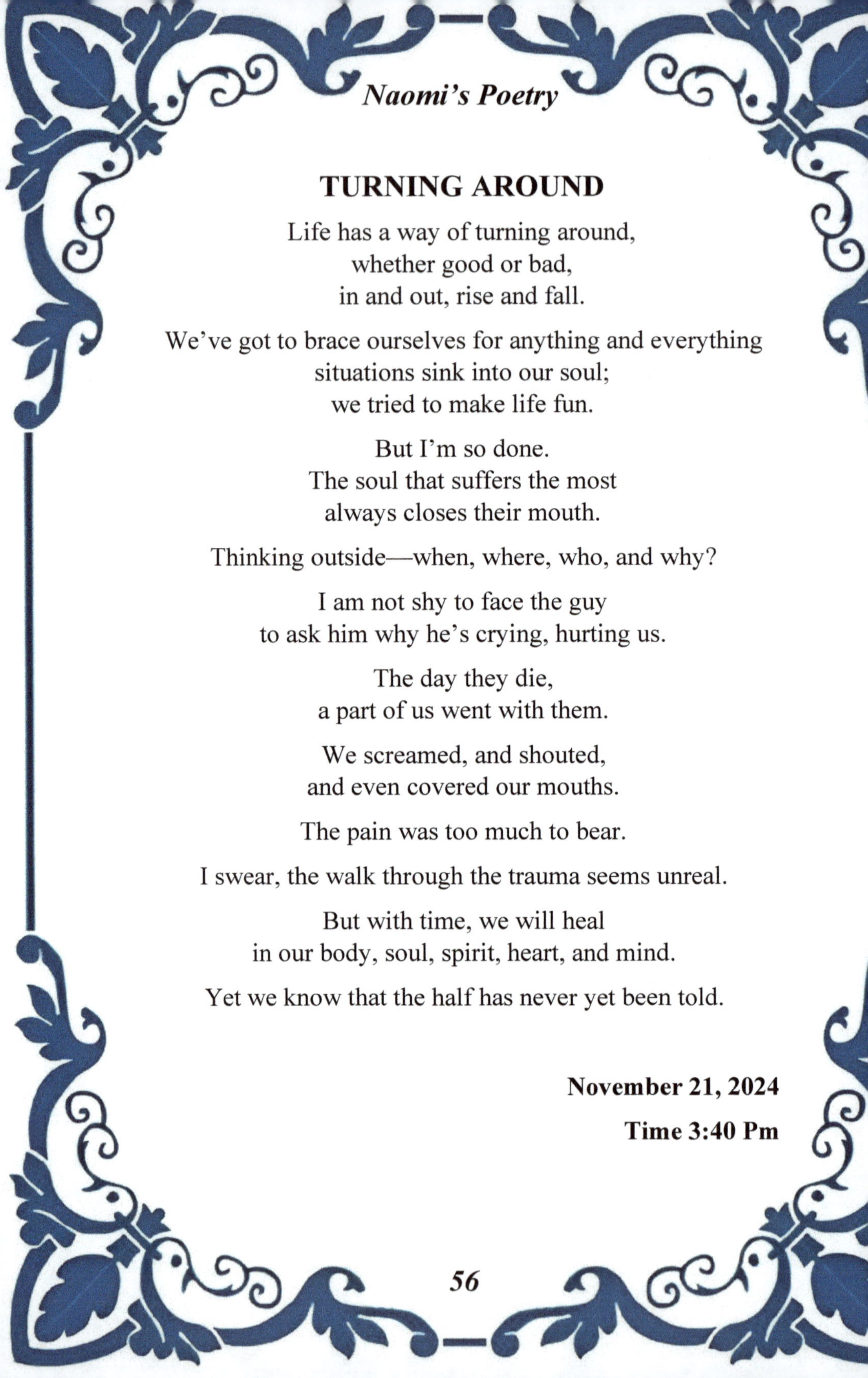

TURNING AROUND

Life has a way of turning around,
whether good or bad,
in and out, rise and fall.

We've got to brace ourselves for anything and everything
situations sink into our soul;
we tried to make life fun.

But I'm so done.
The soul that suffers the most
always closes their mouth.

Thinking outside—when, where, who, and why?

I am not shy to face the guy
to ask him why he's crying, hurting us.

The day they die,
a part of us went with them.

We screamed, and shouted,
and even covered our mouths.

The pain was too much to bear.

I swear, the walk through the trauma seems unreal.

But with time, we will heal
in our body, soul, spirit, heart, and mind.

Yet we know that the half has never yet been told.

November 21, 2024

Time 3:40 Pm

Life turns around,
and with time...
we heal.

LOST IN THE OCEAN

Lost in the ocean as my thoughts flash to land,
looking all around—there's no one or nothing to hold on to.

The hope for rescue is unsure.
How am I going to reach the shores?
My heart beats like a drum.

Thinking I am lost and done.
God, this is not fun.

There is no way to run as the waves get higher.
The current gains its strength, pulling me down,
screaming loudly while trying to save myself in the deep.

Sooner or later, I will have to keep looking for help
in the middle of the deep.

There came a big wave,
pushing me to shore,

then a boat to take me on a tour.

Thank goodness I am safe from the ocean's floor.

November 19, 2024

Time 4:35 Pm

My strength is hidden
in the I am that I Am

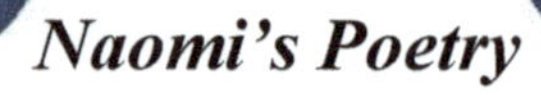

MY WORDS TO MY SON

Son it is so hard to be living without you, my love.

I am no longer the same mom you knew,

my heart has been ripped to pieces.

My life has been difficult.

My mind is not in a good place.

Nothing can change my emotions except if I should see and
hold you in my arms again

Remember you were like oxygen to my body and this
cannot be a case study.

Son I'm struggling in all aspect of my life,

all I'm asking you to do is to please come back,

the day you passed my life has stopped!!

The reality is mocking me

and depression is knocking me,

post trauma is laughing at me.

Son how I'm supposed to be?

Your first cry broke me and told me to be strong.

The day you left my world turned grey how could you do
this to me?

The pain touches my soul so deep that I can't even sleep,

I stayed up and weep.

You were so sweet and this is all I have to keep.

November 22, 2024

Time 12:00 Am

The day you passed,
My life stopped

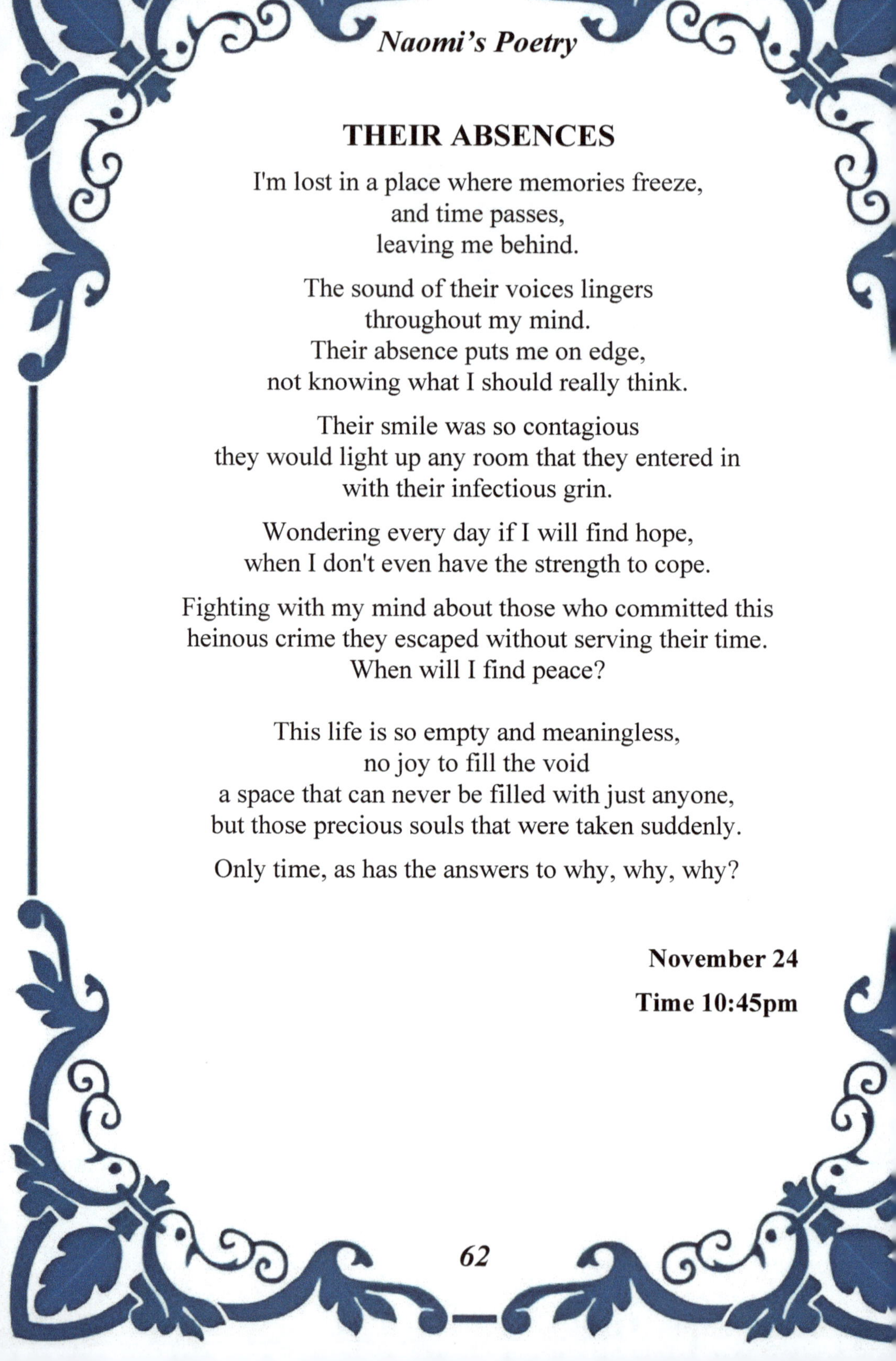

THEIR ABSENCES

I'm lost in a place where memories freeze,
and time passes,
leaving me behind.

The sound of their voices lingers
throughout my mind.
Their absence puts me on edge,
not knowing what I should really think.

Their smile was so contagious
they would light up any room that they entered in
with their infectious grin.

Wondering every day if I will find hope,
when I don't even have the strength to cope.

Fighting with my mind about those who committed this
heinous crime they escaped without serving their time.
When will I find peace?

This life is so empty and meaningless,
no joy to fill the void
a space that can never be filled with just anyone,
but those precious souls that were taken suddenly.

Only time, as has the answers to why, why, why?

November 24

Time 10:45pm

Naomi

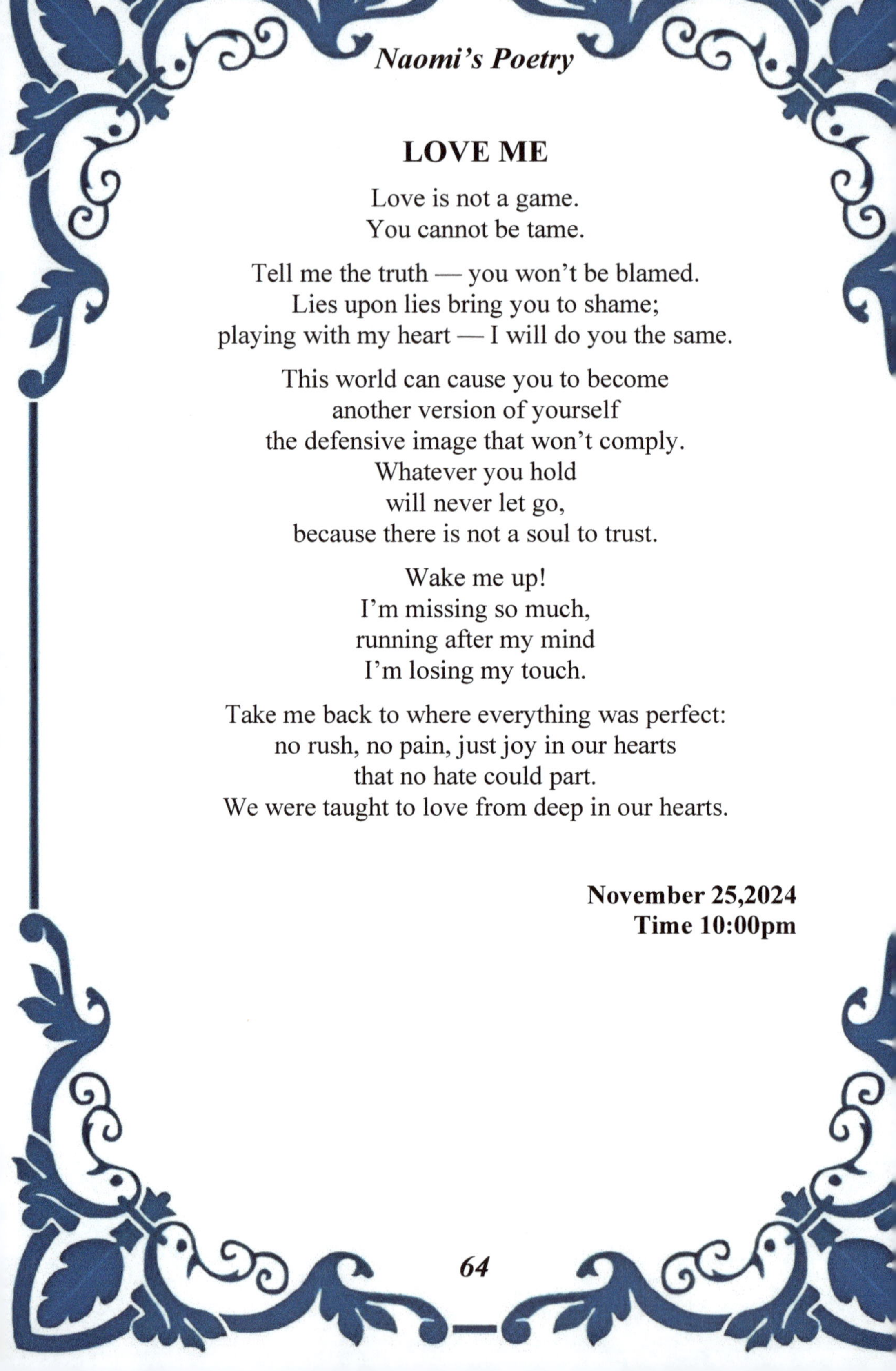

LOVE ME

Love is not a game.
You cannot be tame.

Tell me the truth — you won't be blamed.
Lies upon lies bring you to shame;
playing with my heart — I will do you the same.

This world can cause you to become
another version of yourself
the defensive image that won't comply.
Whatever you hold
will never let go,
because there is not a soul to trust.

Wake me up!
I'm missing so much,
running after my mind
I'm losing my touch.

Take me back to where everything was perfect:
no rush, no pain, just joy in our hearts
that no hate could part.
We were taught to love from deep in our hearts.

November 25,2024
Time 10:00pm

Love is not a game...
wake me up,
I'm missing so much.

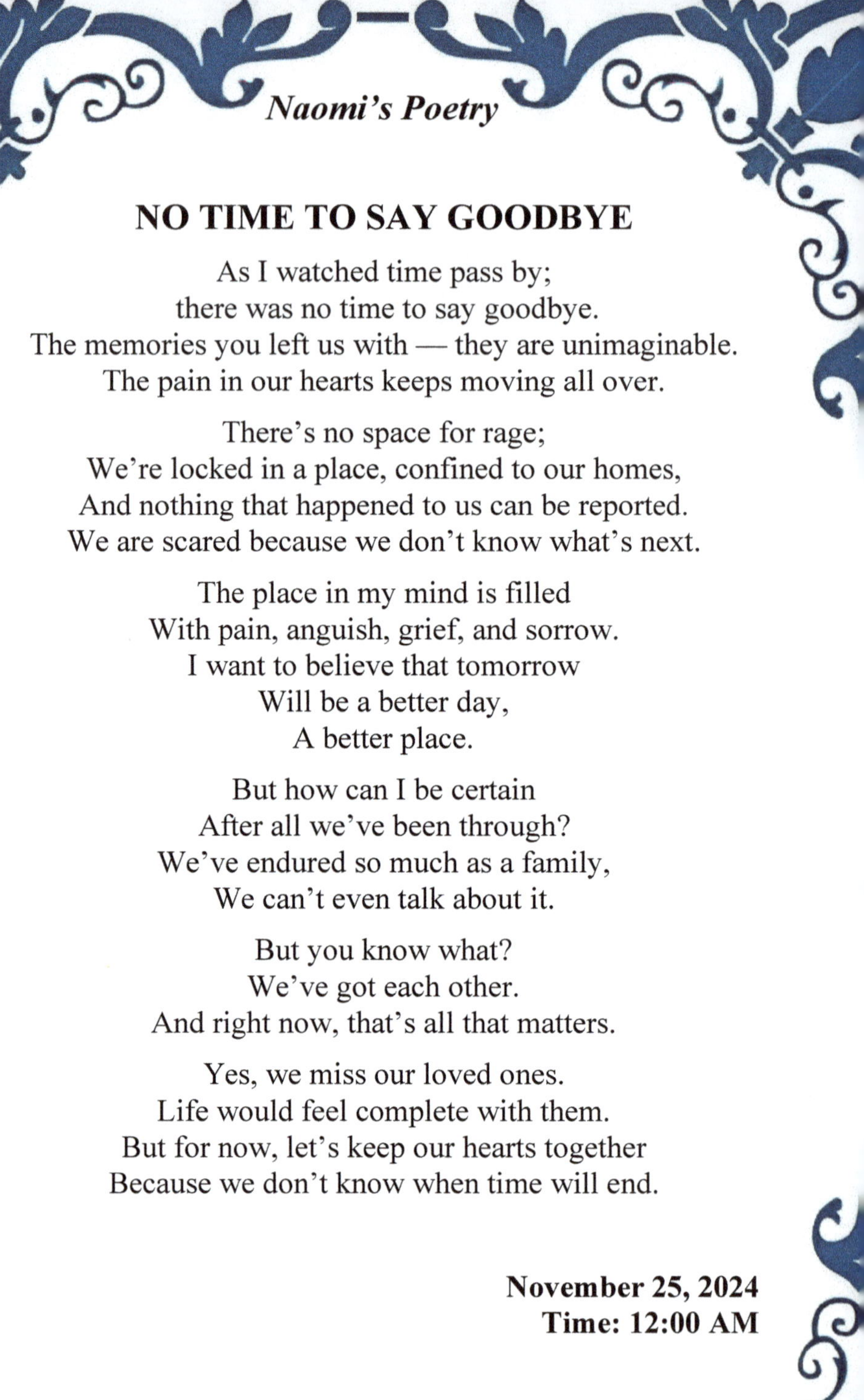

NO TIME TO SAY GOODBYE

As I watched time pass by;
there was no time to say goodbye.
The memories you left us with — they are unimaginable.
The pain in our hearts keeps moving all over.

There's no space for rage;
We're locked in a place, confined to our homes,
And nothing that happened to us can be reported.
We are scared because we don't know what's next.

The place in my mind is filled
With pain, anguish, grief, and sorrow.
I want to believe that tomorrow
Will be a better day,
A better place.

But how can I be certain
After all we've been through?
We've endured so much as a family,
We can't even talk about it.

But you know what?
We've got each other.
And right now, that's all that matters.

Yes, we miss our loved ones.
Life would feel complete with them.
But for now, let's keep our hearts together
Because we don't know when time will end.

November 25, 2024
Time: 12:00 AM

As I watched time pass by;
there wes no time to say goodbye,

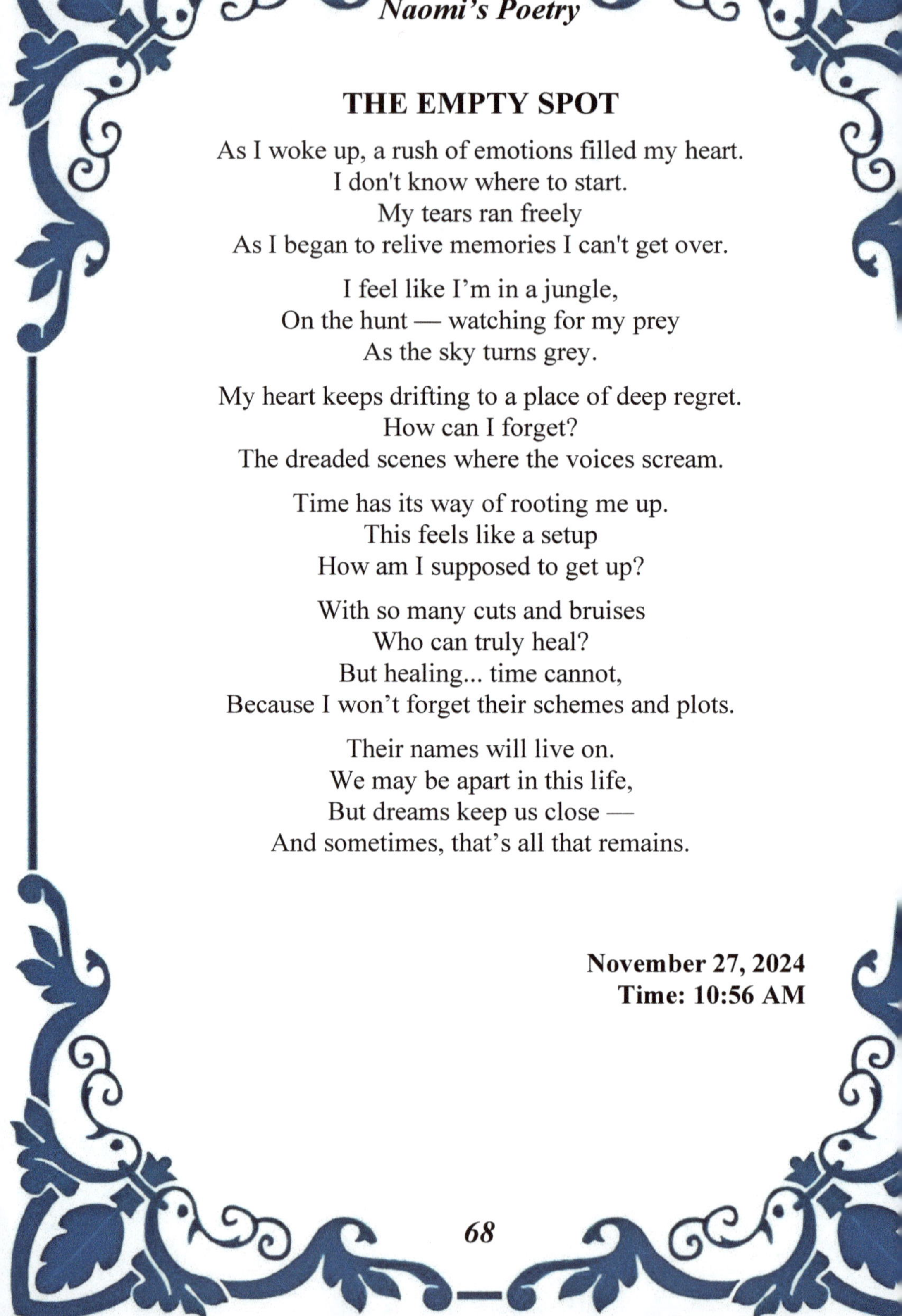

THE EMPTY SPOT

As I woke up, a rush of emotions filled my heart.
I don't know where to start.
My tears ran freely
As I began to relive memories I can't get over.

I feel like I'm in a jungle,
On the hunt — watching for my prey
As the sky turns grey.

My heart keeps drifting to a place of deep regret.
How can I forget?
The dreaded scenes where the voices scream.

Time has its way of rooting me up.
This feels like a setup
How am I supposed to get up?

With so many cuts and bruises
Who can truly heal?
But healing... time cannot,
Because I won't forget their schemes and plots.

Their names will live on.
We may be apart in this life,
But dreams keep us close —
And sometimes, that's all that remains.

November 27, 2024
Time: 10:56 AM

My heart keeps drifting
to a place of
deep regret.

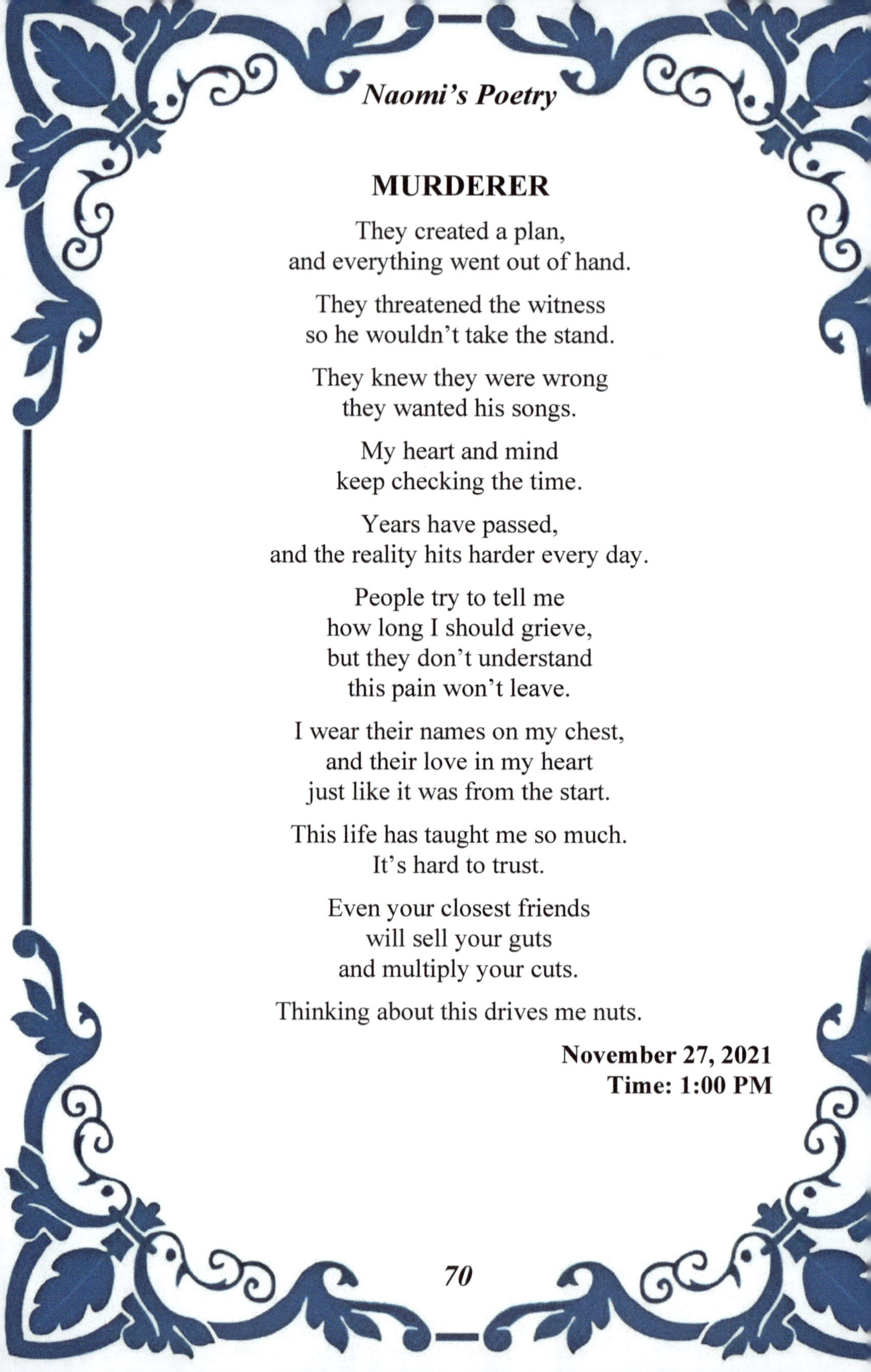

MURDERER

They created a plan,
and everything went out of hand.

They threatened the witness
so he wouldn't take the stand.

They knew they were wrong
they wanted his songs.

My heart and mind
keep checking the time.

Years have passed,
and the reality hits harder every day.

People try to tell me
how long I should grieve,
but they don't understand
this pain won't leave.

I wear their names on my chest,
and their love in my heart
just like it was from the start.

This life has taught me so much.
It's hard to trust.

Even your closest friends
will sell your guts
and multiply your cuts.

Thinking about this drives me nuts.

November 27, 2021
Time: 1:00 PM

I WEAR THEIR NAMES
MY CHEST. AN MY THEIR
HEIR LOVE IN MY HEART.

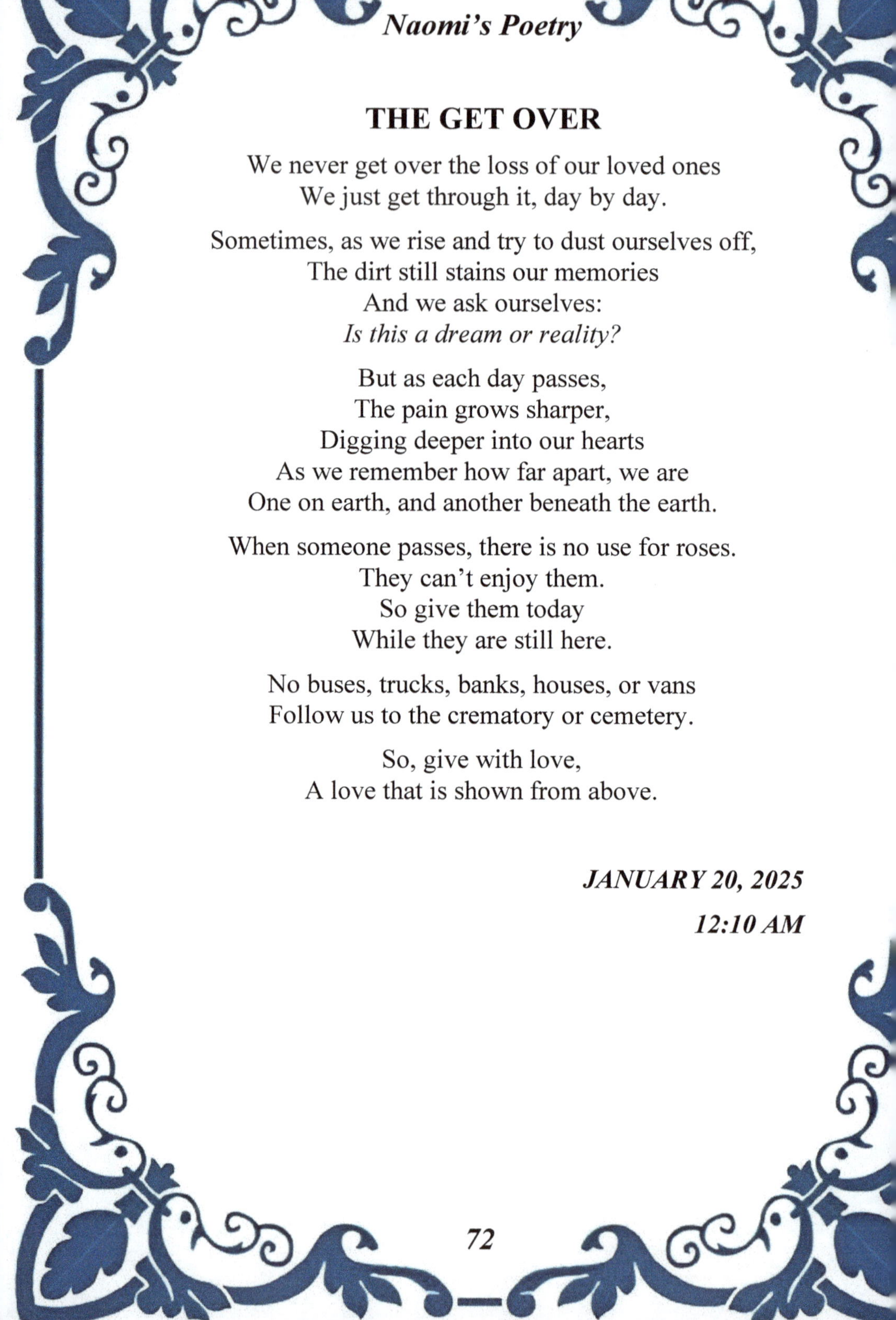

THE GET OVER

We never get over the loss of our loved ones
We just get through it, day by day.

Sometimes, as we rise and try to dust ourselves off,
The dirt still stains our memories
And we ask ourselves:
Is this a dream or reality?

But as each day passes,
The pain grows sharper,
Digging deeper into our hearts
As we remember how far apart, we are
One on earth, and another beneath the earth.

When someone passes, there is no use for roses.
They can't enjoy them.
So give them today
While they are still here.

No buses, trucks, banks, houses, or vans
Follow us to the crematory or cemetery.

So, give with love,
A love that is shown from above.

JANUARY 20, 2025

12:10 AM

WE NEVER GET OVR THE
LOSS of OUR LOVED ONES —
WE JUST GET THROUGH IT,
DAY BY DAY.

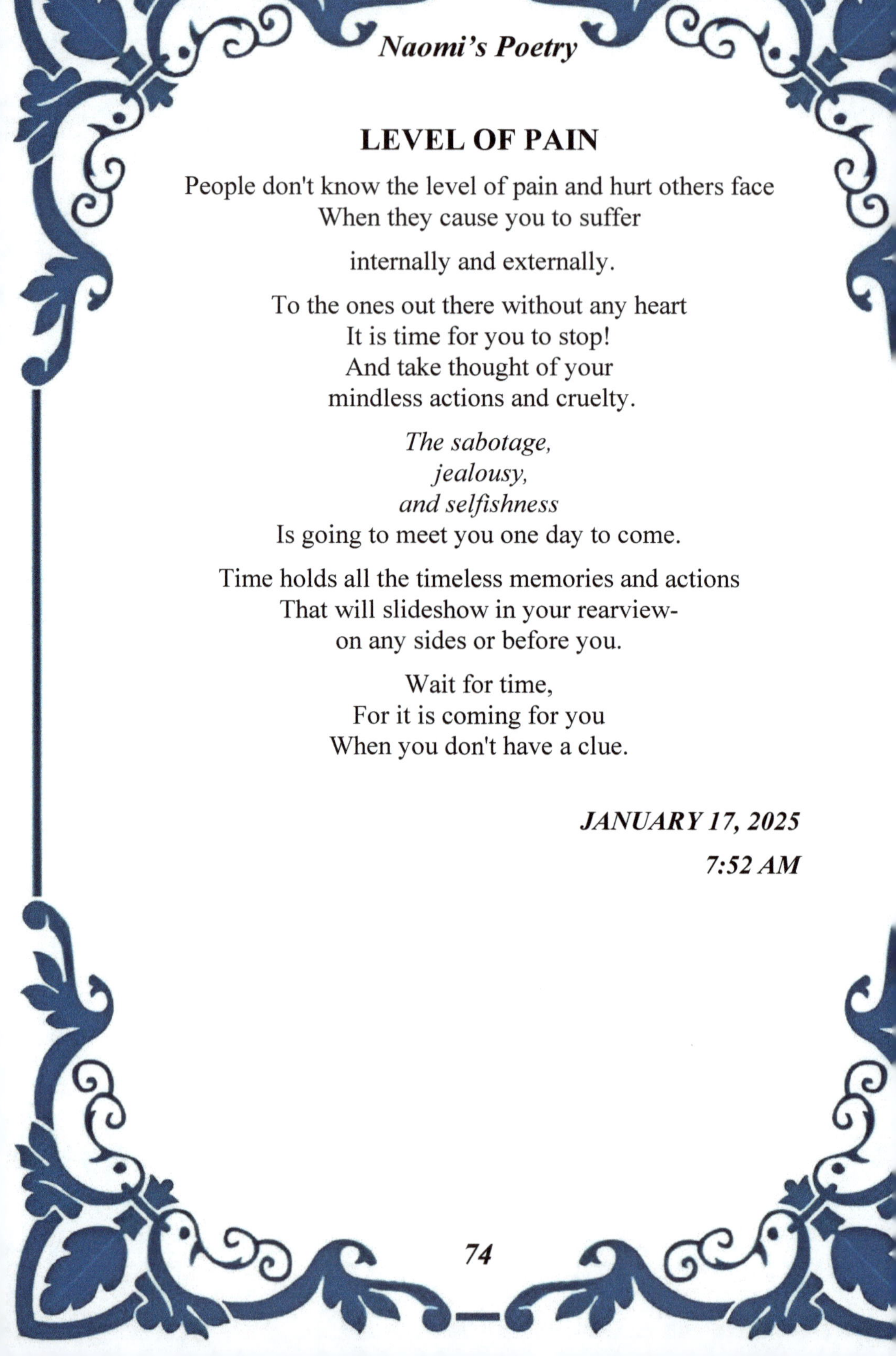

LEVEL OF PAIN

People don't know the level of pain and hurt others face
When they cause you to suffer

internally and externally.

To the ones out there without any heart
It is time for you to stop!
And take thought of your
mindless actions and cruelty.

The sabotage,
jealousy,
and selfishness
Is going to meet you one day to come.

Time holds all the timeless memories and actions
That will slideshow in your rearview-
on any sides or before you.

Wait for time,
For it is coming for you
When you don't have a clue.

JANUARY 17, 2025

7:52 AM

People don't know
the Level of Pain and
Hurt Others Face

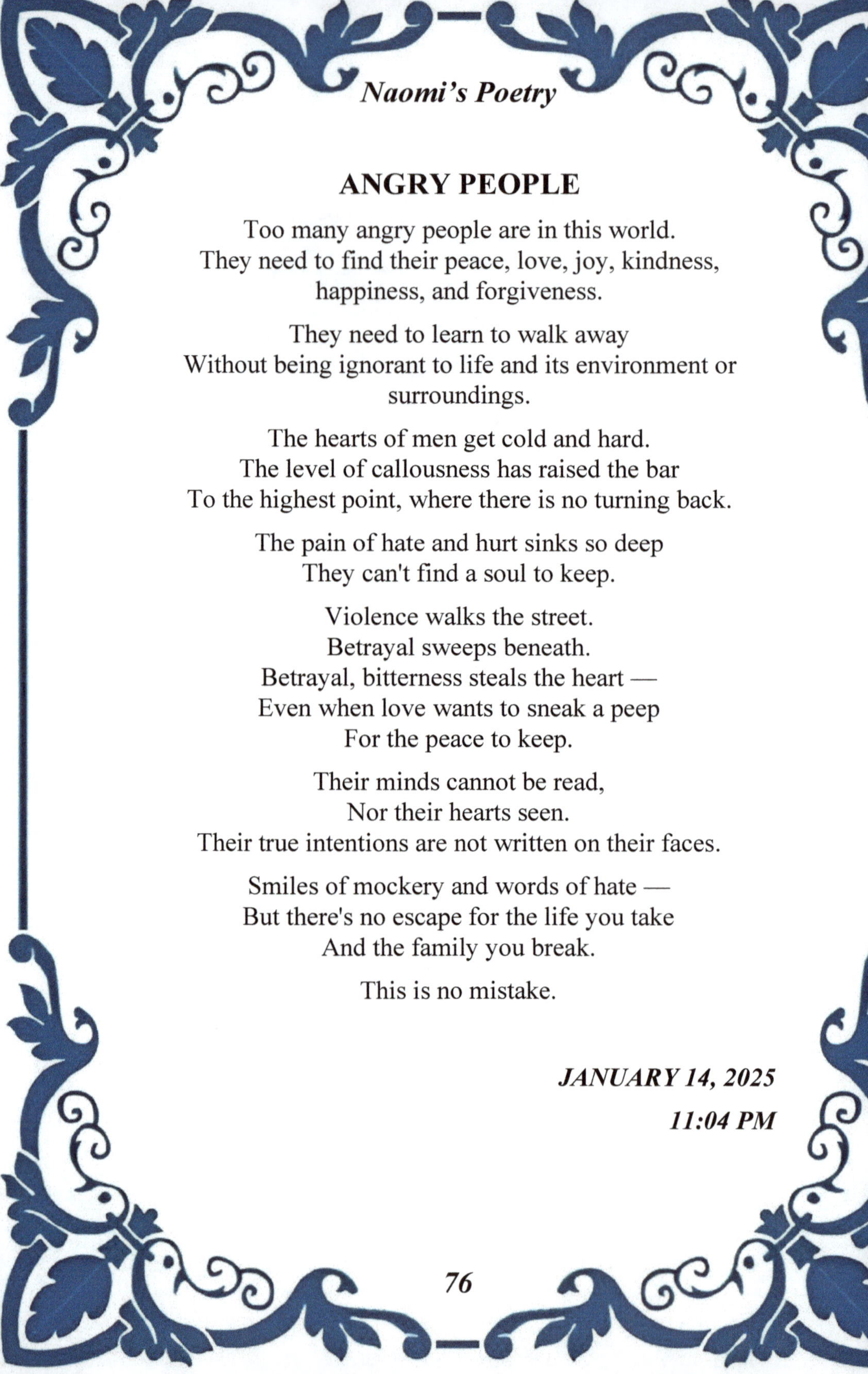

ANGRY PEOPLE

Too many angry people are in this world.
They need to find their peace, love, joy, kindness,
happiness, and forgiveness.

They need to learn to walk away
Without being ignorant to life and its environment or
surroundings.

The hearts of men get cold and hard.
The level of callousness has raised the bar
To the highest point, where there is no turning back.

The pain of hate and hurt sinks so deep
They can't find a soul to keep.

Violence walks the street.
Betrayal sweeps beneath.
Betrayal, bitterness steals the heart —
Even when love wants to sneak a peep
For the peace to keep.

Their minds cannot be read,
Nor their hearts seen.
Their true intentions are not written on their faces.

Smiles of mockery and words of hate —
But there's no escape for the life you take
And the family you break.

This is no mistake.

JANUARY 14, 2025
11:04 PM

TOO MANY
ANGRY PEOPLE
ARE IN THIS WORLD

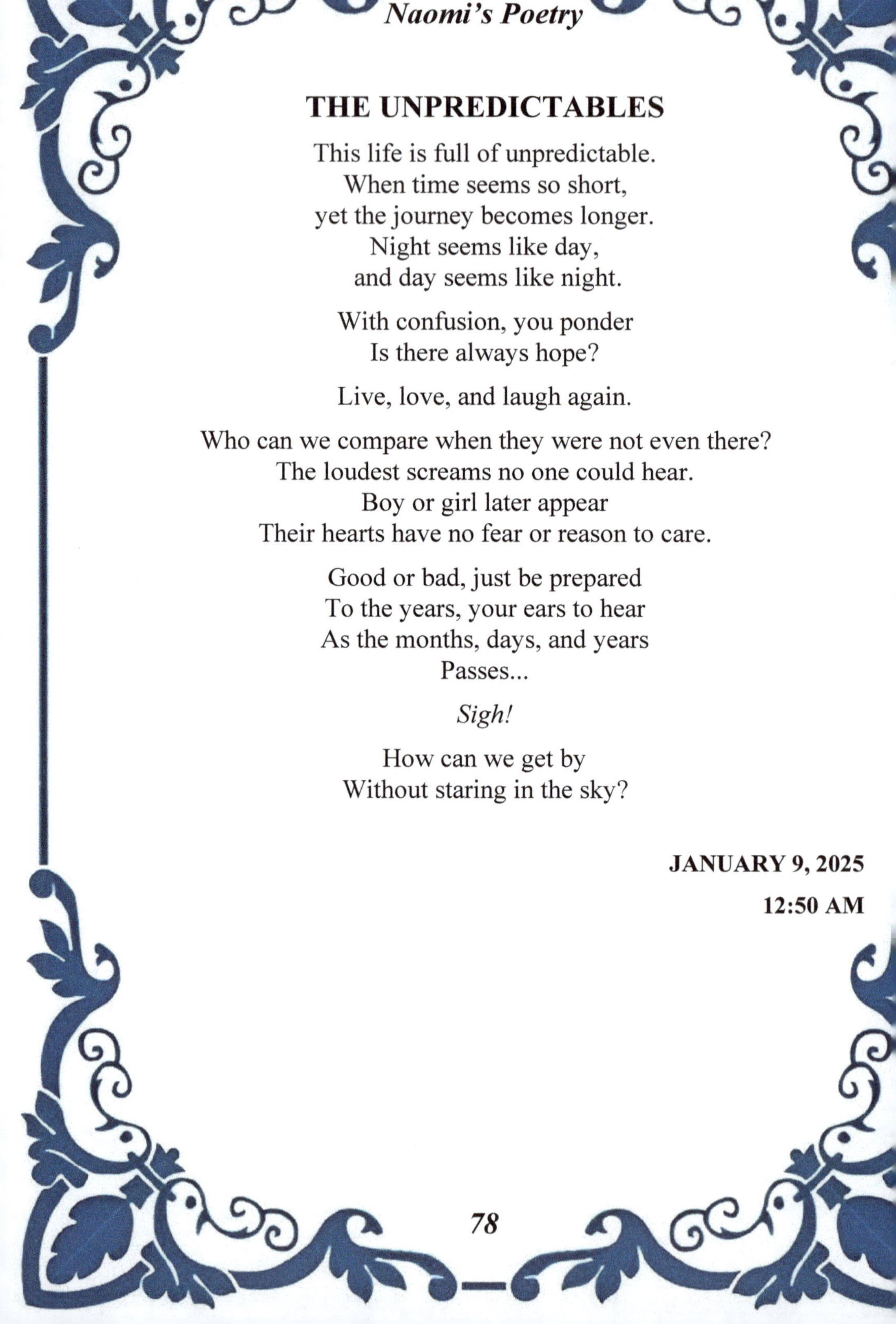

THE UNPREDICTABLES

This life is full of unpredictable.
When time seems so short,
yet the journey becomes longer.
Night seems like day,
and day seems like night.

With confusion, you ponder
Is there always hope?

Live, love, and laugh again.

Who can we compare when they were not even there?
The loudest screams no one could hear.
Boy or girl later appear
Their hearts have no fear or reason to care.

Good or bad, just be prepared
To the years, your ears to hear
As the months, days, and years
Passes...

Sigh!

How can we get by
Without staring in the sky?

JANUARY 9, 2025

12:50 AM

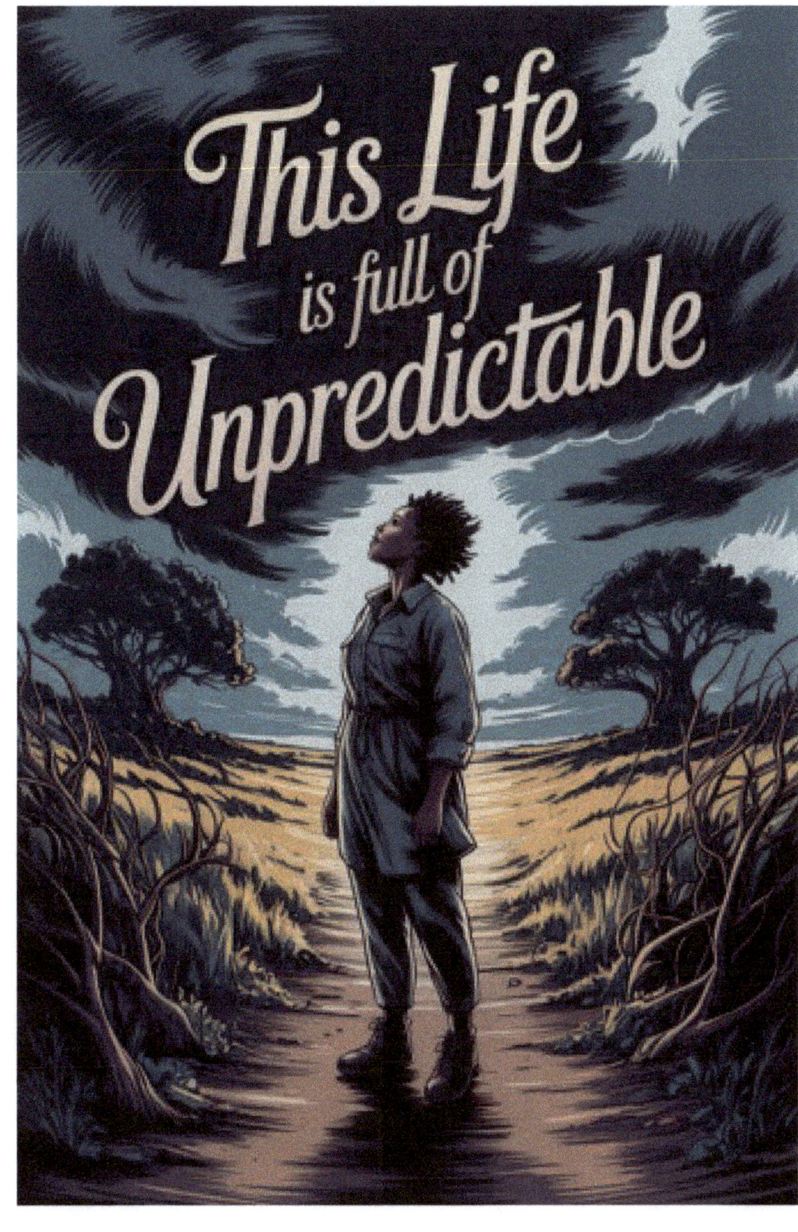

This Life
is full of
Unpredictable

BROKEN FOUNDATION

We were not rich, but we were satisfied with what we have.
We were not jealous of anyone or anything.
We used to gather together to celebrate our own,
While we still have life.

Flipping through the pages of life,
We were not anticipating the worst.

My articulation is not clear on how to explain everything.
The fracture in the foundation of our family is hard to mend.

Since the family splits apart,
We have to think positively
The best choice to make.

It is like a whirlwind of anger, grief,
Sorrow, rage, and pain.

The assault on my family was a bitter and grudgeful one
A grim of dents into our faces.

The betrayal stung us all over.
We have been consumed by pain.

Our loyalty, kindness, love, and caring heart
Led us not to observe those deceptive faces.

Mother's Day, birthdays, holidays,
And special occasions, (*You guys will be missed*)
The depth of our pain sometimes has to be masked.

Our lives felt dark and lonely.
This dreaded revelation combs through our bones.

The weight of conspiracy towards my family
Grows more unbearable, unimaginable,
Uncomfortable, and unforgettable.
We mourn every day.

JANUARY 8, 2024

10:00 PM

Naomi

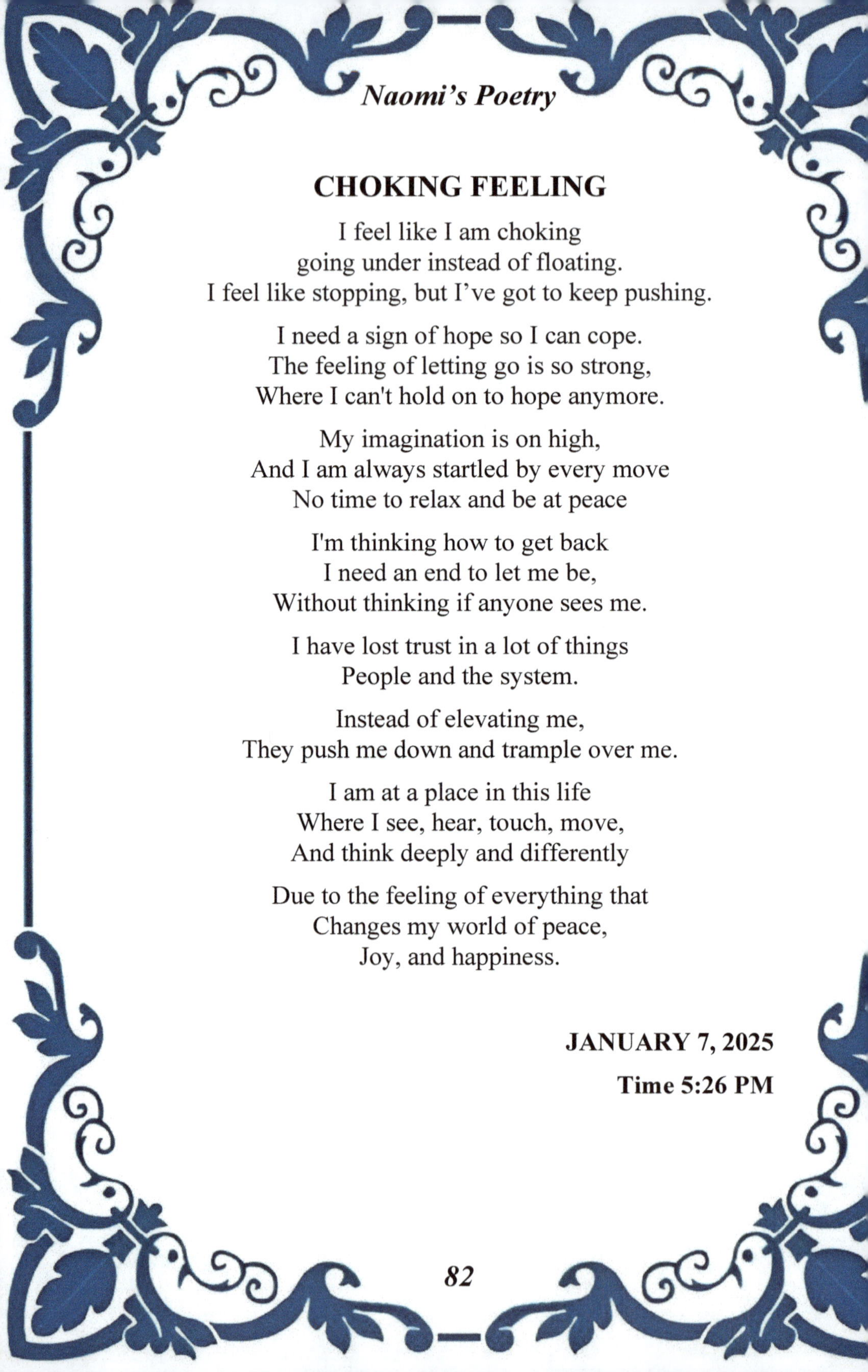

CHOKING FEELING

I feel like I am choking
going under instead of floating.
I feel like stopping, but I've got to keep pushing.

I need a sign of hope so I can cope.
The feeling of letting go is so strong,
Where I can't hold on to hope anymore.

My imagination is on high,
And I am always startled by every move
No time to relax and be at peace

I'm thinking how to get back
I need an end to let me be,
Without thinking if anyone sees me.

I have lost trust in a lot of things
People and the system.

Instead of elevating me,
They push me down and trample over me.

I am at a place in this life
Where I see, hear, touch, move,
And think deeply and differently

Due to the feeling of everything that
Changes my world of peace,
Joy, and happiness.

JANUARY 7, 2025

Time 5:26 PM

I feel like i am choking —
going under instead of floating

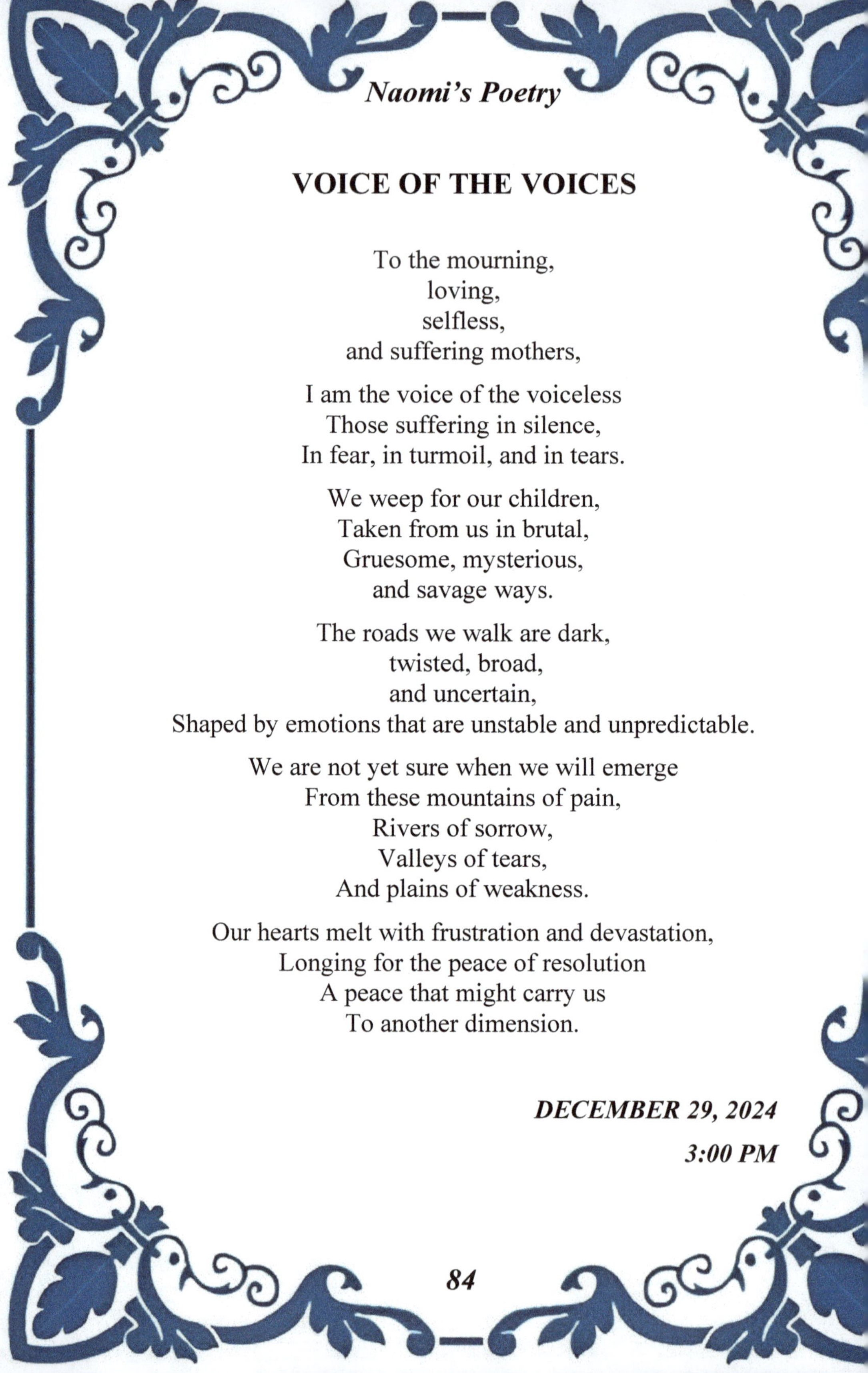

VOICE OF THE VOICES

To the mourning,
loving,
selfless,
and suffering mothers,

I am the voice of the voiceless
Those suffering in silence,
In fear, in turmoil, and in tears.

We weep for our children,
Taken from us in brutal,
Gruesome, mysterious,
and savage ways.

The roads we walk are dark,
twisted, broad,
and uncertain,
Shaped by emotions that are unstable and unpredictable.

We are not yet sure when we will emerge
From these mountains of pain,
Rivers of sorrow,
Valleys of tears,
And plains of weakness.

Our hearts melt with frustration and devastation,
Longing for the peace of resolution
A peace that might carry us
To another dimension.

DECEMBER 29, 2024

3:00 PM

I AM THE
VOICE
OF THE
VOICELESS

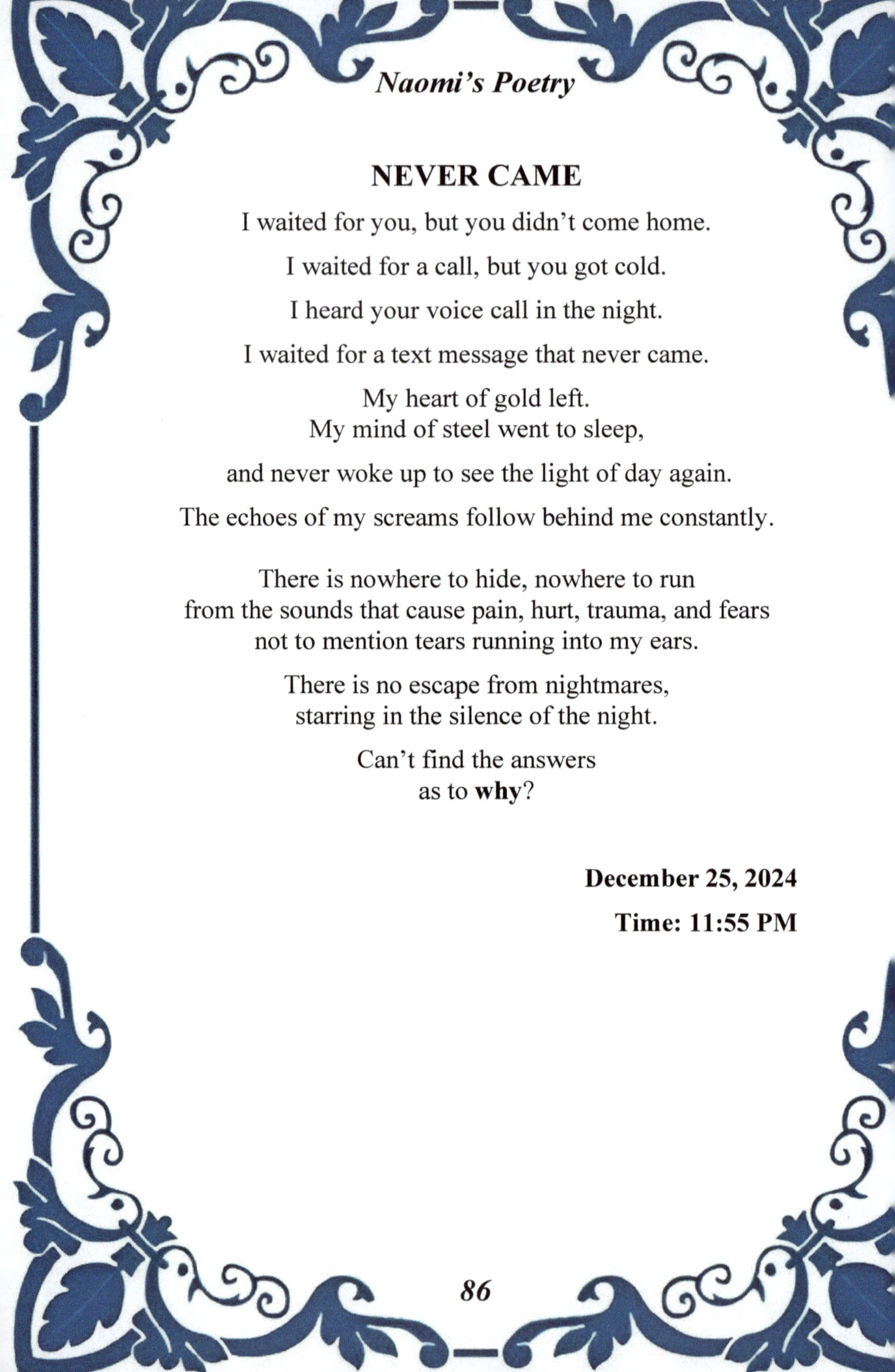

NEVER CAME

I waited for you, but you didn't come home.

I waited for a call, but you got cold.

I heard your voice call in the night.

I waited for a text message that never came.

My heart of gold left.
My mind of steel went to sleep,

and never woke up to see the light of day again.

The echoes of my screams follow behind me constantly.

There is nowhere to hide, nowhere to run
from the sounds that cause pain, hurt, trauma, and fears
not to mention tears running into my ears.

There is no escape from nightmares,
starring in the silence of the night.

Can't find the answers
as to **why**?

December 25, 2024

Time: 11:55 PM

I waited for you,
but you di dddn't
come home.

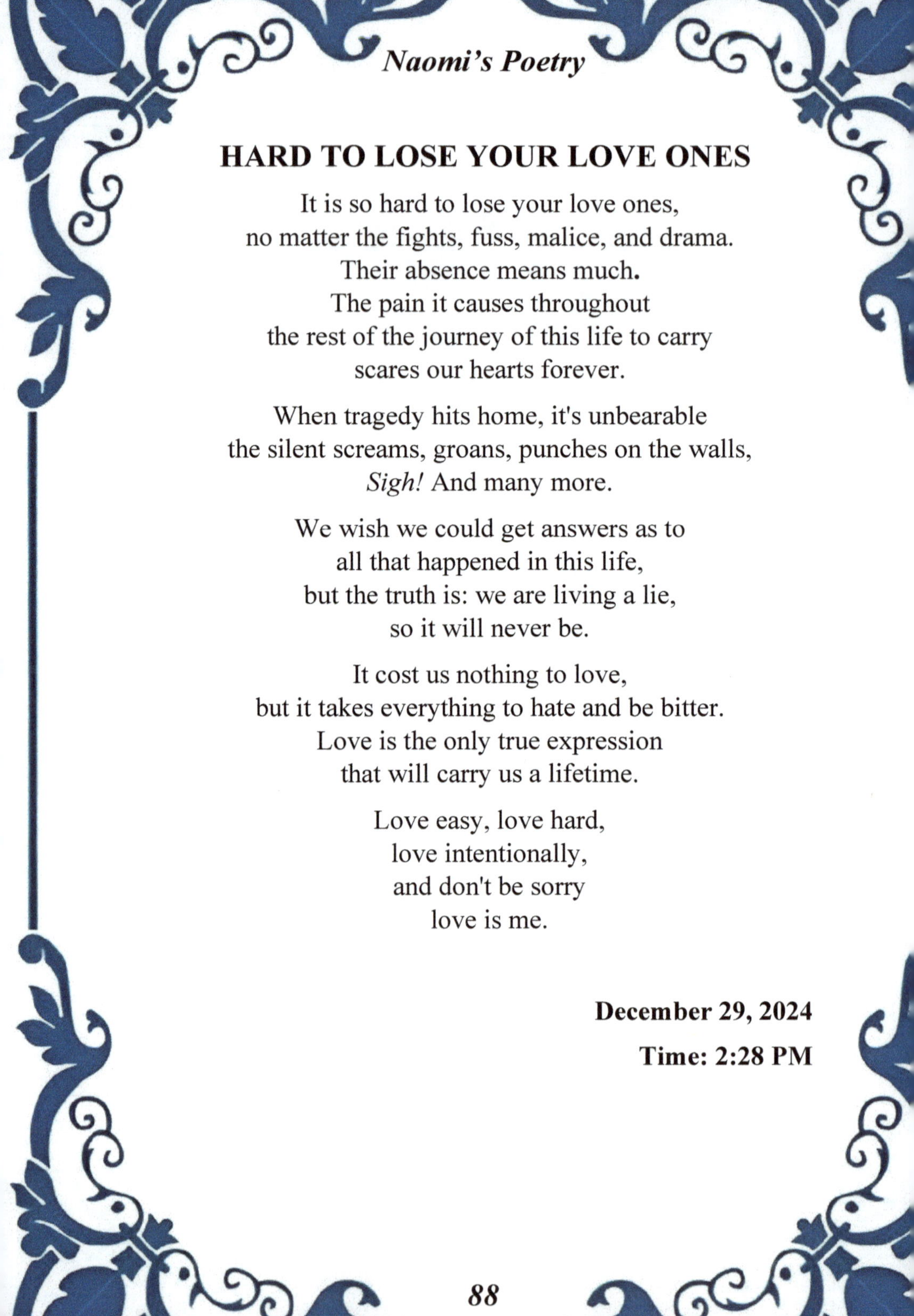

HARD TO LOSE YOUR LOVE ONES

It is so hard to lose your love ones,
no matter the fights, fuss, malice, and drama.
Their absence means much.
The pain it causes throughout
the rest of the journey of this life to carry
scares our hearts forever.

When tragedy hits home, it's unbearable
the silent screams, groans, punches on the walls,
Sigh! And many more.

We wish we could get answers as to
all that happened in this life,
but the truth is: we are living a lie,
so it will never be.

It cost us nothing to love,
but it takes everything to hate and be bitter.
Love is the only true expression
that will carry us a lifetime.

Love easy, love hard,
love intentionally,
and don't be sorry
love is me.

December 29, 2024

Time: 2:28 PM

HARD TO LOSE
YOUR LOVED ONES

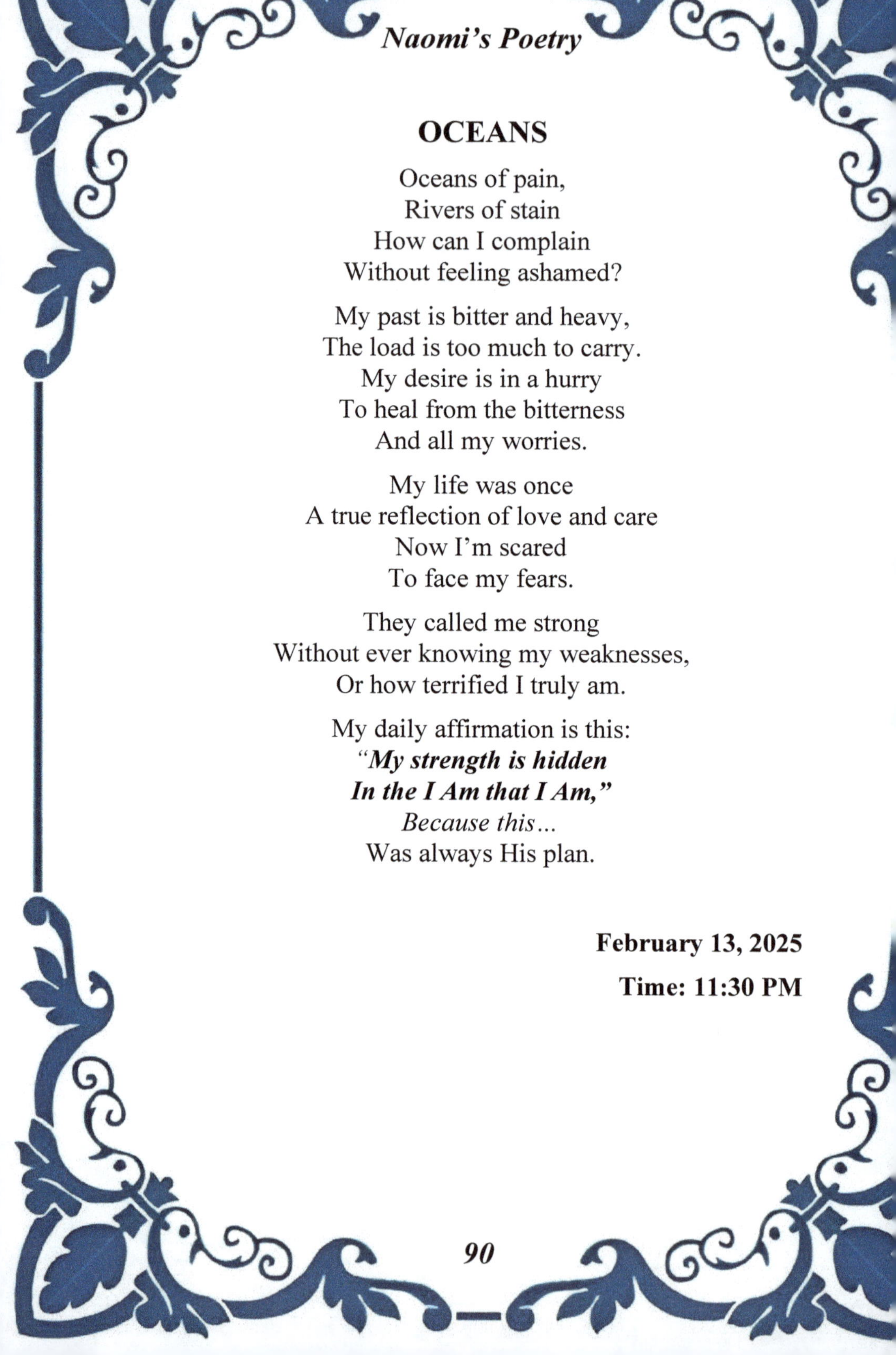

OCEANS

Oceans of pain,
Rivers of stain
How can I complain
Without feeling ashamed?

My past is bitter and heavy,
The load is too much to carry.
My desire is in a hurry
To heal from the bitterness
And all my worries.

My life was once
A true reflection of love and care
Now I'm scared
To face my fears.

They called me strong
Without ever knowing my weaknesses,
Or how terrified I truly am.

My daily affirmation is this:
***"My strength is hidden
In the I Am that I Am,"***
Because this…
Was always His plan.

February 13, 2025
Time: 11:30 PM

My strength is hidden
in the I am that I Am

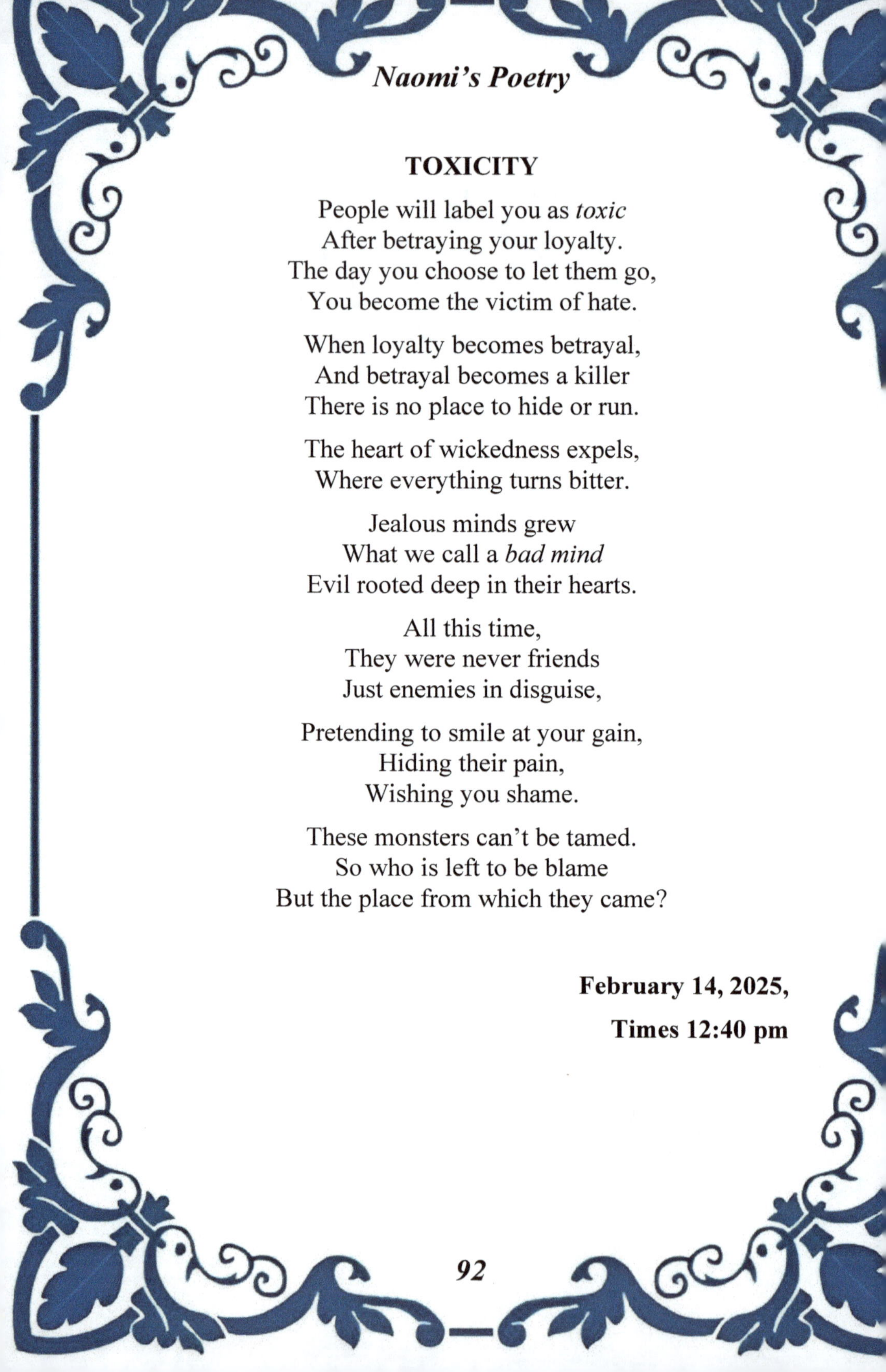

TOXICITY

People will label you as *toxic*
After betraying your loyalty.
The day you choose to let them go,
You become the victim of hate.

When loyalty becomes betrayal,
And betrayal becomes a killer
There is no place to hide or run.

The heart of wickedness expels,
Where everything turns bitter.

Jealous minds grew
What we call a *bad mind*
Evil rooted deep in their hearts.

All this time,
They were never friends
Just enemies in disguise,

Pretending to smile at your gain,
Hiding their pain,
Wishing you shame.

These monsters can't be tamed.
So who is left to be blame
But the place from which they came?

February 14, 2025,

Times 12:40 pm

LIFE HAPPENS

In the worst moments of one's life.
The pain that weakens you,
Tears you apart
Shuts down your heart,
Body, mind, and soul.

You feel like you have no control.
I'm ripped to pieces every day,
Wondering what to say,
When depression keeps pressing on my mind
And the only thought is:
Give in… let depression win.

But there's a song
That you and I can sing
And a word God gave
To help us win.

After that…
We'll be flying on His wings,
Singing with the angels,
On streets of gold
We made it.

February 15, 2025

Time: 11:07 PM

When depression keeps
pressing on my mind

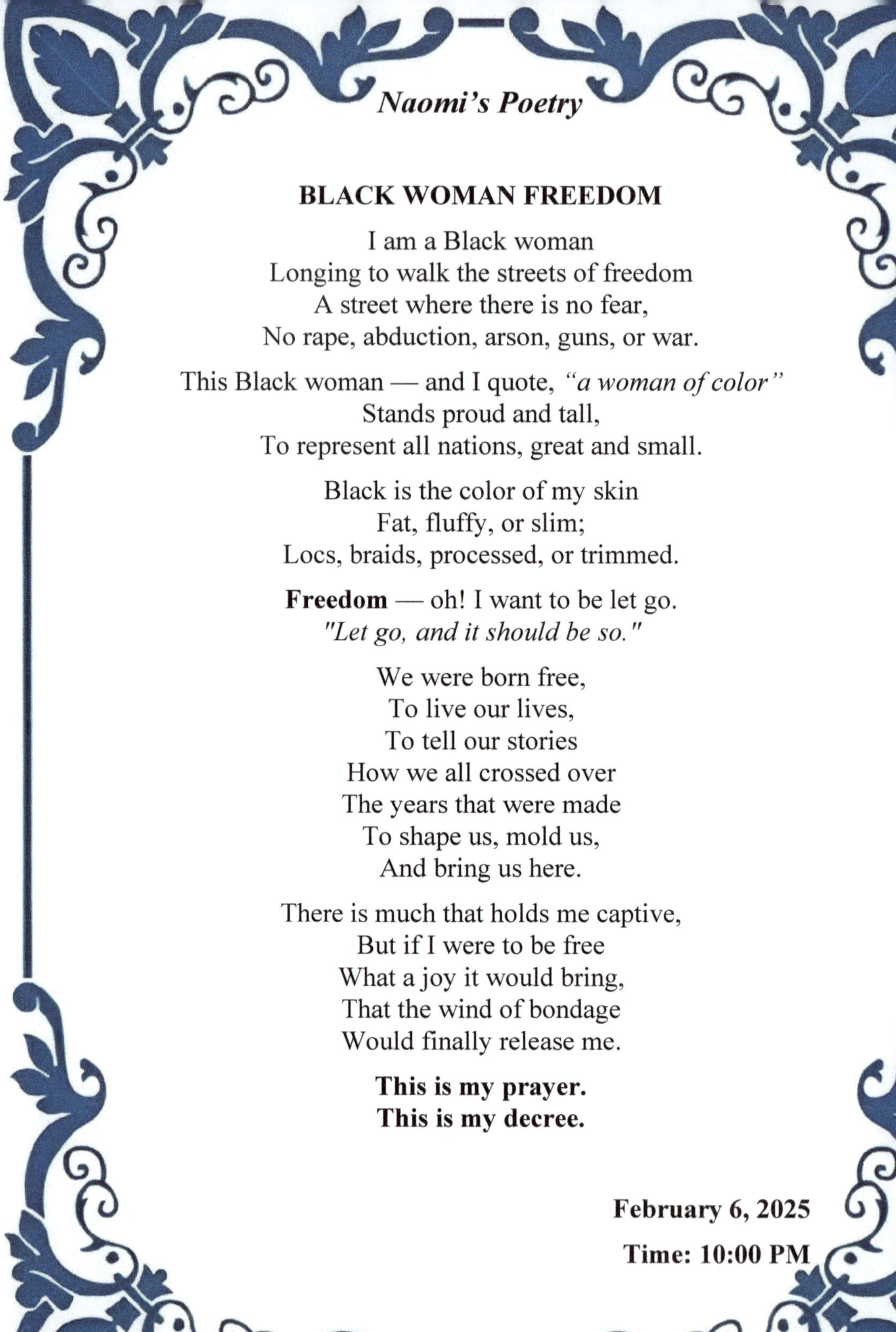

BLACK WOMAN FREEDOM

I am a Black woman
Longing to walk the streets of freedom
A street where there is no fear,
No rape, abduction, arson, guns, or war.

This Black woman — and I quote, *"a woman of color"*
Stands proud and tall,
To represent all nations, great and small.

Black is the color of my skin
Fat, fluffy, or slim;
Locs, braids, processed, or trimmed.

Freedom — oh! I want to be let go.
"Let go, and it should be so."

We were born free,
To live our lives,
To tell our stories
How we all crossed over
The years that were made
To shape us, mold us,
And bring us here.

There is much that holds me captive,
But if I were to be free
What a joy it would bring,
That the wind of bondage
Would finally release me.

This is my prayer.
This is my decree.

February 6, 2025

Time: 10:00 PM

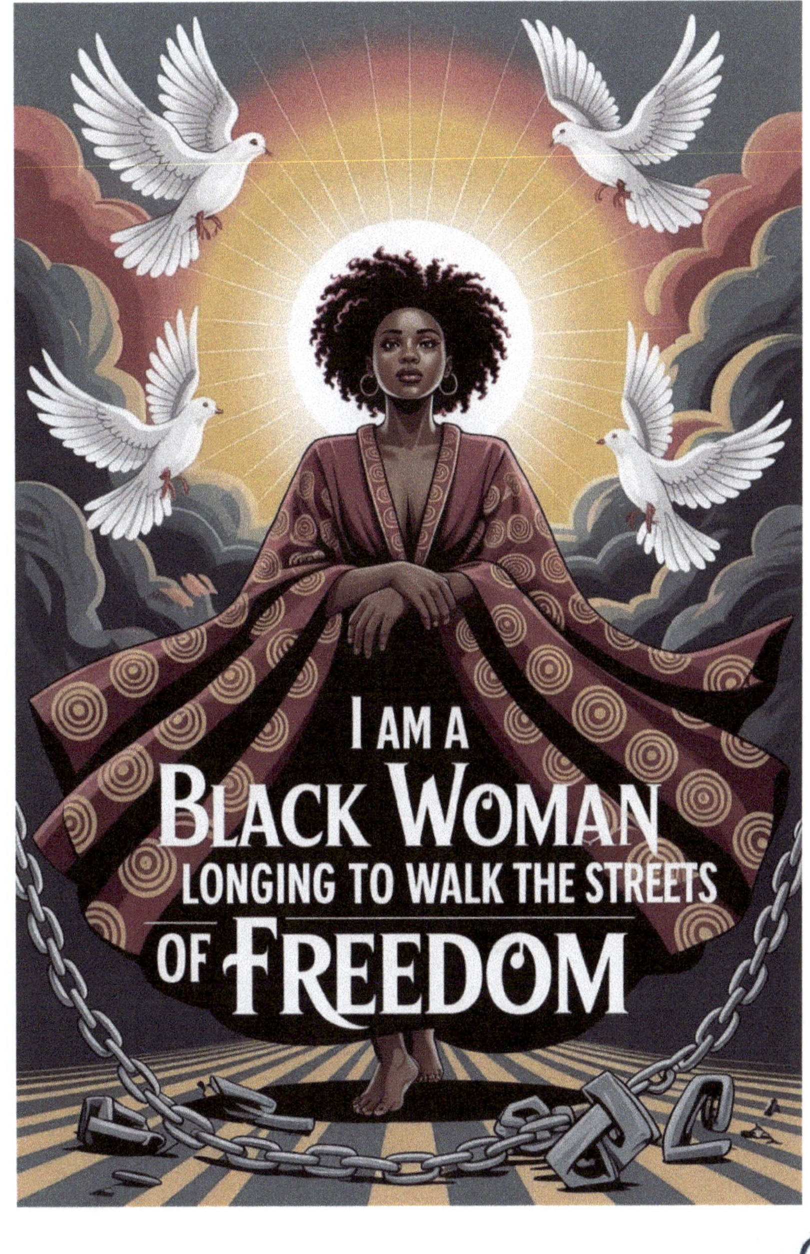
I AM A
BLACK WOMAN
LONGING TO WALK THE STREETS
OF FREEDOM

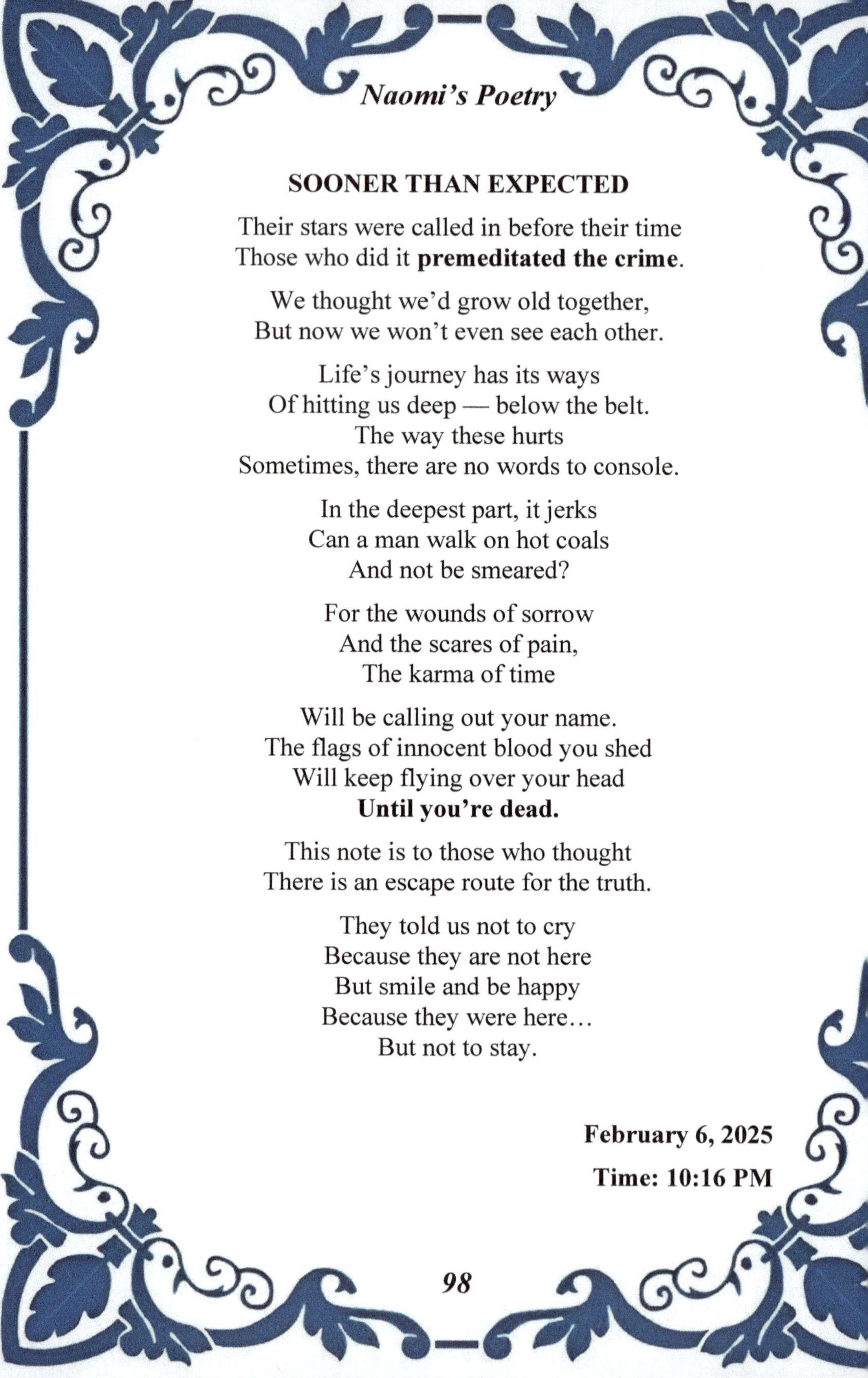

SOONER THAN EXPECTED

Their stars were called in before their time
Those who did it **premeditated the crime**.

We thought we'd grow old together,
But now we won't even see each other.

Life's journey has its ways
Of hitting us deep — below the belt.
The way these hurts
Sometimes, there are no words to console.

In the deepest part, it jerks
Can a man walk on hot coals
And not be smeared?

For the wounds of sorrow
And the scares of pain,
The karma of time

Will be calling out your name.
The flags of innocent blood you shed
Will keep flying over your head
Until you're dead.

This note is to those who thought
There is an escape route for the truth.

They told us not to cry
Because they are not here
But smile and be happy
Because they were here…
But not to stay.

February 6, 2025
Time: 10:16 PM

"Their stars were called in before their time —
but the truth will always rise with them."

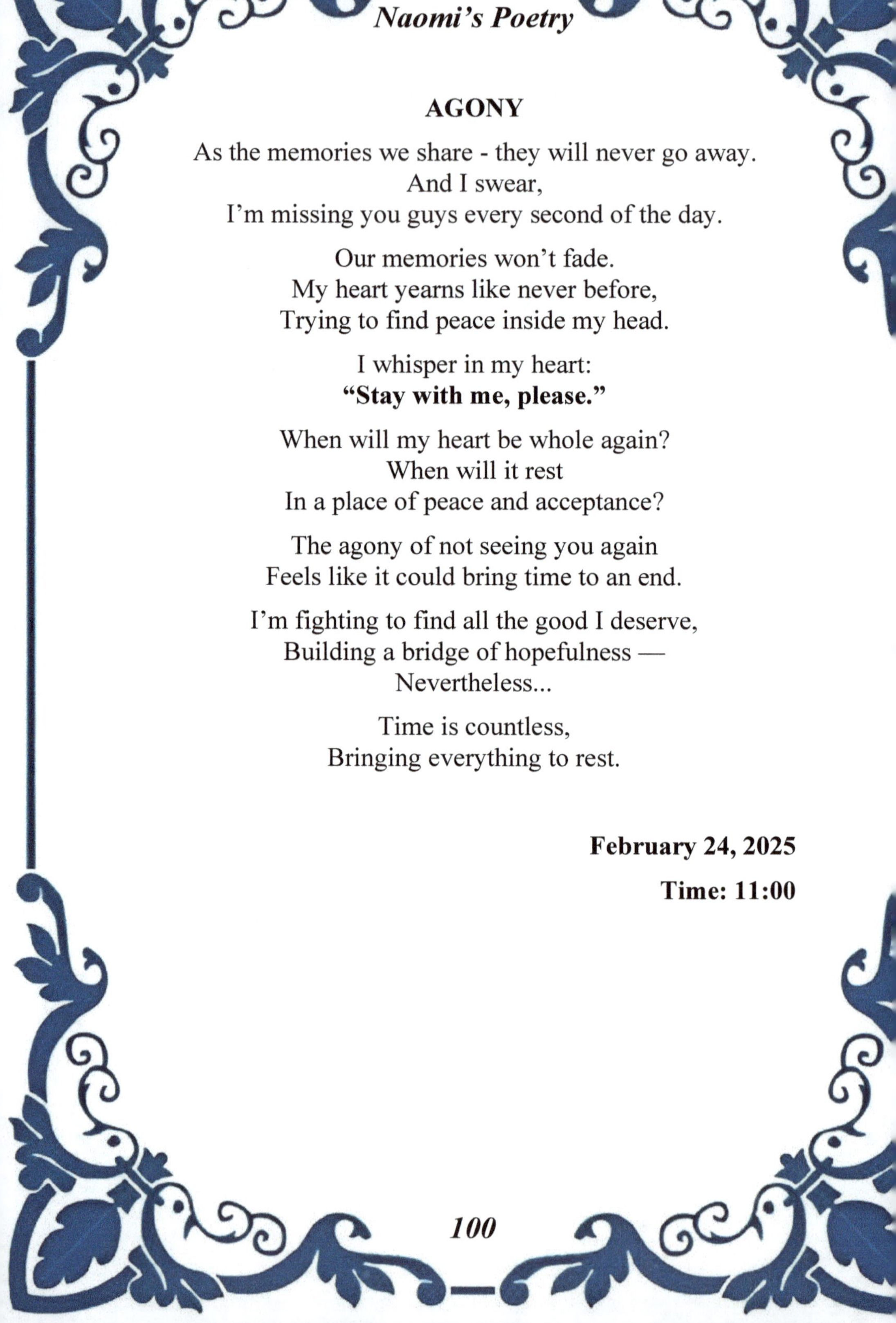

AGONY

As the memories we share - they will never go away.
And I swear,
I'm missing you guys every second of the day.

Our memories won't fade.
My heart yearns like never before,
Trying to find peace inside my head.

I whisper in my heart:
"Stay with me, please."

When will my heart be whole again?
When will it rest
In a place of peace and acceptance?

The agony of not seeing you again
Feels like it could bring time to an end.

I'm fighting to find all the good I deserve,
Building a bridge of hopefulness —
Nevertheless...

Time is countless,
Bringing everything to rest.

February 24, 2025

Time: 11:00

The agony of missing you buidges betwen pain and hope.

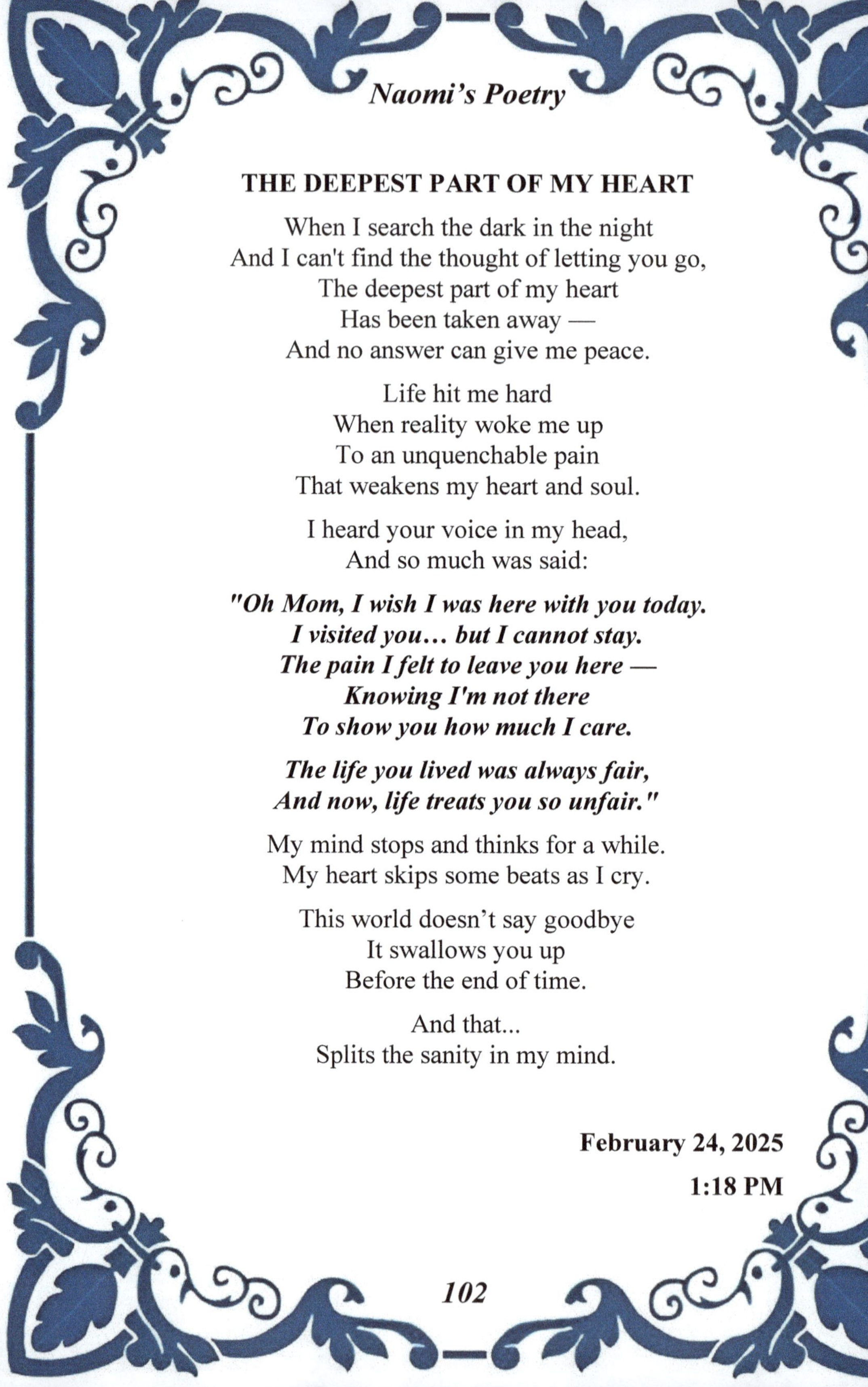

THE DEEPEST PART OF MY HEART

When I search the dark in the night
And I can't find the thought of letting you go,
The deepest part of my heart
Has been taken away —
And no answer can give me peace.

Life hit me hard
When reality woke me up
To an unquenchable pain
That weakens my heart and soul.

I heard your voice in my head,
And so much was said:

*"Oh Mom, I wish I was here with you today.
I visited you… but I cannot stay.
The pain I felt to leave you here —
Knowing I'm not there
To show you how much I care.*

*The life you lived was always fair,
And now, life treats you so unfair."*

My mind stops and thinks for a while.
My heart skips some beats as I cry.

This world doesn't say goodbye
It swallows you up
Before the end of time.

And that...
Splits the sanity in my mind.

February 24, 2025

1:18 PM

The deepest part of
my heart was taken,
away, yet your
voice still stays

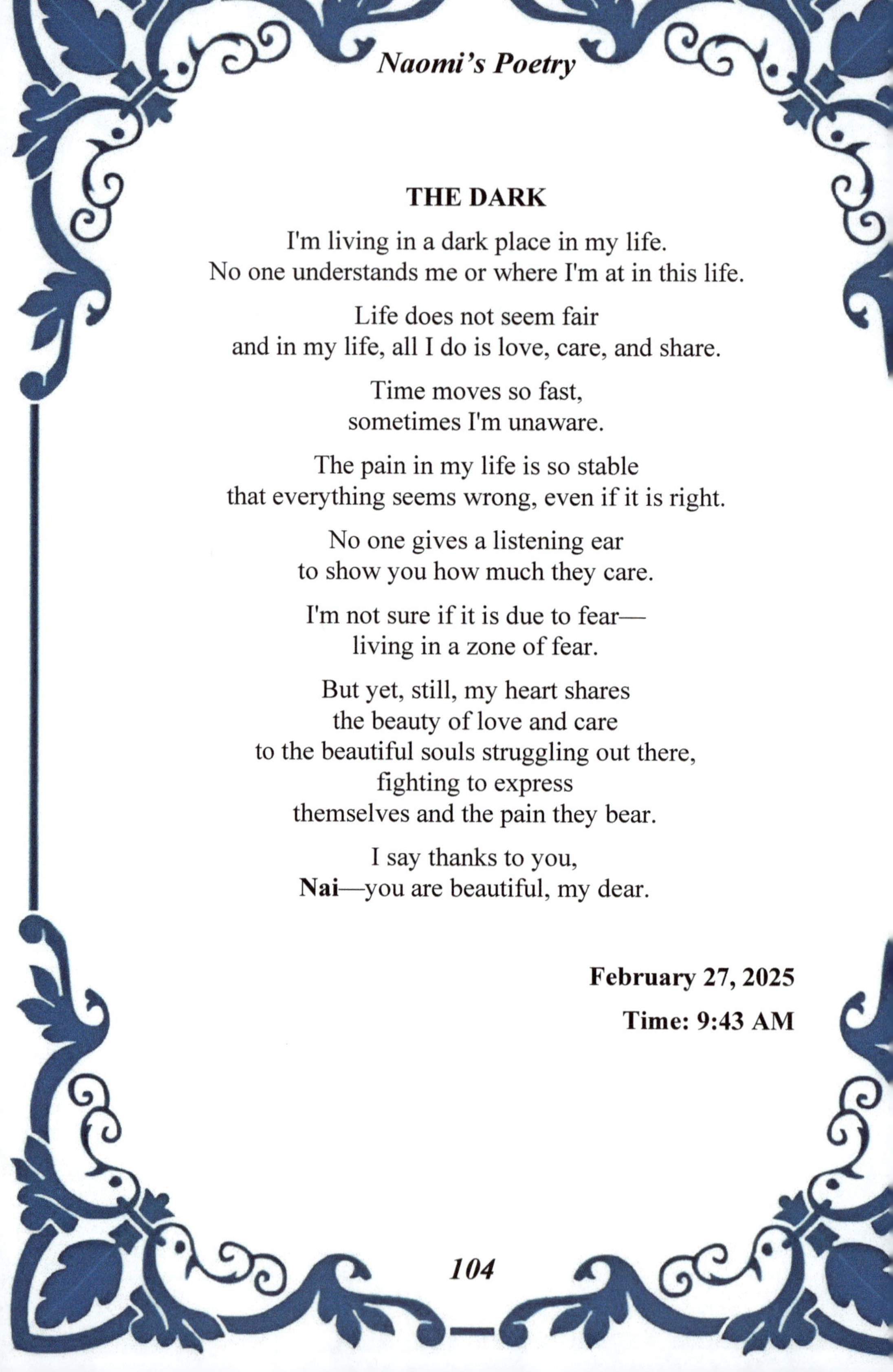

THE DARK

I'm living in a dark place in my life.
No one understands me or where I'm at in this life.

Life does not seem fair
and in my life, all I do is love, care, and share.

Time moves so fast,
sometimes I'm unaware.

The pain in my life is so stable
that everything seems wrong, even if it is right.

No one gives a listening ear
to show you how much they care.

I'm not sure if it is due to fear—
living in a zone of fear.

But yet, still, my heart shares
the beauty of love and care
to the beautiful souls struggling out there,
fighting to express
themselves and the pain they bear.

I say thanks to you,
Nai—you are beautiful, my dear.

February 27, 2025

Time: 9:43 AM

Even in the dark,
my heart still shares love.

TRAUMA

The past will come back to haunt the unflinching killers
of my family.

Trauma has codes that can be seen or heard.
Trauma can live secretly in you
and play the tune of a psychopath.

Trauma is deep, painful, and sometimes remorseful.
Traumas are unseen and unheard.
Trauma can speak in silence.

Look, hear, and feel.
Use your imagination, feelings, and emotions
as you can always see, hear, and feel.
Trauma is a ***Monster***.

Understanding can live in a dark place
and that is the only place you might feel safe.

The thumping of your heart
that gives that sound when you are afraid,
lonely, and scared…
You are startled by every move.

Not living—just existing in memories,
A pain to dangle and tangle with.

We want to be ourselves,
but trauma is at every door you open,
and every lock you turn
facing you in this cold and painful world.

February 27, 2025

Time: 6:45 PM

TRAUMA IS A MONSTER, …
YET FACE EVERY DOOR,
FEAR, PAIN, LOSS,
PAIN PAIN LOSS,
SURVIVE

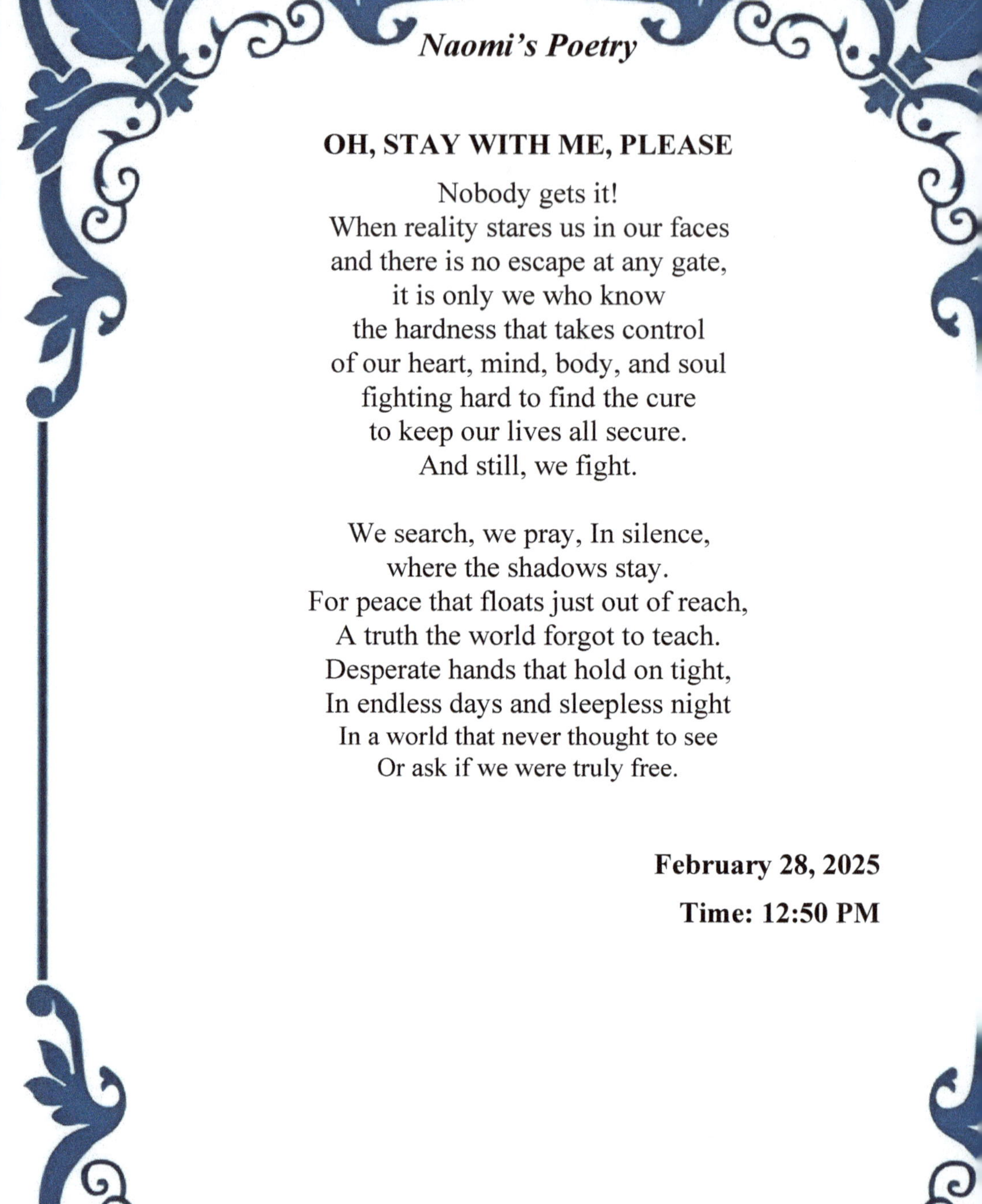

OH, STAY WITH ME, PLEASE

Nobody gets it!
When reality stares us in our faces
and there is no escape at any gate,
it is only we who know
the hardness that takes control
of our heart, mind, body, and soul
fighting hard to find the cure
to keep our lives all secure.
And still, we fight.

We search, we pray, In silence,
where the shadows stay.
For peace that floats just out of reach,
A truth the world forgot to teach.
Desperate hands that hold on tight,
In endless days and sleepless night
In a world that never thought to see
Or ask if we were truly free.

February 28, 2025
Time: 12:50 PM

NOBODY GETS IT --
YET STILL,
I FIGHT TO BE FREE

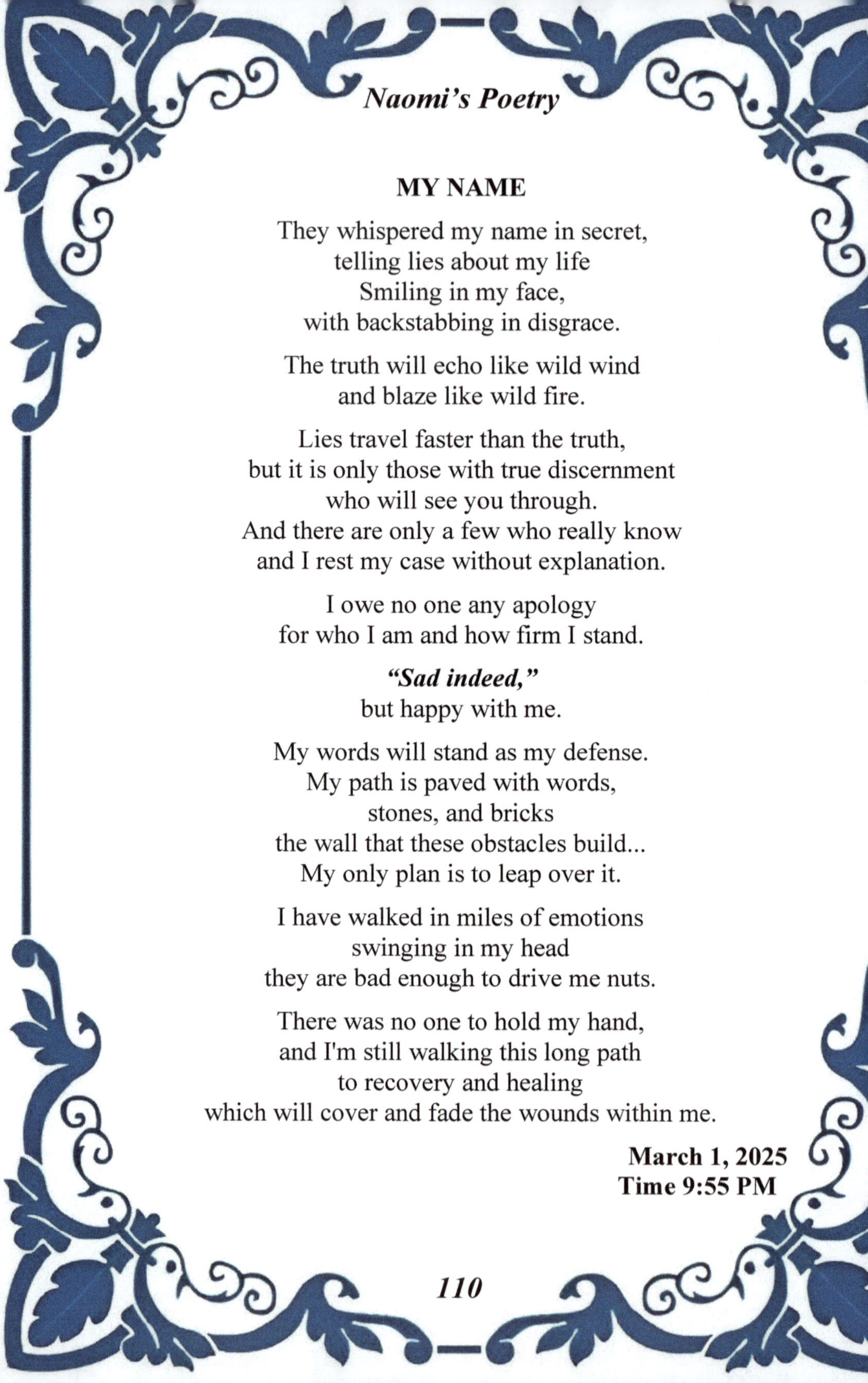

Naomi's Poetry

MY NAME

They whispered my name in secret,
telling lies about my life
Smiling in my face,
with backstabbing in disgrace.

The truth will echo like wild wind
and blaze like wild fire.

Lies travel faster than the truth,
but it is only those with true discernment
who will see you through.
And there are only a few who really know
and I rest my case without explanation.

I owe no one any apology
for who I am and how firm I stand.

"Sad indeed,"
but happy with me.

My words will stand as my defense.
My path is paved with words,
stones, and bricks
the wall that these obstacles build...
My only plan is to leap over it.

I have walked in miles of emotions
swinging in my head
they are bad enough to drive me nuts.

There was no one to hold my hand,
and I'm still walking this long path
to recovery and healing
which will cover and fade the wounds within me.

March 1, 2025
Time 9:55 PM

110

Lonely, Broken Mother
— is that my name?

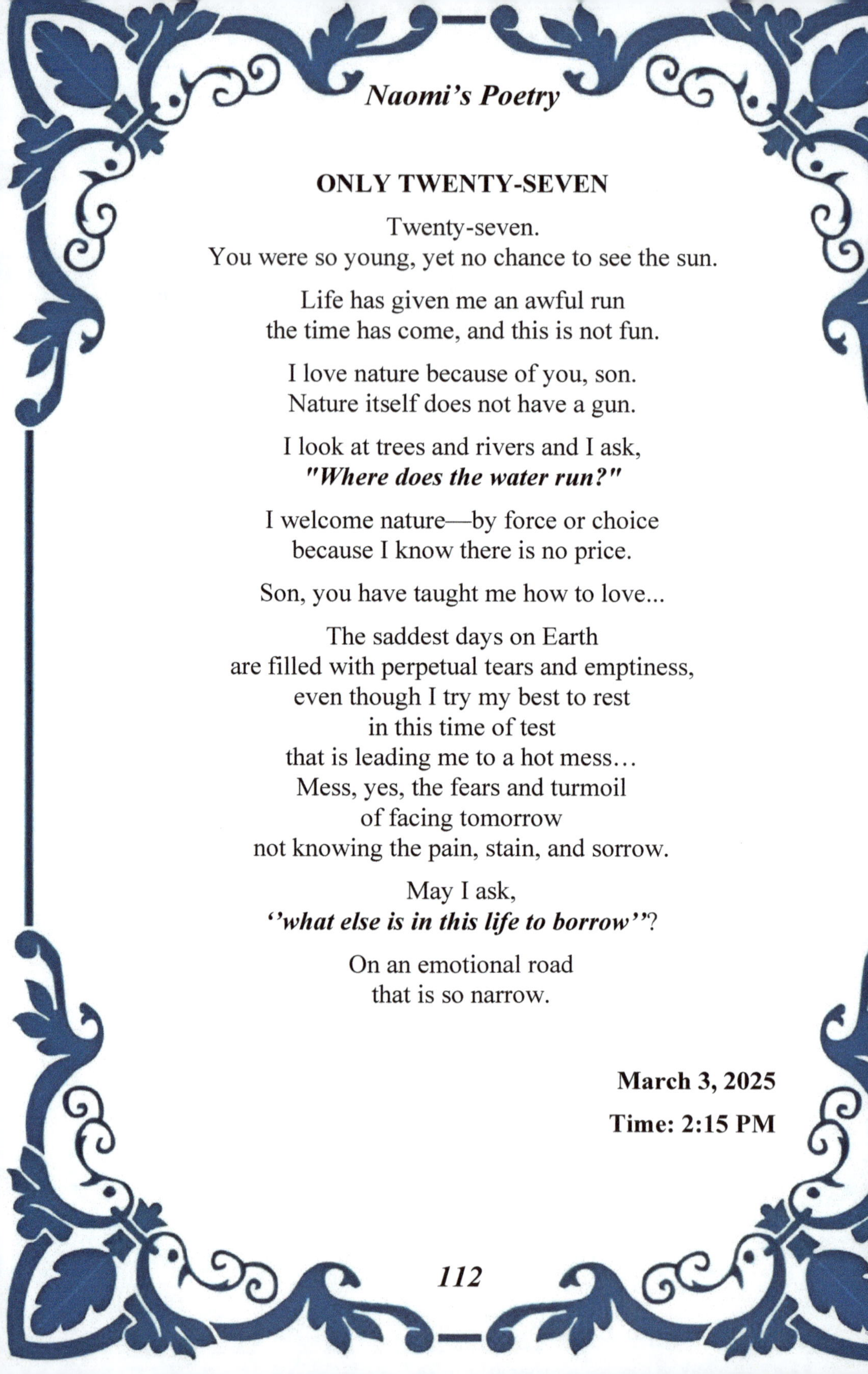
Naomi's Poetry

ONLY TWENTY-SEVEN

Twenty-seven.
You were so young, yet no chance to see the sun.

Life has given me an awful run
the time has come, and this is not fun.

I love nature because of you, son.
Nature itself does not have a gun.

I look at trees and rivers and I ask,
"Where does the water run?"

I welcome nature—by force or choice
because I know there is no price.

Son, you have taught me how to love...

The saddest days on Earth
are filled with perpetual tears and emptiness,
even though I try my best to rest
in this time of test
that is leading me to a hot mess…
Mess, yes, the fears and turmoil
of facing tomorrow
not knowing the pain, stain, and sorrow.

May I ask,
''what else is in this life to borrow''?

On an emotional road
that is so narrow.

March 3, 2025

Time: 2:15 PM

112

You were so young,
yet no chance to see the sun.

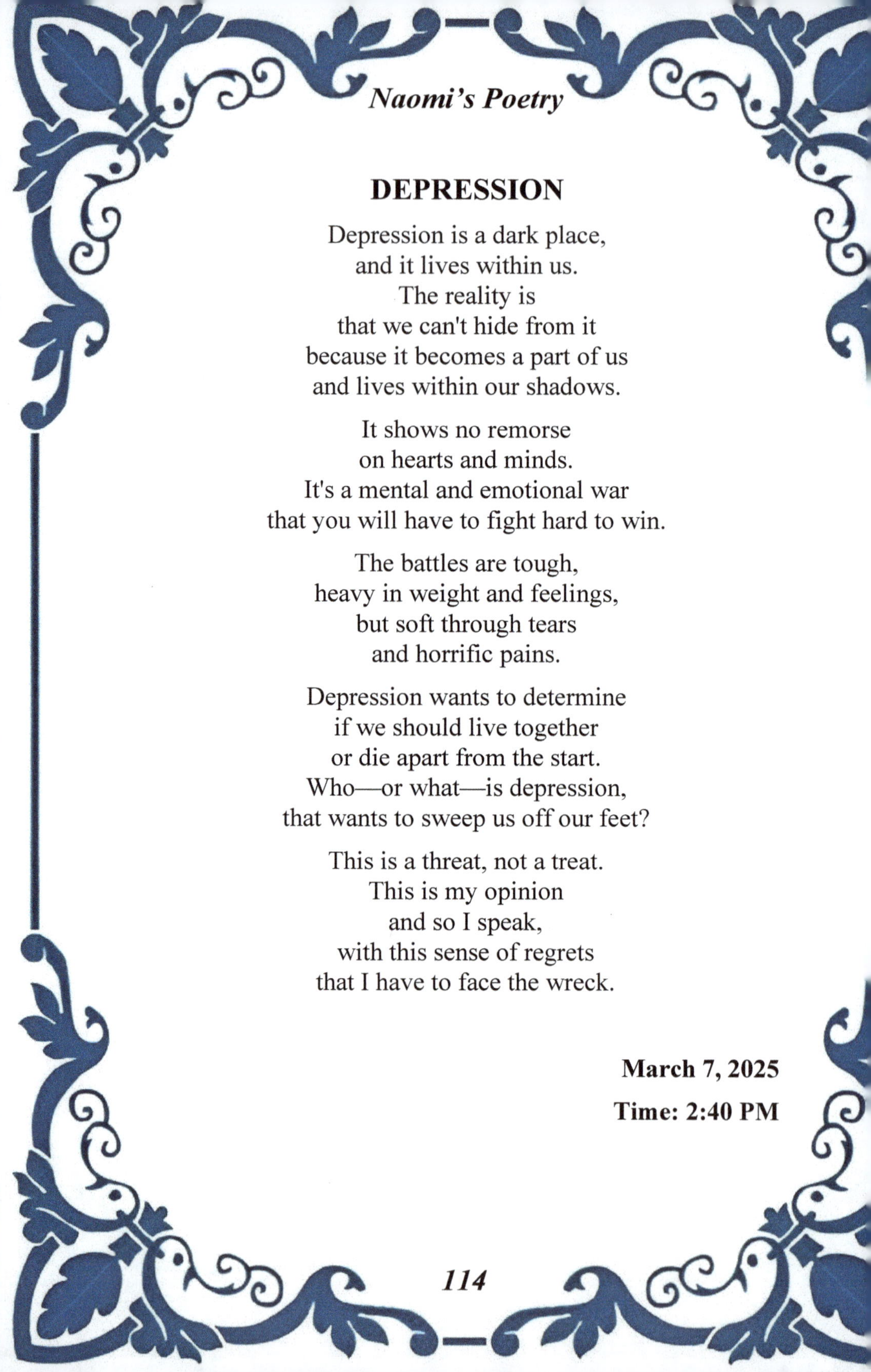

DEPRESSION

Depression is a dark place,
and it lives within us.
The reality is
that we can't hide from it
because it becomes a part of us
and lives within our shadows.

It shows no remorse
on hearts and minds.
It's a mental and emotional war
that you will have to fight hard to win.

The battles are tough,
heavy in weight and feelings,
but soft through tears
and horrific pains.

Depression wants to determine
if we should live together
or die apart from the start.
Who—or what—is depression,
that wants to sweep us off our feet?

This is a threat, not a treat.
This is my opinion
and so I speak,
with this sense of regrets
that I have to face the wreck.

March 7, 2025
Time: 2:40 PM

Depression
is a dark place....
a mental and emotional war

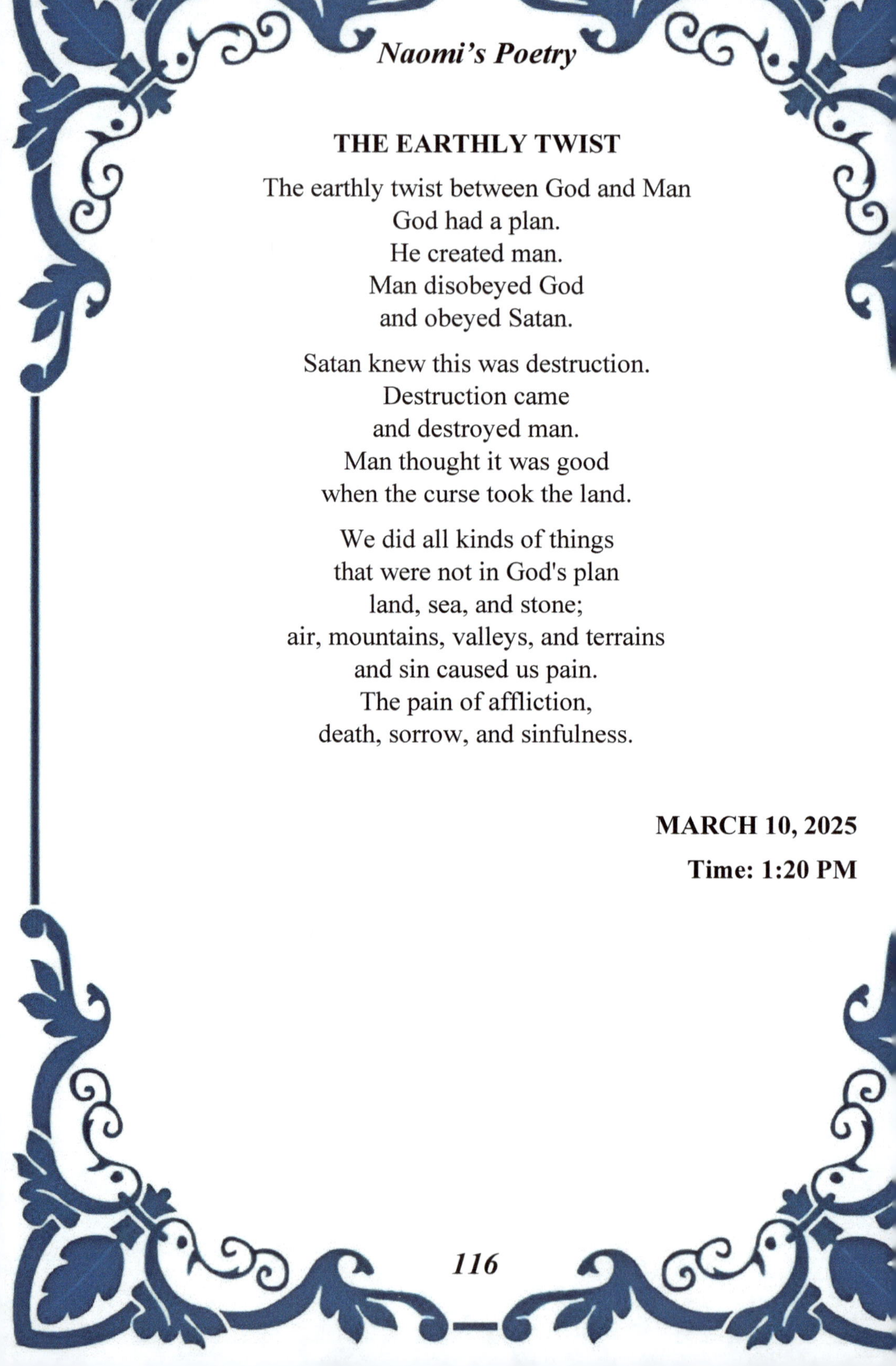

THE EARTHLY TWIST

The earthly twist between God and Man
God had a plan.
He created man.
Man disobeyed God
and obeyed Satan.

Satan knew this was destruction.
Destruction came
and destroyed man.
Man thought it was good
when the curse took the land.

We did all kinds of things
that were not in God's plan
land, sea, and stone;
air, mountains, valleys, and terrains
and sin caused us pain.
The pain of affliction,
death, sorrow, and sinfulness.

MARCH 10, 2025

Time: 1:20 PM

THE EARTHLY TWIST
GOD AND DAYS
MAN
DESTRUCTION (AND
DESTROYED MAN)
MAN

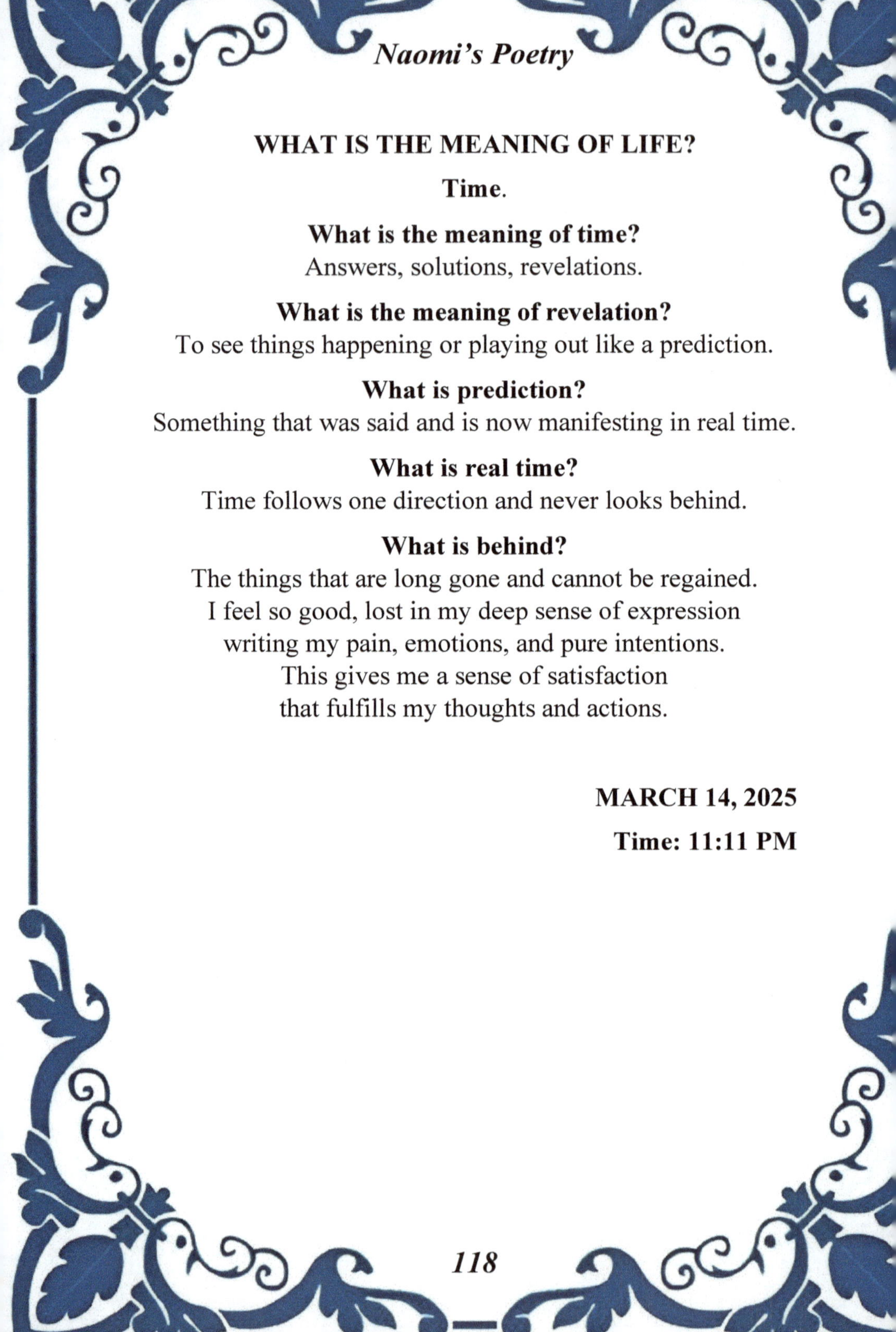

WHAT IS THE MEANING OF LIFE?

Time.

What is the meaning of time?
Answers, solutions, revelations.

What is the meaning of revelation?
To see things happening or playing out like a prediction.

What is prediction?
Something that was said and is now manifesting in real time.

What is real time?
Time follows one direction and never looks behind.

What is behind?
The things that are long gone and cannot be regained.
I feel so good, lost in my deep sense of expression
writing my pain, emotions, and pure intentions.
This gives me a sense of satisfaction
that fulfills my thoughts and actions.

MARCH 14, 2025

Time: 11:11 PM

Time
follows
one
Direction
and never
looks
behind

CAN NEVER BE ERASED

The things that can never be erased are the calls,
the time, the scene, the rumors, the dates, the year and
years,
their voices, their love, their kindness, their image, their
memories, their smiles, their words, their favorite colors,
their fragrances, their attitude — that no one can substitute.
Don't call January — it scars my memory.
Don't call February — it bruises my sanity.

Don't call April — it has torn me apart.
Don't call may — I don't have words to say.
Don't call June — it rips my womb.
The room of screams, tears, silence, sighs, and
isolation tells it all. I accepted denial and denied acceptance.
Victory was defeated when you both left, and defeat won
because they both did not come back.

They left without a notice.
Why am I living a lie? And the truth is buried
somewhere around the corner
peeping, laughing, mocking,
and rejoicing that no one knows. This is so surreal.

March 15, 2025

time: 6:26 pm

JANUARY
JUNE
The things that can
never ... ...
ther their smiles,
their memories.

Naomi's Poetry

THE MEMORIES WE SHARE

As the memories we share, they will never go away,

And I swear,
I'm missing you guys every second of the day.
Our memories won't fade.
My heart yearns like never
before, trying to find peace inside my head.
"I whisper in my heart, 'stay with me, please.'" nobody gets
it when reality stares you in the face, and there
is no escape at any gate.

It is only you who knows the
hardness that takes control of the mind, body, and soul.
I try to take long showers to ease my trauma,
pain, and depression — wanting to suppress my emotions.
But as the water runs on my body, that is when
all my memories appear — crazy.

I cried and cry for some relief.
Oh, help me please!
reminisce on the past,
as I struggle with the present,
thinking if my future ends.

I always see things
as pending due to life's journey and atrocities.

MARCH 14, 2025

TIME: 10:58 PM

Naomi

GRIEF

Grief is a wound that lives deep within the heart,
body, spirit, mind, and soul.

We are so deeply wounded,
and our hearts are pounded.
They were innocent and defenseless.
Every day, we've been wondering:
Where are they?

This wound cannot be measured in size,
and the pain cannot be weighed on a scale from 1 to 10.

This life has no guarantee of tomorrow,
for the mysteries of tomorrow are in His hands.
The step we take might be quicksand—
for only God knows how long we can stand.

Pointing to reality,
our steps are numbered in His hands.
Looking for time to spend
sailing along life's oceans,
praying for the best
during life's biggest regrets.

MARCH 20, 2025
TIME: 3:13 PM

Grief is a wound that lives
within the heart, body,
spirit, mind, and soul.

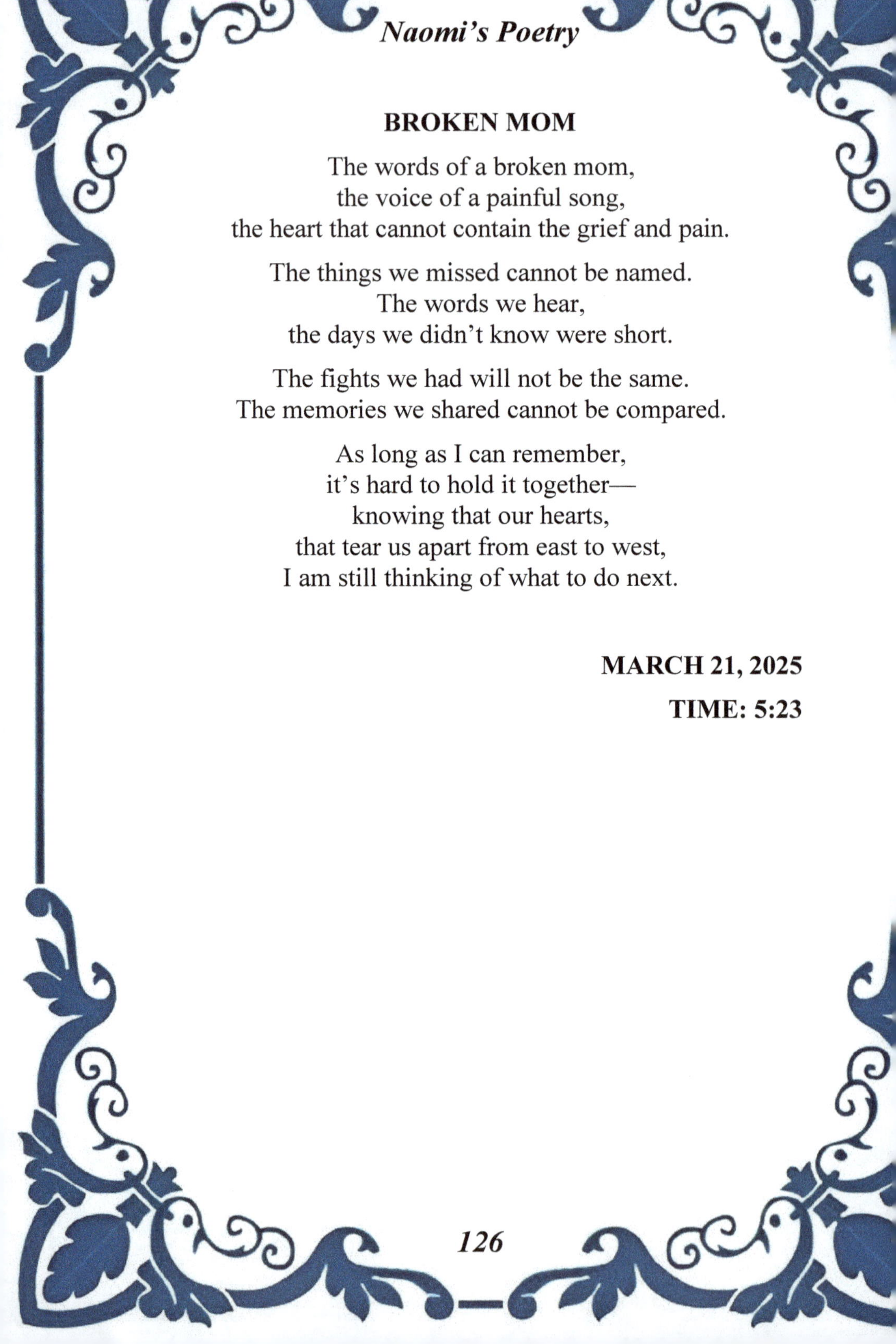

BROKEN MOM

The words of a broken mom,
the voice of a painful song,
the heart that cannot contain the grief and pain.

The things we missed cannot be named.
The words we hear,
the days we didn't know were short.

The fights we had will not be the same.
The memories we shared cannot be compared.

As long as I can remember,
it's hard to hold it together—
knowing that our hearts,
that tear us apart from east to west,
I am still thinking of what to do next.

MARCH 21, 2025
TIME: 5:23

"THE WORDS OF A BROKEN MOM,
THE VOICE OF A PAINFUL SONG."

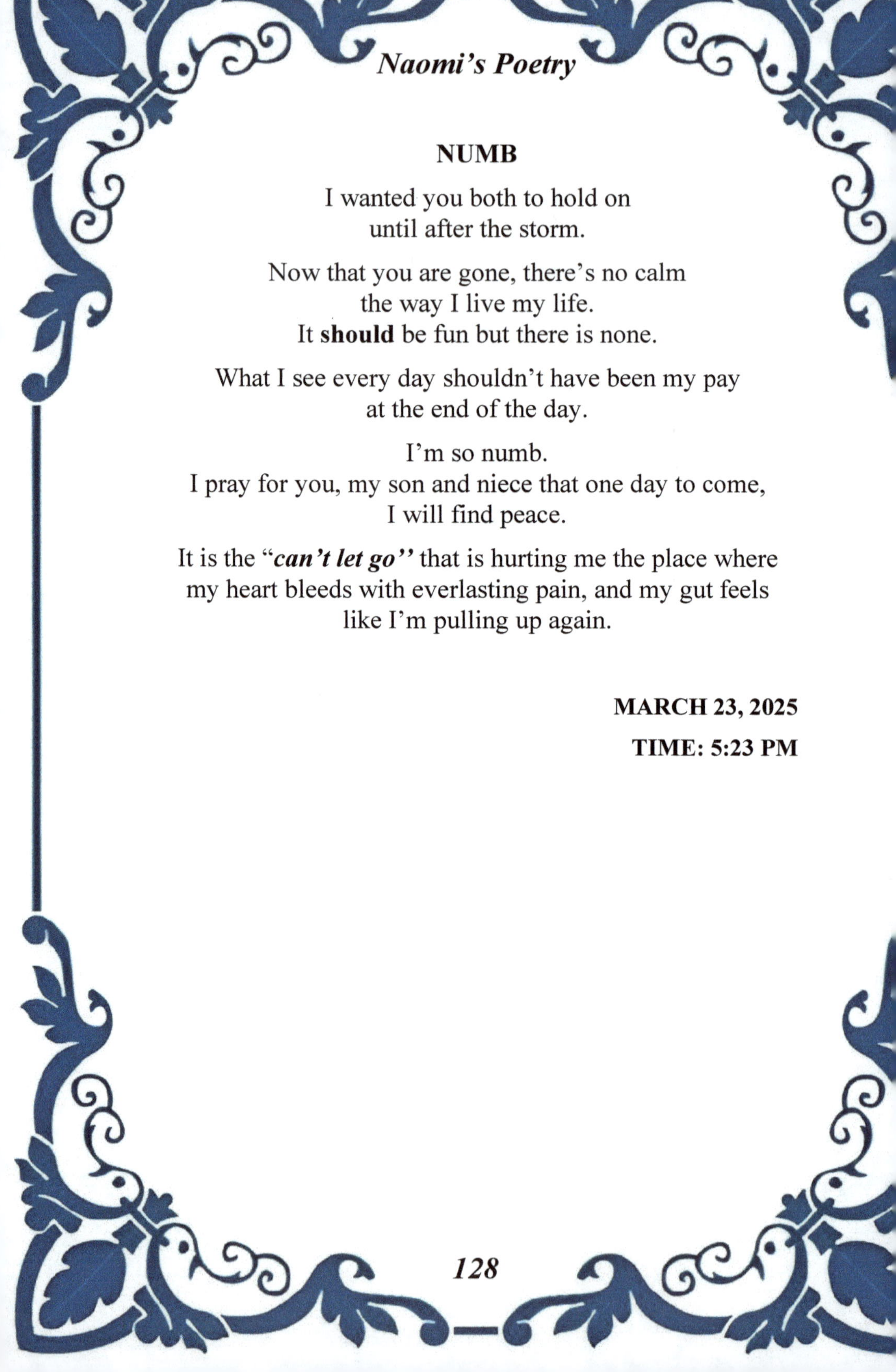

NUMB

I wanted you both to hold on
until after the storm.

Now that you are gone, there's no calm
the way I live my life.
It **should** be fun but there is none.

What I see every day shouldn't have been my pay
at the end of the day.

I'm so numb.
I pray for you, my son and niece that one day to come,
I will find peace.

It is the *"can't let go"* that is hurting me the place where
my heart bleeds with everlasting pain, and my gut feels
like I'm pulling up again.

MARCH 23, 2025

TIME: 5:23 PM

I'm so numb.
I pray for you,
my son and niece.

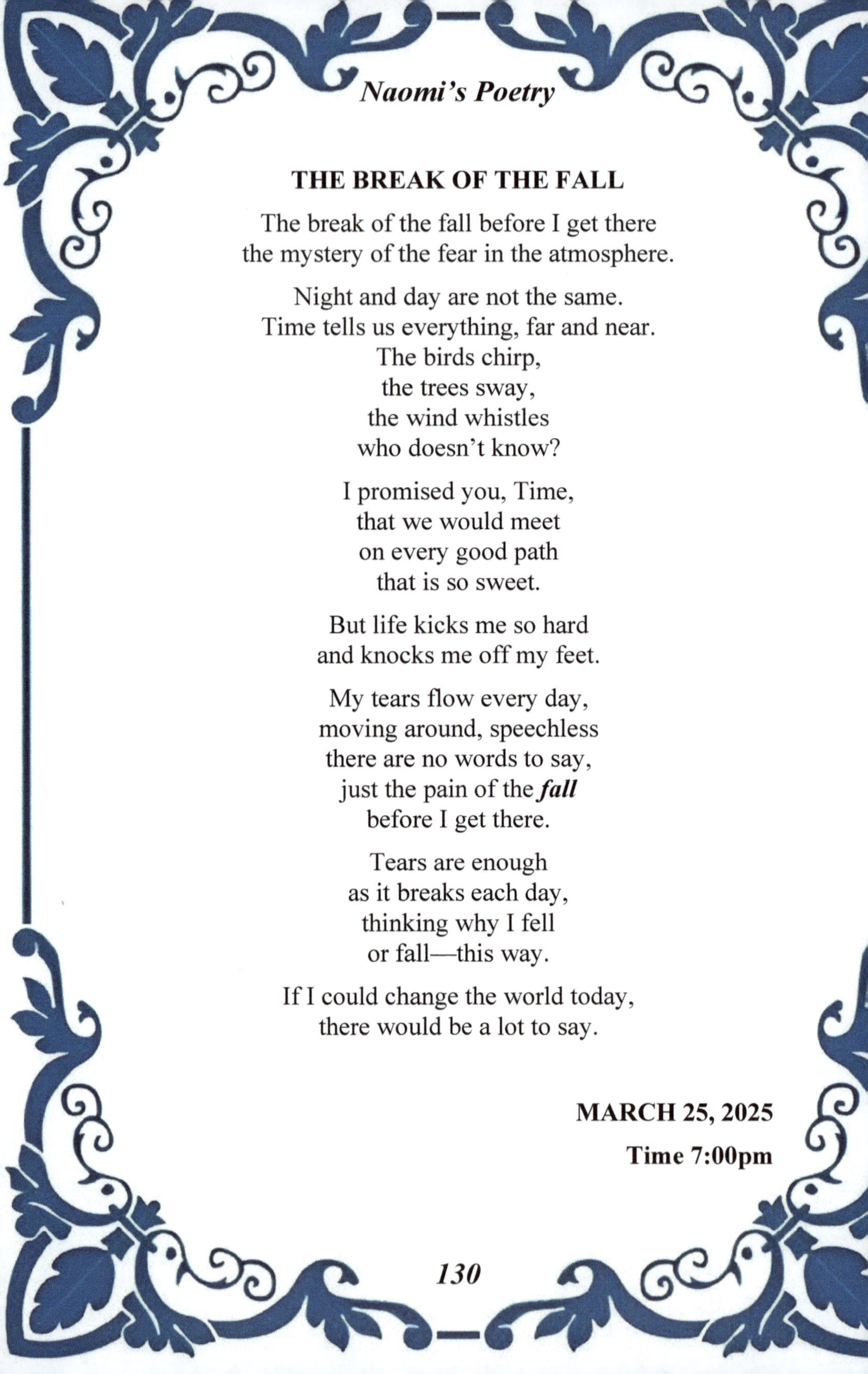

THE BREAK OF THE FALL

The break of the fall before I get there
the mystery of the fear in the atmosphere.

Night and day are not the same.
Time tells us everything, far and near.
The birds chirp,
the trees sway,
the wind whistles
who doesn't know?

I promised you, Time,
that we would meet
on every good path
that is so sweet.

But life kicks me so hard
and knocks me off my feet.

My tears flow every day,
moving around, speechless
there are no words to say,
just the pain of the ***fall***
before I get there.

Tears are enough
as it breaks each day,
thinking why I fell
or fall—this way.

If I could change the world today,
there would be a lot to say.

MARCH 25, 2025

Time 7:00pm

...My tears flow every day
Just the pain of the fall
before I get there

Naomi's Poetry

YESTERDAY

Yesterday, I asked Today what Tomorrow looks like.
Yesterday shook its head,
trying to figure out Today
and wondering about Tomorrow.

I try to press the reset button,
but I am still on hold
due to the uncertainties of Tomorrow.
Today is over.
Tomorrow is not promised.

The ***ifs, buts, does, and the don'ts***

My mind is always on rewind,
pause, and playback mode.
Tomorrow is on the clock.
Who knows that?

Sit and watch you will get the shock
that everything happens on the clock.
I tried to hold on to Today,
but Tomorrow told me:
"The secret of everything is time."

MARCH 27, 2025

TIME: 9:45 PM

Yesterday,
Today,
Tomorrow
Yesterday, I asked today
what tomorrow looks like.

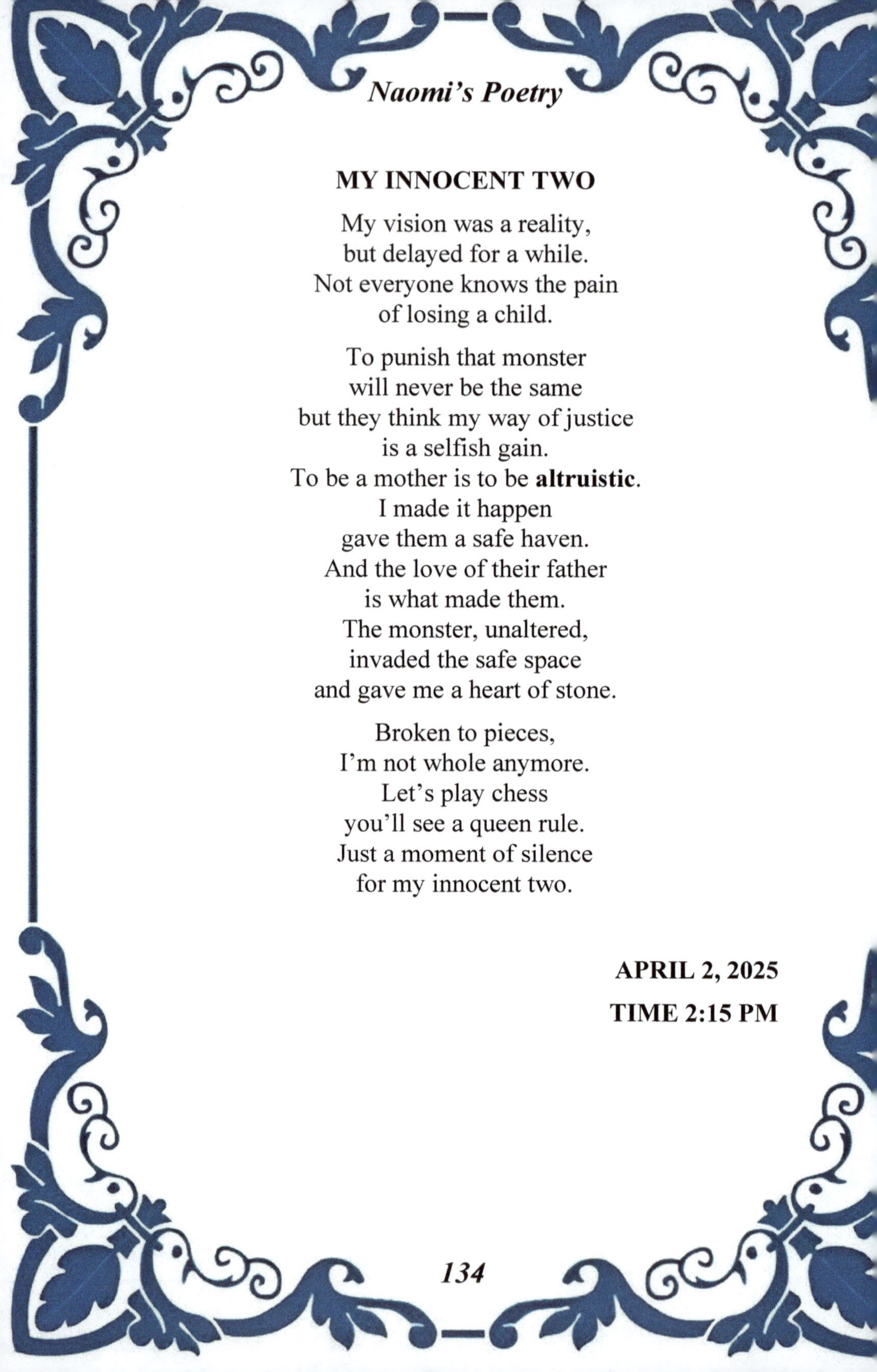

MY INNOCENT TWO

My vision was a reality,
but delayed for a while.
Not everyone knows the pain
of losing a child.

To punish that monster
will never be the same
but they think my way of justice
is a selfish gain.
To be a mother is to be **altruistic**.
I made it happen
gave them a safe haven.
And the love of their father
is what made them.
The monster, unaltered,
invaded the safe space
and gave me a heart of stone.

Broken to pieces,
I'm not whole anymore.
Let's play chess
you'll see a queen rule.
Just a moment of silence
for my innocent two.

APRIL 2, 2025

TIME 2:15 PM

Naomi

135

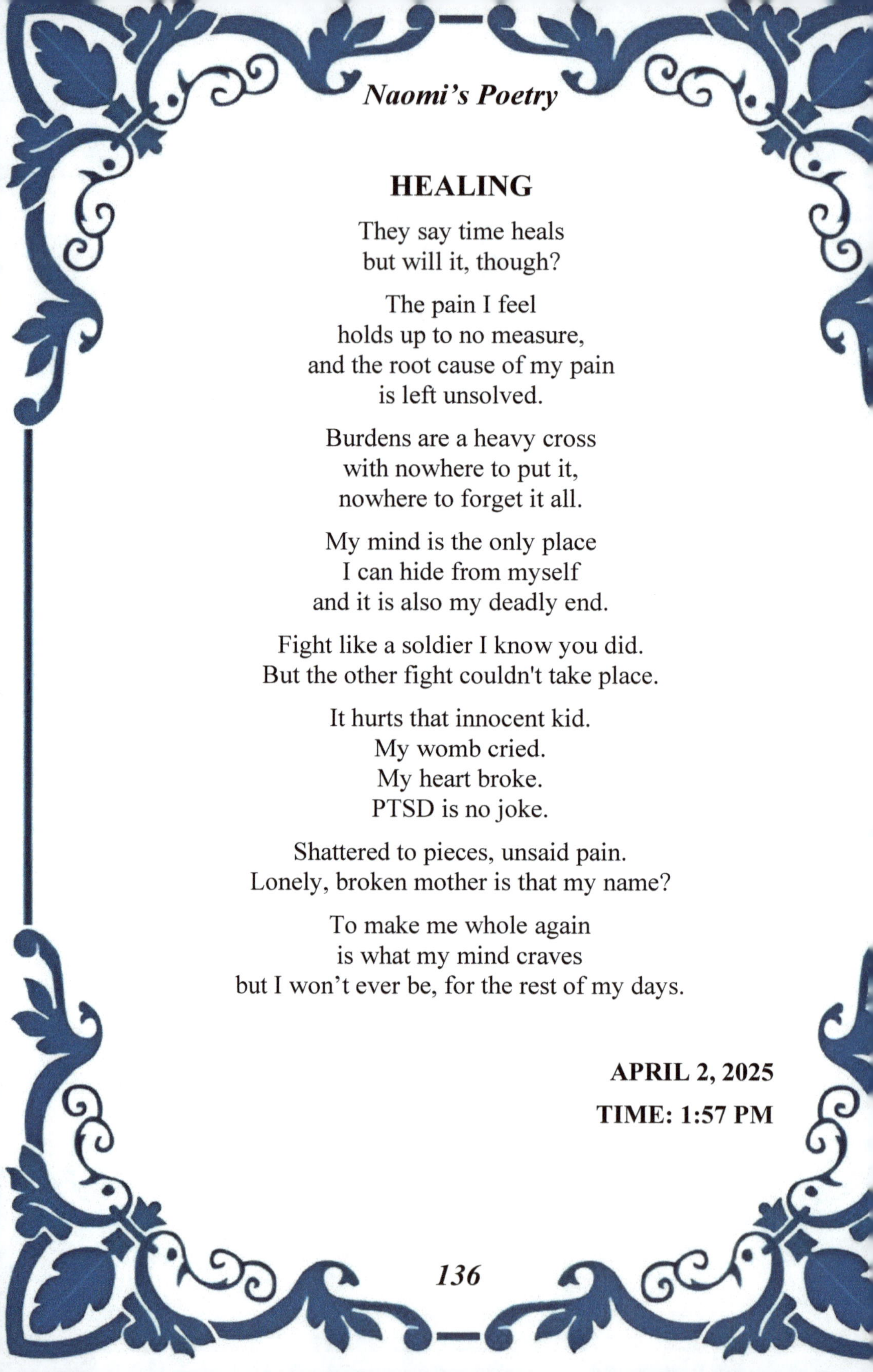

HEALING

They say time heals
but will it, though?

The pain I feel
holds up to no measure,
and the root cause of my pain
is left unsolved.

Burdens are a heavy cross
with nowhere to put it,
nowhere to forget it all.

My mind is the only place
I can hide from myself
and it is also my deadly end.

Fight like a soldier I know you did.
But the other fight couldn't take place.

It hurts that innocent kid.
My womb cried.
My heart broke.
PTSD is no joke.

Shattered to pieces, unsaid pain.
Lonely, broken mother is that my name?

To make me whole again
is what my mind craves
but I won't ever be, for the rest of my days.

APRIL 2, 2025

TIME: 1:57 PM

Naomi

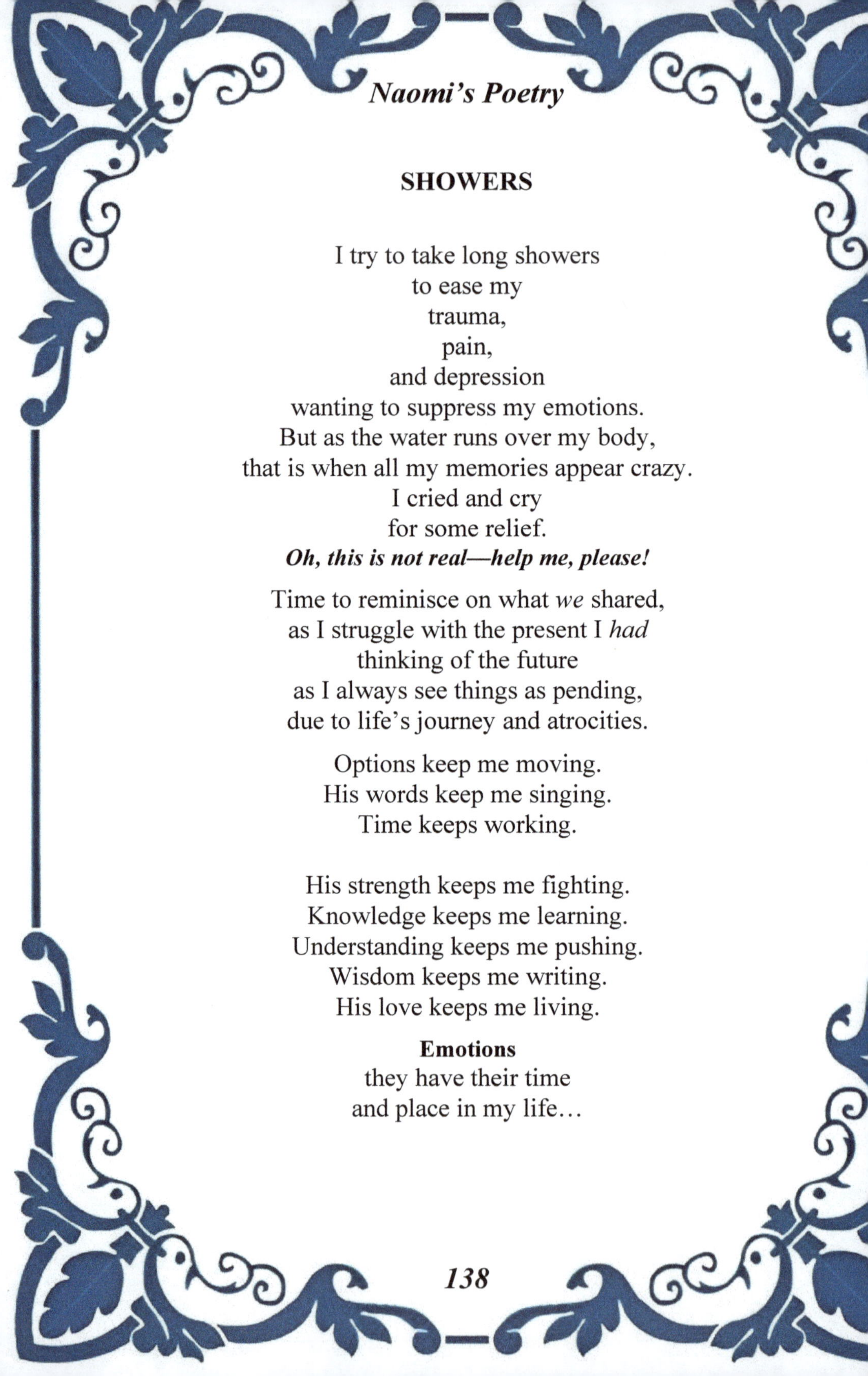

SHOWERS

I try to take long showers
to ease my
trauma,
pain,
and depression
wanting to suppress my emotions.
But as the water runs over my body,
that is when all my memories appear crazy.
I cried and cry
for some relief.
Oh, this is not real—help me, please!

Time to reminisce on what *we* shared,
as I struggle with the present I *had*
thinking of the future
as I always see things as pending,
due to life's journey and atrocities.

Options keep me moving.
His words keep me singing.
Time keeps working.

His strength keeps me fighting.
Knowledge keeps me learning.
Understanding keeps me pushing.
Wisdom keeps me writing.
His love keeps me living.

Emotions
they have their time
and place in my life…

To sink the bow,
everything went under
and now I'm just floating
on what is left to fix.

I am me.

Dec 26, 2024

TIME 2:00 Am 55

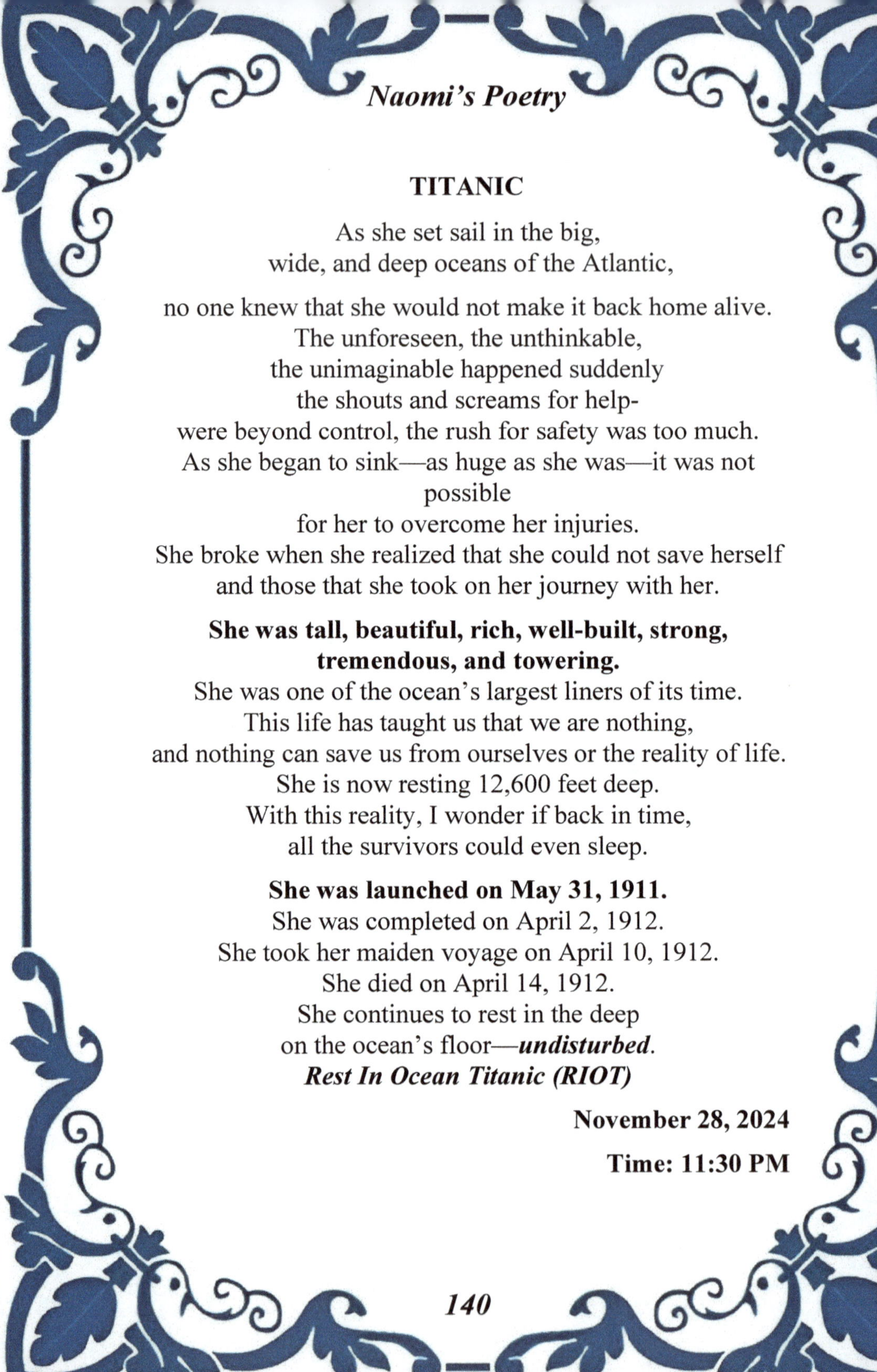

TITANIC

As she set sail in the big,
wide, and deep oceans of the Atlantic,

no one knew that she would not make it back home alive.
The unforeseen, the unthinkable,
the unimaginable happened suddenly
the shouts and screams for help-
were beyond control, the rush for safety was too much.
As she began to sink—as huge as she was—it was not
possible
for her to overcome her injuries.
She broke when she realized that she could not save herself
and those that she took on her journey with her.

**She was tall, beautiful, rich, well-built, strong,
tremendous, and towering.**
She was one of the ocean's largest liners of its time.
This life has taught us that we are nothing,
and nothing can save us from ourselves or the reality of life.
She is now resting 12,600 feet deep.
With this reality, I wonder if back in time,
all the survivors could even sleep.

She was launched on May 31, 1911.
She was completed on April 2, 1912.
She took her maiden voyage on April 10, 1912.
She died on April 14, 1912.
She continues to rest in the deep
on the ocean's floor—***undisturbed***.
Rest In Ocean Titanic (RIOT)

November 28, 2024

Time: 11:30 PM

She continues
to rest in the deep
on ocean's floor
— undisturbed

TEARFUL EYES

I hold no reservation when it comes to love, and tears,
and the care that carry all the spears.
I spent years crying
myself to sleep, and waking up to weep.

Who is there to sweep the joy of peace and love?
Only the One from up above.
I pray for a sign of a dove,

to prove his love.

When my heart whimpers and I begin to
look for support and strength, everyone disappears,
leaving me in despair. When my chest hurts,
I gasp for air, still no one was near,
not even to change a gear.

I struggled with finding peace
and ways to stop my tears.
But naturally, it won't go away.
If my tears could make this world a better place,
it would be a beautiful place.

Make no mistake, my
tears are an expression of mixed emotions.
Sigh!

November 30, 2024

Time: 11 AM

Naomi

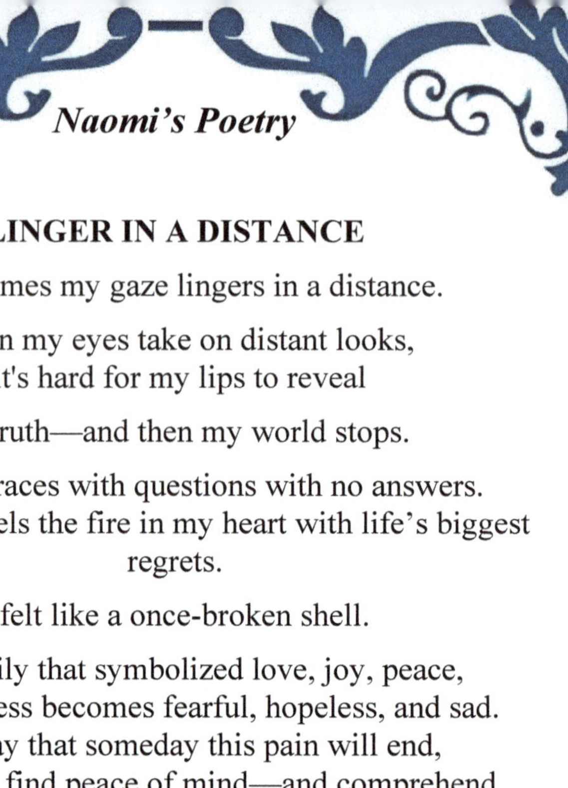

LINGER IN A DISTANCE

Sometimes my gaze lingers in a distance.

When my eyes take on distant looks,
it's hard for my lips to reveal

the truth—and then my world stops.

My heart races with questions with no answers.
These hurt fuels the fire in my heart with life's biggest
regrets.

I felt like a once-broken shell.

The family that symbolized love, joy, peace,
and happiness becomes fearful, hopeless, and sad.
We pray that someday this pain will end,
and we will find peace of mind—and comprehend.

The world feels emptier without you guys.

We treasured your memories in our hearts.
Our repressed feelings need to be unbound
from the shackles of grief and sorrows.

Losing you guys is not the only most painful thing,
but not being able to see you again makes it worse—painful.

We lost moments spent together,
people, places, and things that meant a lot to us.
But you know what?
We are still here, celebrating you guys' love from us.

You will never, ever be forgotten.

December 1, 2024
Time: 10:50 PM

Sometimes
my gaze lingers
in a distance.

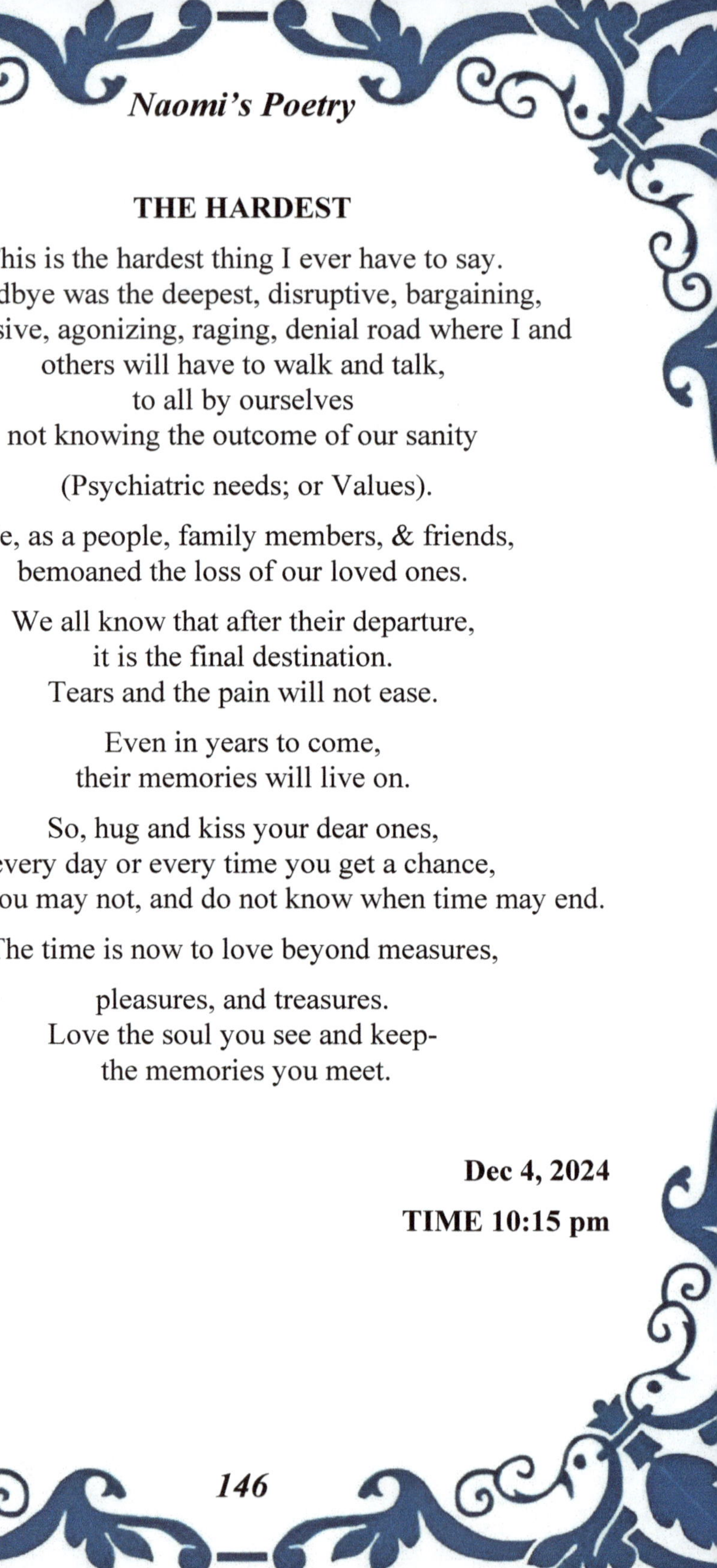

THE HARDEST

This is the hardest thing I ever have to say.
Goodbye was the deepest, disruptive, bargaining,
depressive, agonizing, raging, denial road where I and
others will have to walk and talk,
to all by ourselves
not knowing the outcome of our sanity

(Psychiatric needs; or Values).

We, as a people, family members, & friends,
bemoaned the loss of our loved ones.

We all know that after their departure,
it is the final destination.
Tears and the pain will not ease.

Even in years to come,
their memories will live on.

So, hug and kiss your dear ones,
every day or every time you get a chance,
because you may not, and do not know when time may end.

The time is now to love beyond measures,

pleasures, and treasures.
Love the soul you see and keep-
the memories you meet.

Dec 4, 2024

TIME 10:15 pm

THIS IS THE
HARDEST
THING I EVER
HAVE TO SAY —
GOODBYE.

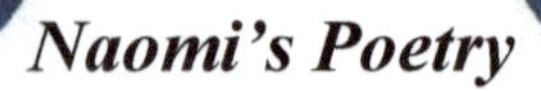

ANTHEM

As the wind of sorrow blew over my country Jamaica.
we stood at attention
as we weep for our youths—at cross roads,
marginalized, murdered,
empty with purpose, mentally enslaved, powerless—
and those who are
scarred with the guilt of bloodstained hands.

Our country's anthem
was a prayer that we used to build on,
but now we've lost it all
to a ***tainted hands and society***
Where right seems wrong,
and wrong seems right.

Our freedom of speech has been taken away.
If we try to complain, our lives are taken away.
The chief cornerstone has been moved,
and now the foundation
set loose.

You have to pick and choose not to get
confused.

Our country's song meant so much to us,
but right now, it has lost its touch.
No one cares about the words that
once stood tall, covering us
as we traveled near and far.

Please
I'm asking us to love
and cease from the hurt that's increasing in us.

Dec 4, 2024

Time 10:40pm 43

Our country's anthem
was a prayer...
but now we've lost it all.

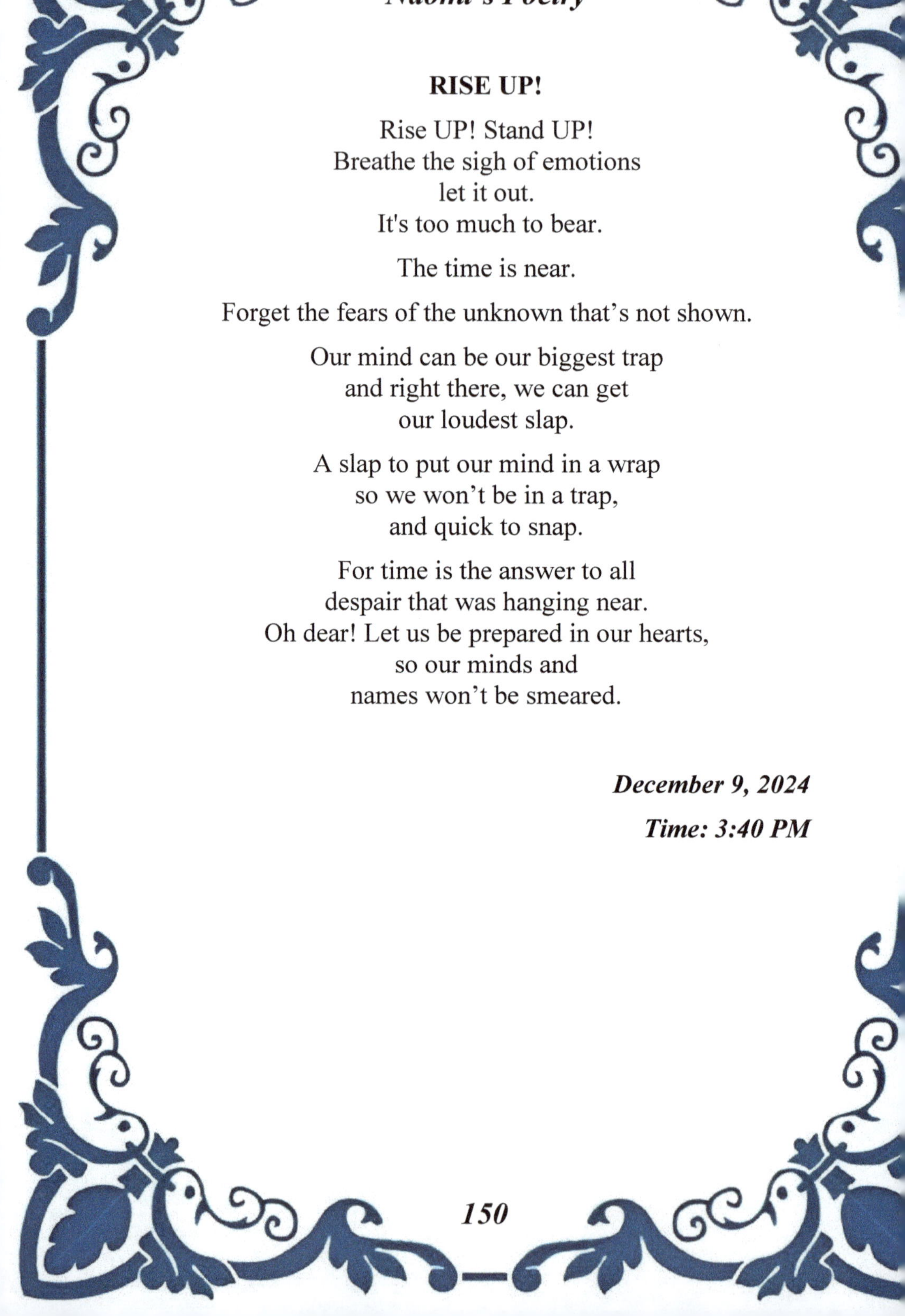

RISE UP!

Rise UP! Stand UP!
Breathe the sigh of emotions
let it out.
It's too much to bear.

The time is near.

Forget the fears of the unknown that's not shown.

Our mind can be our biggest trap
and right there, we can get
our loudest slap.

A slap to put our mind in a wrap
so we won't be in a trap,
and quick to snap.

For time is the answer to all
despair that was hanging near.
Oh dear! Let us be prepared in our hearts,
so our minds and
names won't be smeared.

December 9, 2024

Time: 3:40 PM

RISE UP!
STAND UP!
BREATHE
THE SIGH OF
EMOTIONS --
LET IT OUT.

THE RACE

This race that I am running requires patience, love,
energy, and most of all—prayers.

The body that houses this
resilient soul
needs support in all the allies.
Nevertheless, someday
I must see the finish line,
and find the strength and
courage to push to the end.

And then I will thank
myself for being strong,
determined, dedicated,
and relentless courageous,
brave for making it possible
to win the trophy of triumph or victory.

Let me stand tall,
wave my hands, and be proud
I have won again.

December 9, 2024

Time: 5:45 PM

THIS RACE THAT I AM RUNNING REQUIRES PATIENCE, LOVE, ENERGY, AND MOST OF ALL —
— PRAYERS.

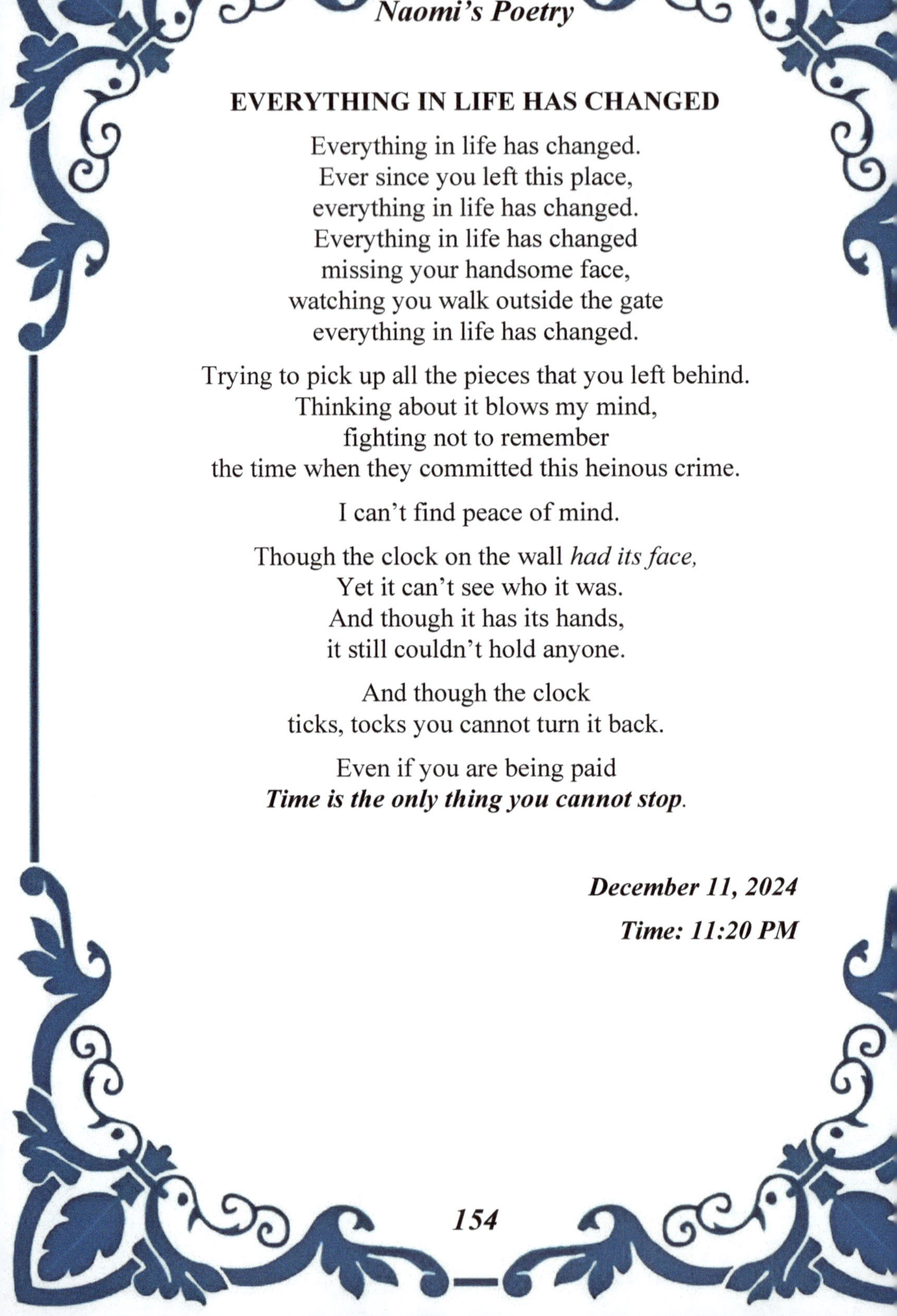

EVERYTHING IN LIFE HAS CHANGED

Everything in life has changed.
Ever since you left this place,
everything in life has changed.
Everything in life has changed
missing your handsome face,
watching you walk outside the gate
everything in life has changed.

Trying to pick up all the pieces that you left behind.
Thinking about it blows my mind,
fighting not to remember
the time when they committed this heinous crime.

I can't find peace of mind.

Though the clock on the wall *had its face,*
Yet it can't see who it was.
And though it has its hands,
it still couldn't hold anyone.

And though the clock
ticks, tocks you cannot turn it back.

Even if you are being paid
Time is the only thing you cannot stop.

December 11, 2024

Time: 11:20 PM

Everything
in life
has changed...
ever since you left
this place.

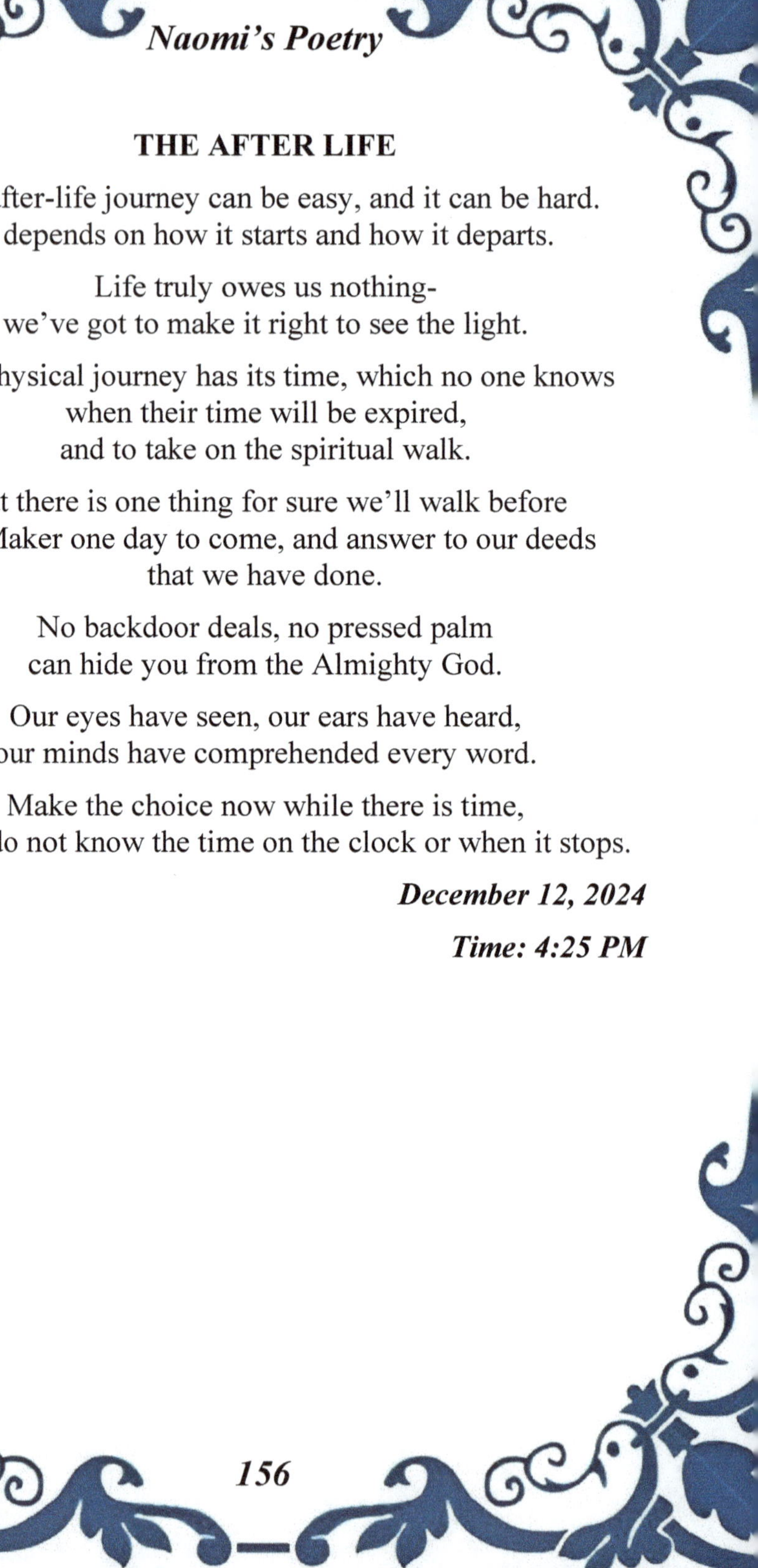

THE AFTER LIFE

The after-life journey can be easy, and it can be hard.
It depends on how it starts and how it departs.

Life truly owes us nothing-
we've got to make it right to see the light.

This physical journey has its time, which no one knows
when their time will be expired,
and to take on the spiritual walk.

But there is one thing for sure we'll walk before
the Maker one day to come, and answer to our deeds
that we have done.

No backdoor deals, no pressed palm
can hide you from the Almighty God.

Our eyes have seen, our ears have heard,
our minds have comprehended every word.

Make the choice now while there is time,
for we do not know the time on the clock or when it stops.

December 12, 2024

Time: 4:25 PM

We'll Walk
Before the Maker
One Day to Come

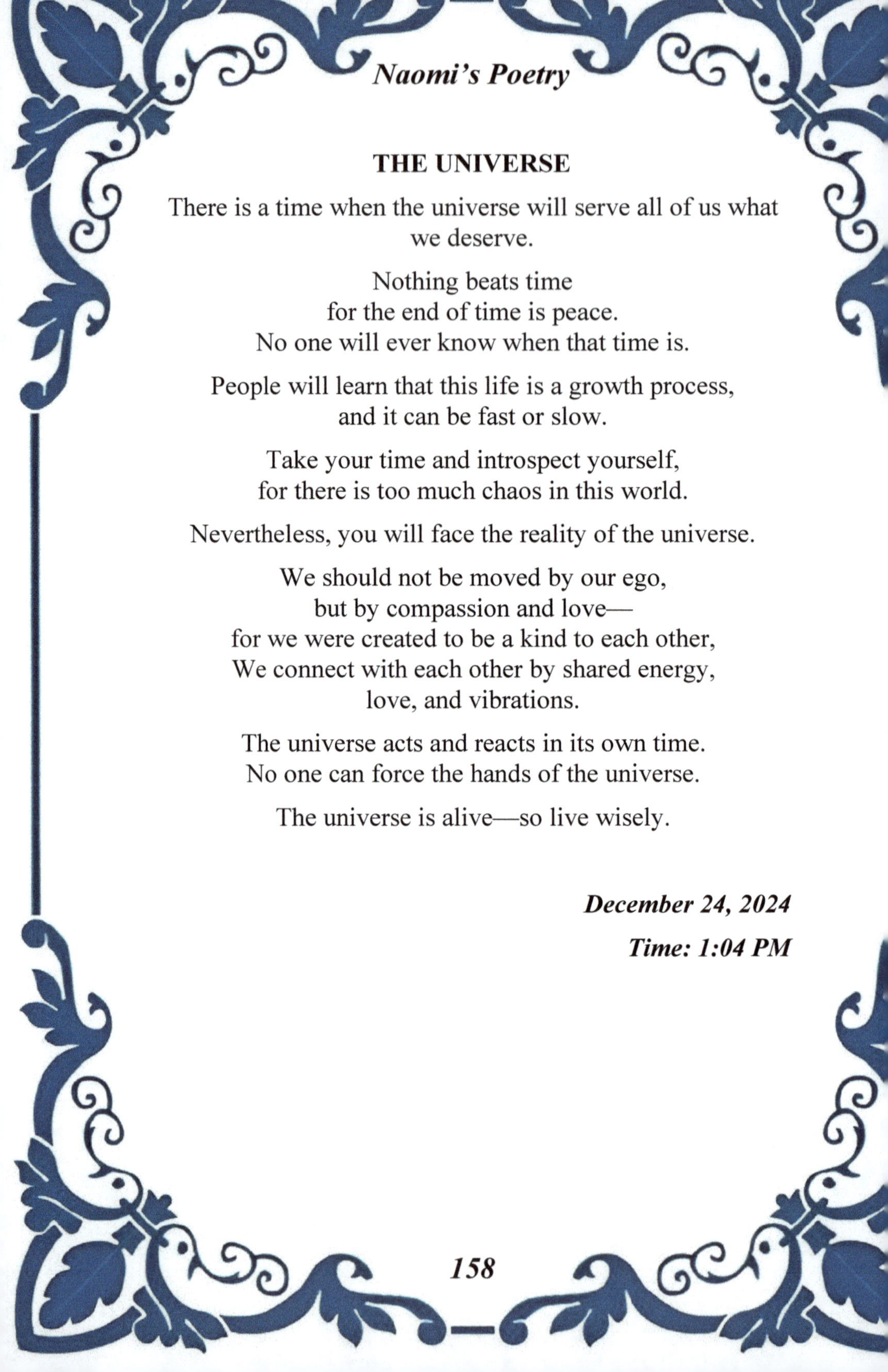

THE UNIVERSE

There is a time when the universe will serve all of us what
we deserve.

Nothing beats time
for the end of time is peace.
No one will ever know when that time is.

People will learn that this life is a growth process,
and it can be fast or slow.

Take your time and introspect yourself,
for there is too much chaos in this world.

Nevertheless, you will face the reality of the universe.

We should not be moved by our ego,
but by compassion and love—
for we were created to be a kind to each other,
We connect with each other by shared energy,
love, and vibrations.

The universe acts and reacts in its own time.
No one can force the hands of the universe.

The universe is alive—so live wisely.

December 24, 2024

Time: 1:04 PM

The Universe
acts and reacts
in its own time

TIME MACHINE

Life is like a time machine
no one knows when, where,
how, and why we face loneliness, struggles, grief, and fears.

It takes our imaginations far and deep
that no one can see the guilt we carry and the load we bear,
capturing the heart-wrenching pain of our past,
dragging it into the present, and afraid of the future.

We carry emotions that are undecided
and will take us a lifetime to decide what we are feeling.

Take us back to when everything was magical and beautiful,
and time was all that we needed.

When everything started great,
and now seems bitter with time.

Everyone and everything will return to their perfect place
and memories.

December 18th, 2024

Time: 8:00 PM

Life is like a time machine ...
capturing the heart-wrenching pain of our past

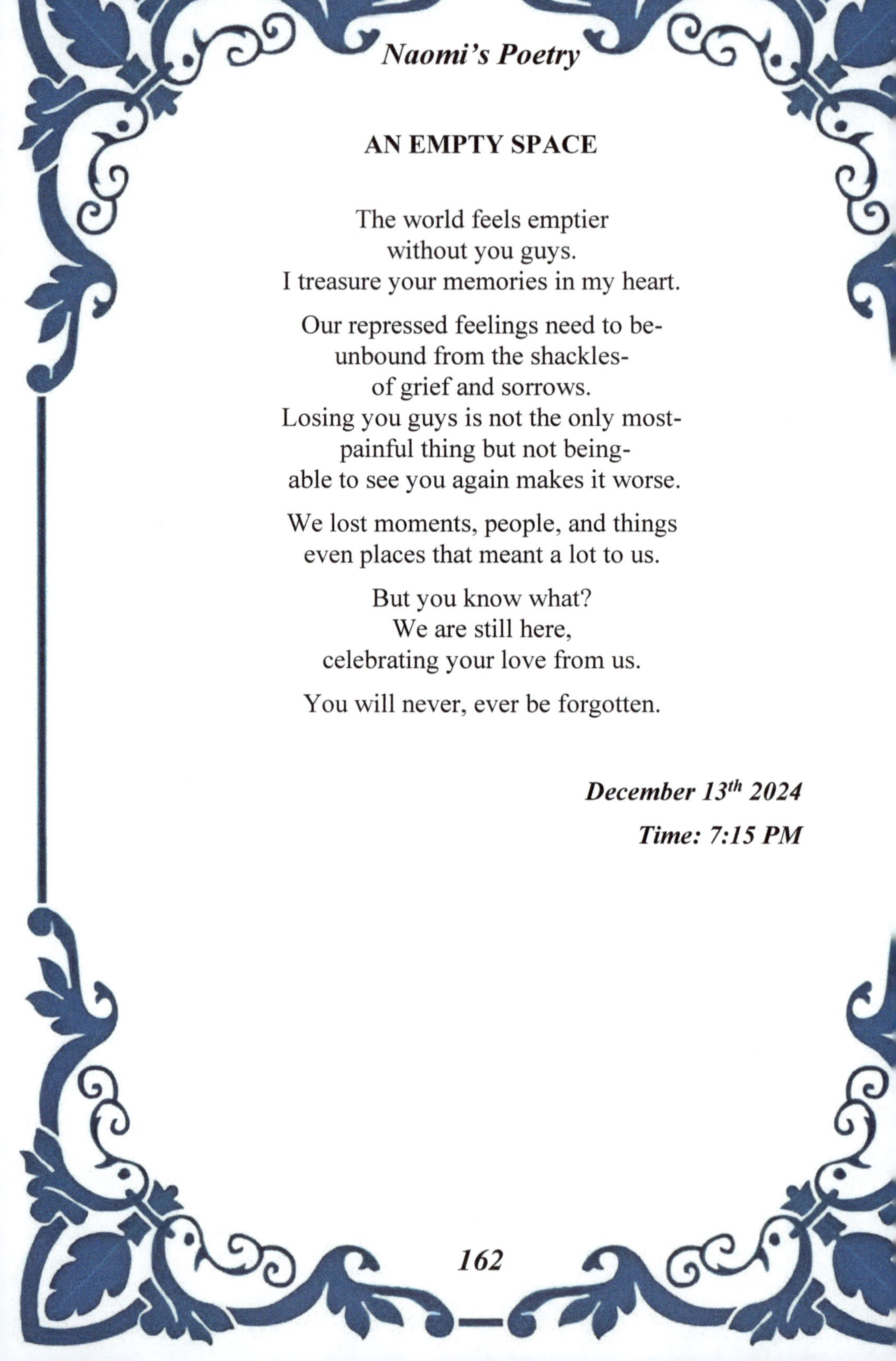

AN EMPTY SPACE

The world feels emptier
without you guys.
I treasure your memories in my heart.

Our repressed feelings need to be-
unbound from the shackles-
of grief and sorrows.
Losing you guys is not the only most-
painful thing but not being-
able to see you again makes it worse.

We lost moments, people, and things
even places that meant a lot to us.

But you know what?
We are still here,
celebrating your love from us.

You will never, ever be forgotten.

December 13th 2024

Time: 7:15 PM

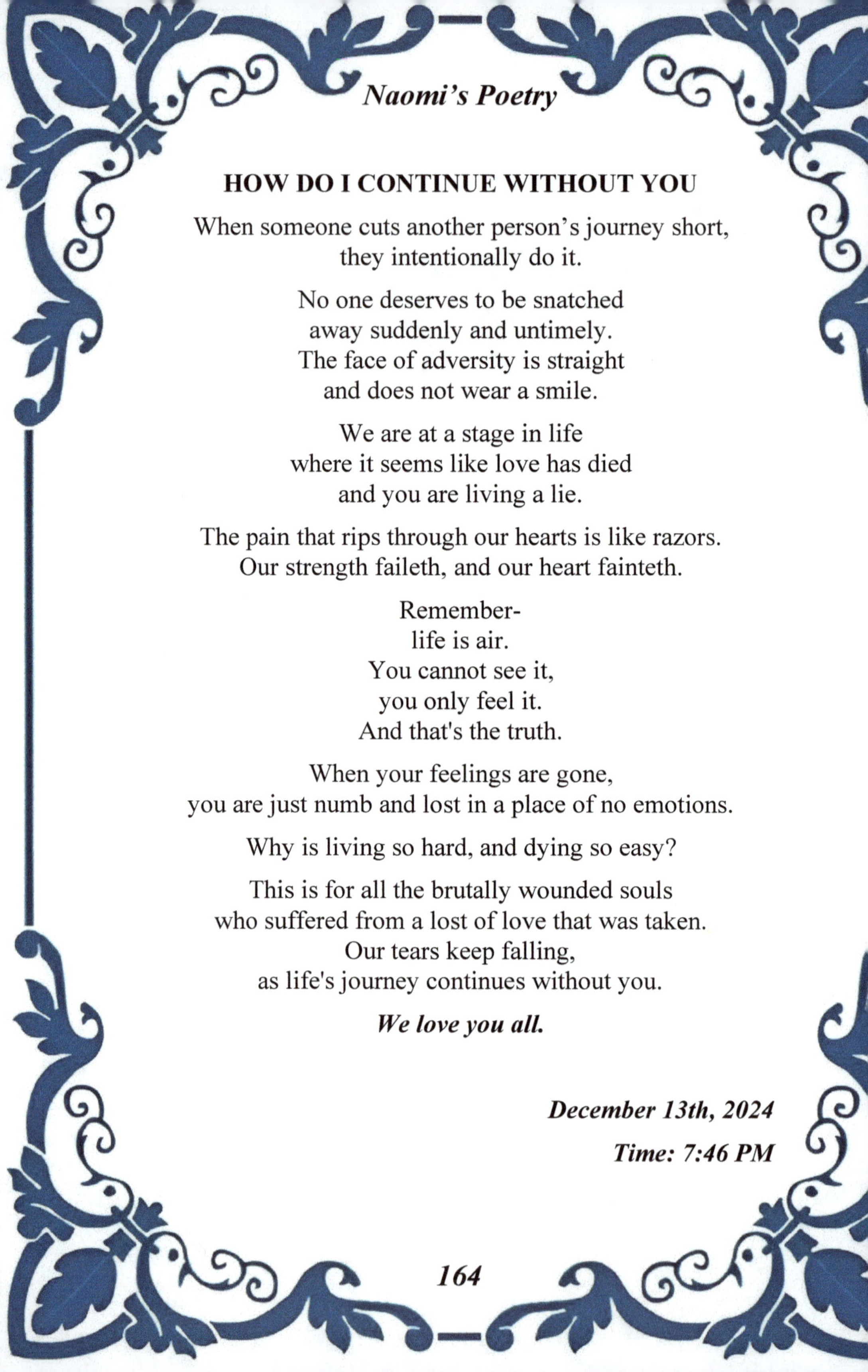

HOW DO I CONTINUE WITHOUT YOU

When someone cuts another person's journey short,
they intentionally do it.

No one deserves to be snatched
away suddenly and untimely.
The face of adversity is straight
and does not wear a smile.

We are at a stage in life
where it seems like love has died
and you are living a lie.

The pain that rips through our hearts is like razors.
Our strength faileth, and our heart fainteth.

Remember-
life is air.
You cannot see it,
you only feel it.
And that's the truth.

When your feelings are gone,
you are just numb and lost in a place of no emotions.

Why is living so hard, and dying so easy?

This is for all the brutally wounded souls
who suffered from a lost of love that was taken.
Our tears keep falling,
as life's journey continues without you.

We love you all.

December 13th, 2024

Time: 7:46 PM

HOW DO I CONTINUE WITHOUT YOU

When someone cuts another person's journey short,
they intentionally do it.
No one deserves to be snatched
away suddenly and untimely.
The face of adversity is straight
and does not wear a smile.
We are at a stage in life
where it seems like love has died
and you are living a lie.
The pain that rips through our hearts
is like razors.
Our strength faileth, and our heart fainteth
Remember-
life is air.
You cannot see it,
you only feel it.
And that's the truth.
When your feelings
are gone, you are just
numb and lost in
place of no emotions.
Why is living so hard,
and dying so easy?
This is for all the brutally
wounded souls
who suffered feeling lost of
love that was taken.
Our tears keep falling,
as life's journey continues without you.

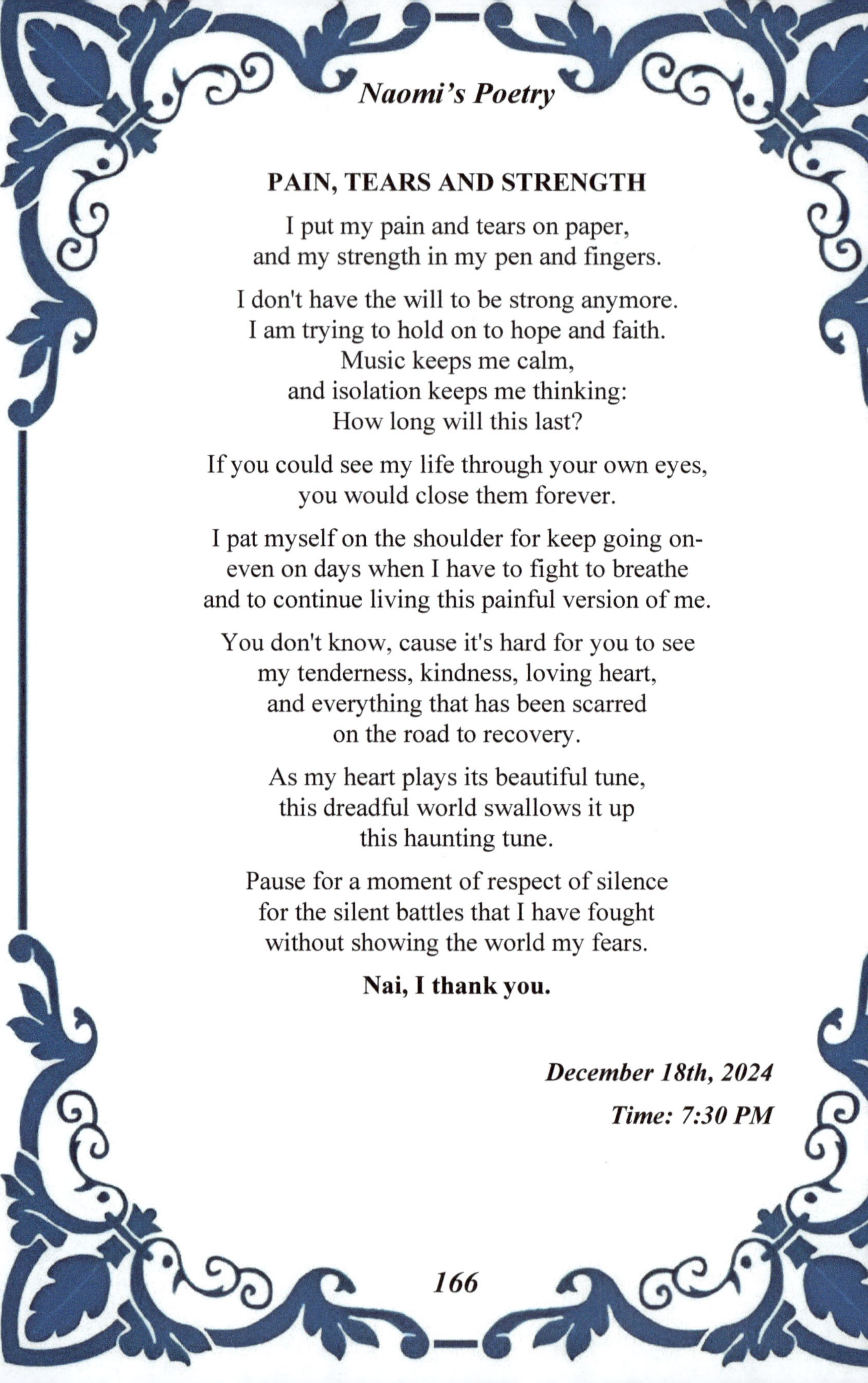

PAIN, TEARS AND STRENGTH

I put my pain and tears on paper,
and my strength in my pen and fingers.

I don't have the will to be strong anymore.
I am trying to hold on to hope and faith.
Music keeps me calm,
and isolation keeps me thinking:
How long will this last?

If you could see my life through your own eyes,
you would close them forever.

I pat myself on the shoulder for keep going on-
even on days when I have to fight to breathe
and to continue living this painful version of me.

You don't know, cause it's hard for you to see
my tenderness, kindness, loving heart,
and everything that has been scarred
on the road to recovery.

As my heart plays its beautiful tune,
this dreadful world swallows it up
this haunting tune.

Pause for a moment of respect of silence
for the silent battles that I have fought
without showing the world my fears.

Nai, I thank you.

December 18th, 2024

Time: 7:30 PM

I put my pain and tears on paper,
and my strength in my pen fingers.

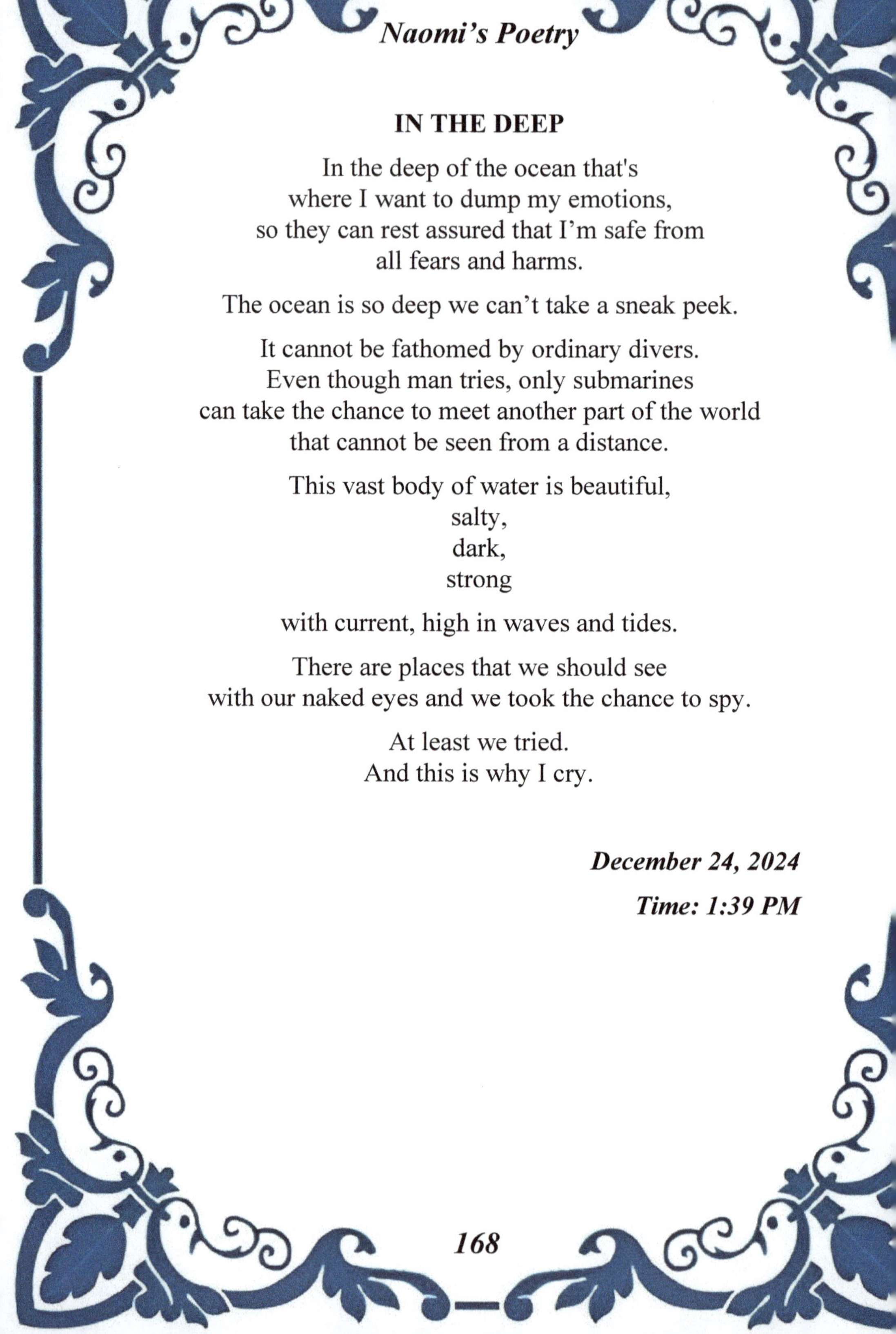

IN THE DEEP

In the deep of the ocean that's
where I want to dump my emotions,
so they can rest assured that I'm safe from
all fears and harms.

The ocean is so deep we can't take a sneak peek.

It cannot be fathomed by ordinary divers.
Even though man tries, only submarines
can take the chance to meet another part of the world
that cannot be seen from a distance.

This vast body of water is beautiful,
salty,
dark,
strong

with current, high in waves and tides.

There are places that we should see
with our naked eyes and we took the chance to spy.

At least we tried.
And this is why I cry.

December 24, 2024

Time: 1:39 PM

Crying
Worry
Isolation
Frustration
Depression
Pain
Page

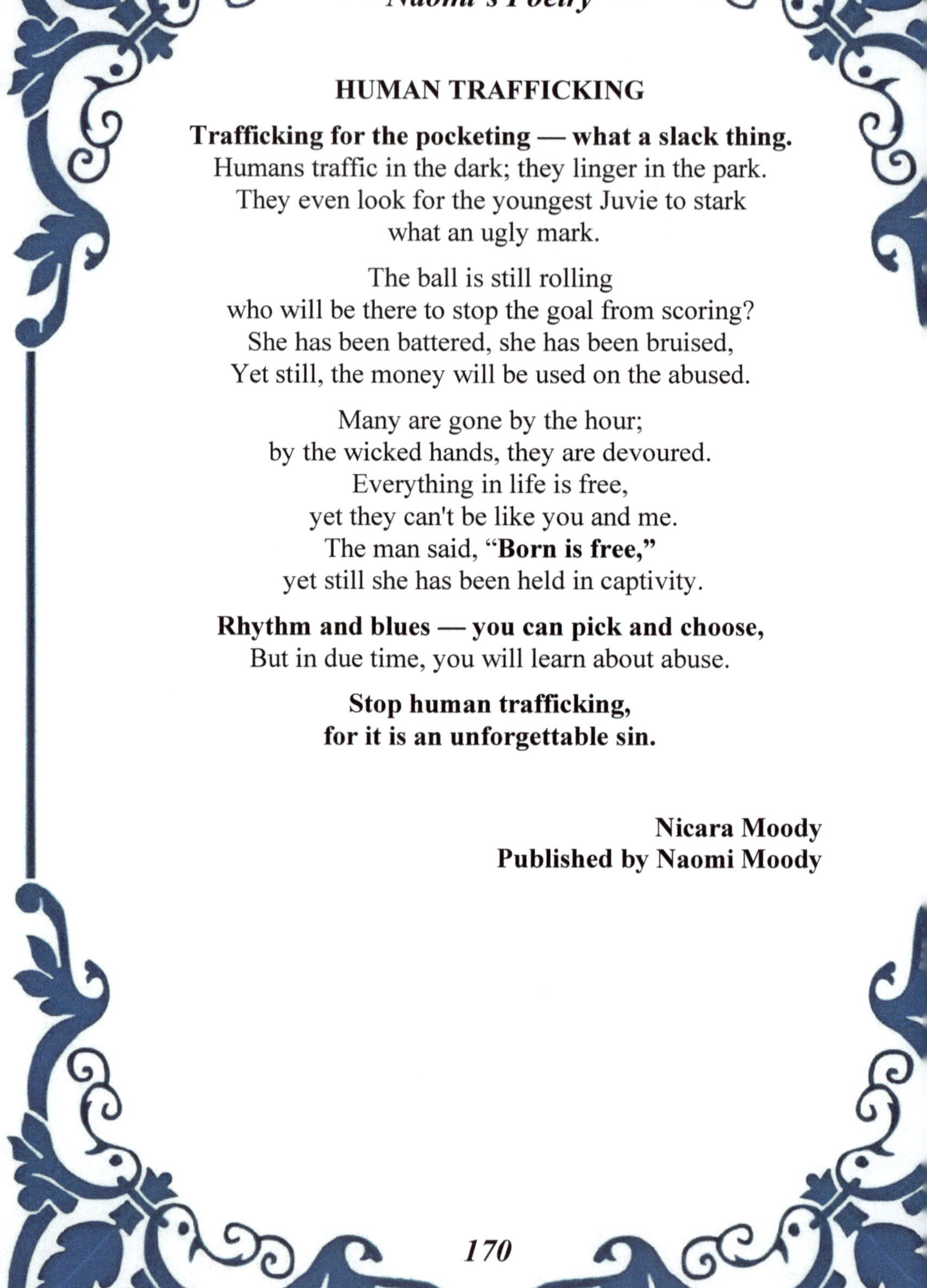

HUMAN TRAFFICKING

Trafficking for the pocketing — what a slack thing.
Humans traffic in the dark; they linger in the park.
They even look for the youngest Juvie to stark
what an ugly mark.

The ball is still rolling
who will be there to stop the goal from scoring?
She has been battered, she has been bruised,
Yet still, the money will be used on the abused.

Many are gone by the hour;
by the wicked hands, they are devoured.
Everything in life is free,
yet they can't be like you and me.
The man said, **"Born is free,"**
yet still she has been held in captivity.

Rhythm and blues — you can pick and choose,
But in due time, you will learn about abuse.

Stop human trafficking,
for it is an unforgettable sin.

Nicara Moody
Published by Naomi Moody

STOP
HUMAN TRFFICING
WILLPREVAIL
DIATNICNT
POLICE FOLRY
POLIICACRCE

HUMAN TRAFFICKING

They took her just yesterday, just to get pay.
They didn't think about the life of a next day Nancy.
They called her
she was used and abused by men of all demeanor.
She screamed and shouted for help,
but instead, they wanted her dead.

They took her pride, innocence, integrity
all that she holds.

Human trafficking
"These men need to stop defending this thing!"
Look at your
mom,
sisters,
nieces,
nephews,
brothers, and fathers.

(***Hehe***) Story comes to bump — finally, they catch the prey
that thought that he would have gotten away.

No, my dear! It isn't here to stay!

Human traffickers must not get away.

Written by Naomi Bent Moody

June 8, 2018

HUMAN TRAFFICKING MUST END
STOP SELLING LIVES FOR MONEY

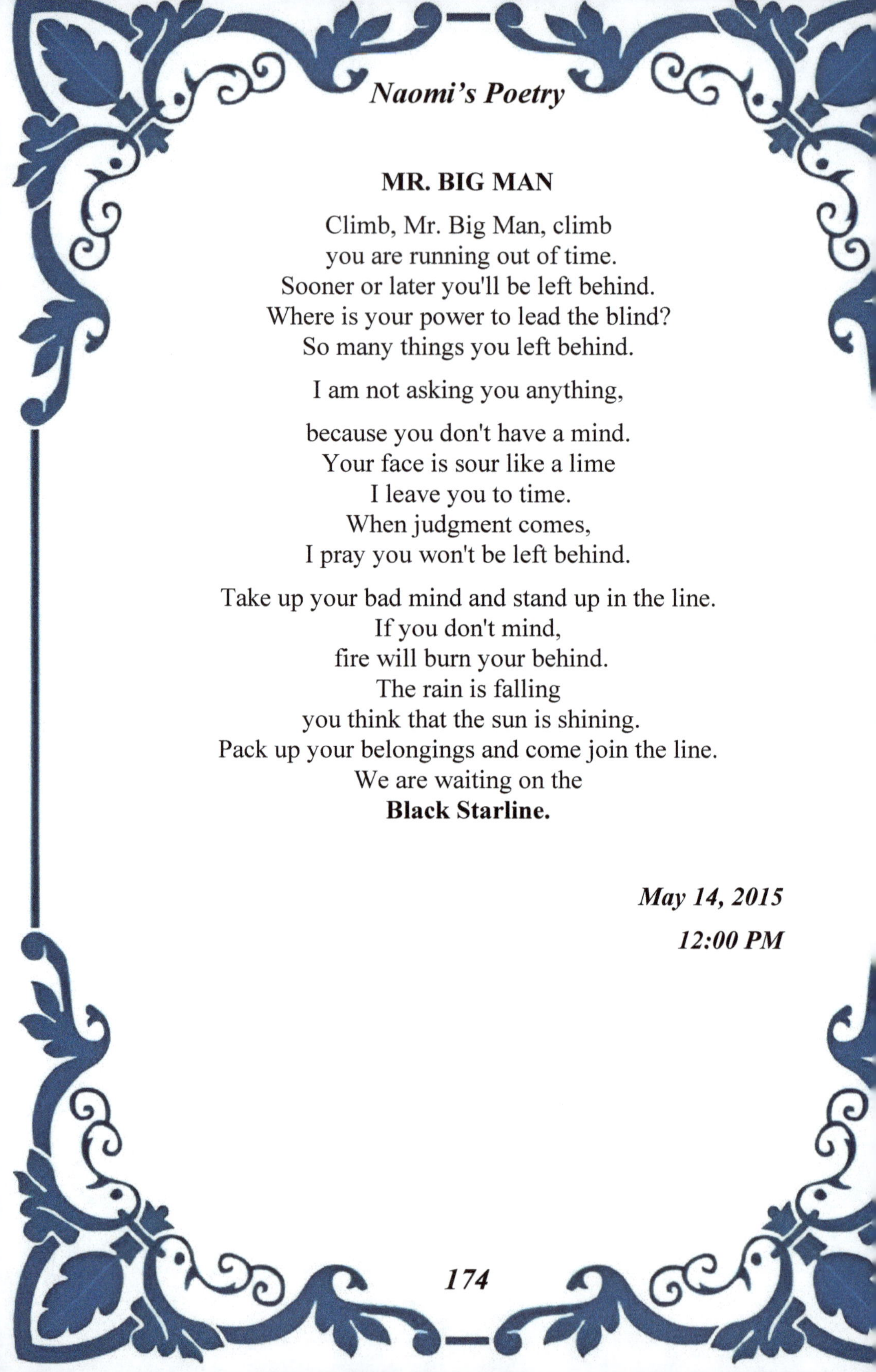

Naomi's Poetry

MR. BIG MAN

Climb, Mr. Big Man, climb
you are running out of time.
Sooner or later you'll be left behind.
Where is your power to lead the blind?
So many things you left behind.

I am not asking you anything,

because you don't have a mind.
Your face is sour like a lime
I leave you to time.
When judgment comes,
I pray you won't be left behind.

Take up your bad mind and stand up in the line.
If you don't mind,
fire will burn your behind.
The rain is falling
you think that the sun is shining.
Pack up your belongings and come join the line.
We are waiting on the
Black Starline.

May 14, 2015
12:00 PM

174

Climb, Mr. Big man, climb ---
You are running out of time.

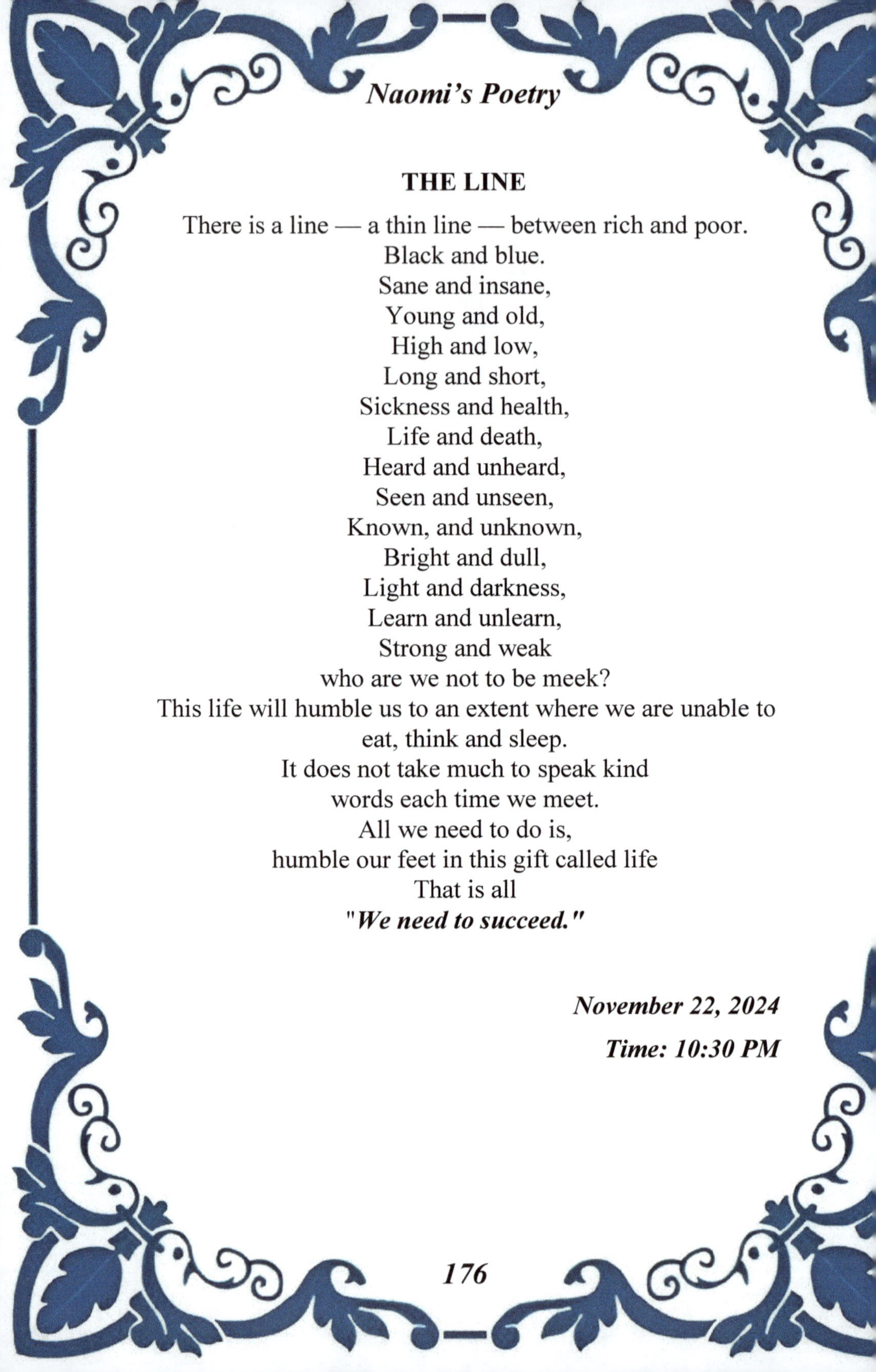

THE LINE

There is a line — a thin line — between rich and poor.
Black and blue.
Sane and insane,
Young and old,
High and low,
Long and short,
Sickness and health,
Life and death,
Heard and unheard,
Seen and unseen,
Known, and unknown,
Bright and dull,
Light and darkness,
Learn and unlearn,
Strong and weak
who are we not to be meek?
This life will humble us to an extent where we are unable to
eat, think and sleep.
It does not take much to speak kind
words each time we meet.
All we need to do is,
humble our feet in this gift called life
That is all
"We need to succeed."

November 22, 2024

Time: 10:30 PM

The Line...
Life will humble us all.

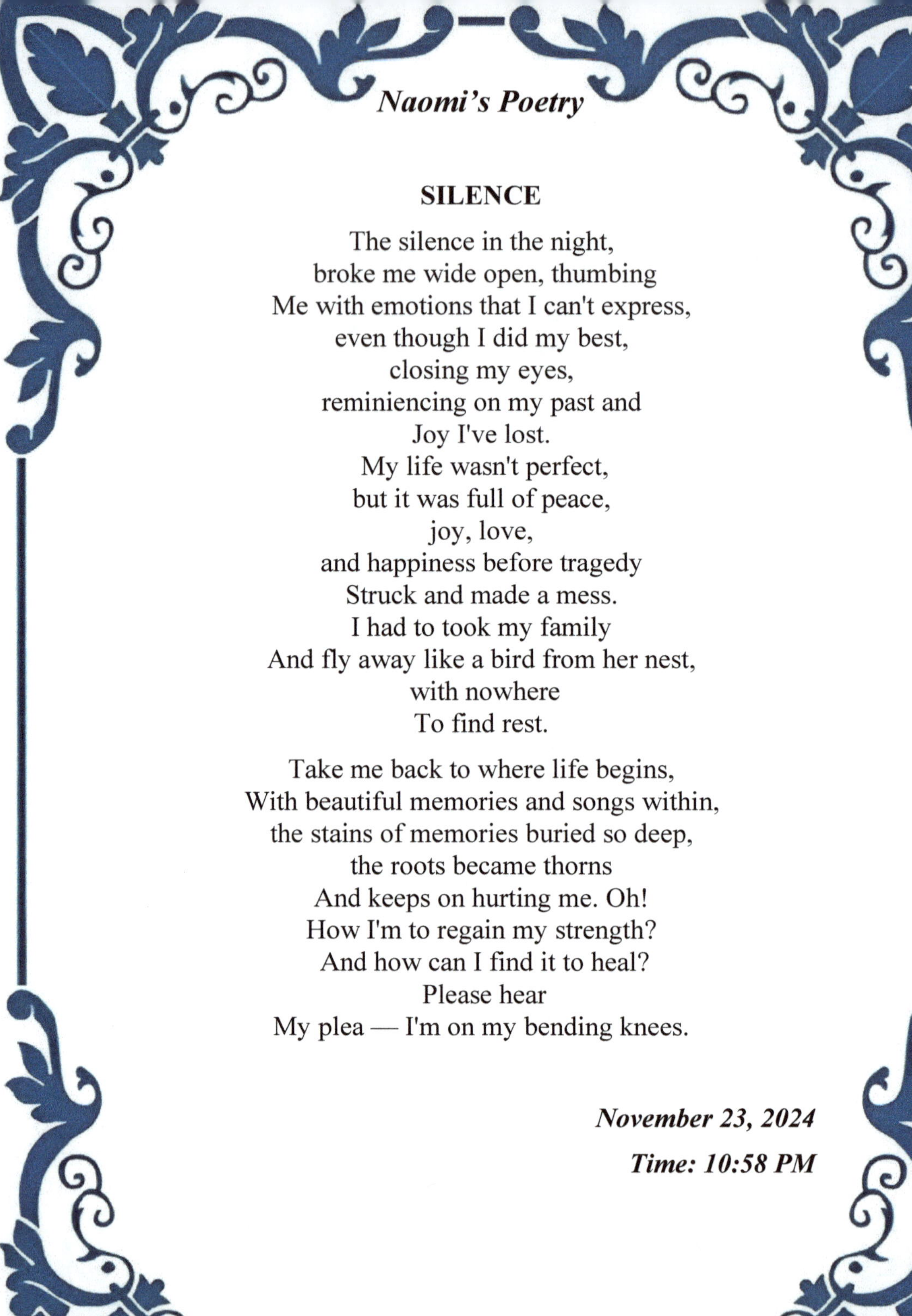

SILENCE

The silence in the night,
broke me wide open, thumbing
Me with emotions that I can't express,
even though I did my best,
closing my eyes,
reminiencing on my past and
Joy I've lost.
My life wasn't perfect,
but it was full of peace,
joy, love,
and happiness before tragedy
Struck and made a mess.
I had to took my family
And fly away like a bird from her nest,
with nowhere
To find rest.

Take me back to where life begins,
With beautiful memories and songs within,
the stains of memories buried so deep,
the roots became thorns
And keeps on hurting me. Oh!
How I'm to regain my strength?
And how can I find it to heal?
Please hear
My plea — I'm on my bending knees.

November 23, 2024

Time: 10:58 PM

Silence

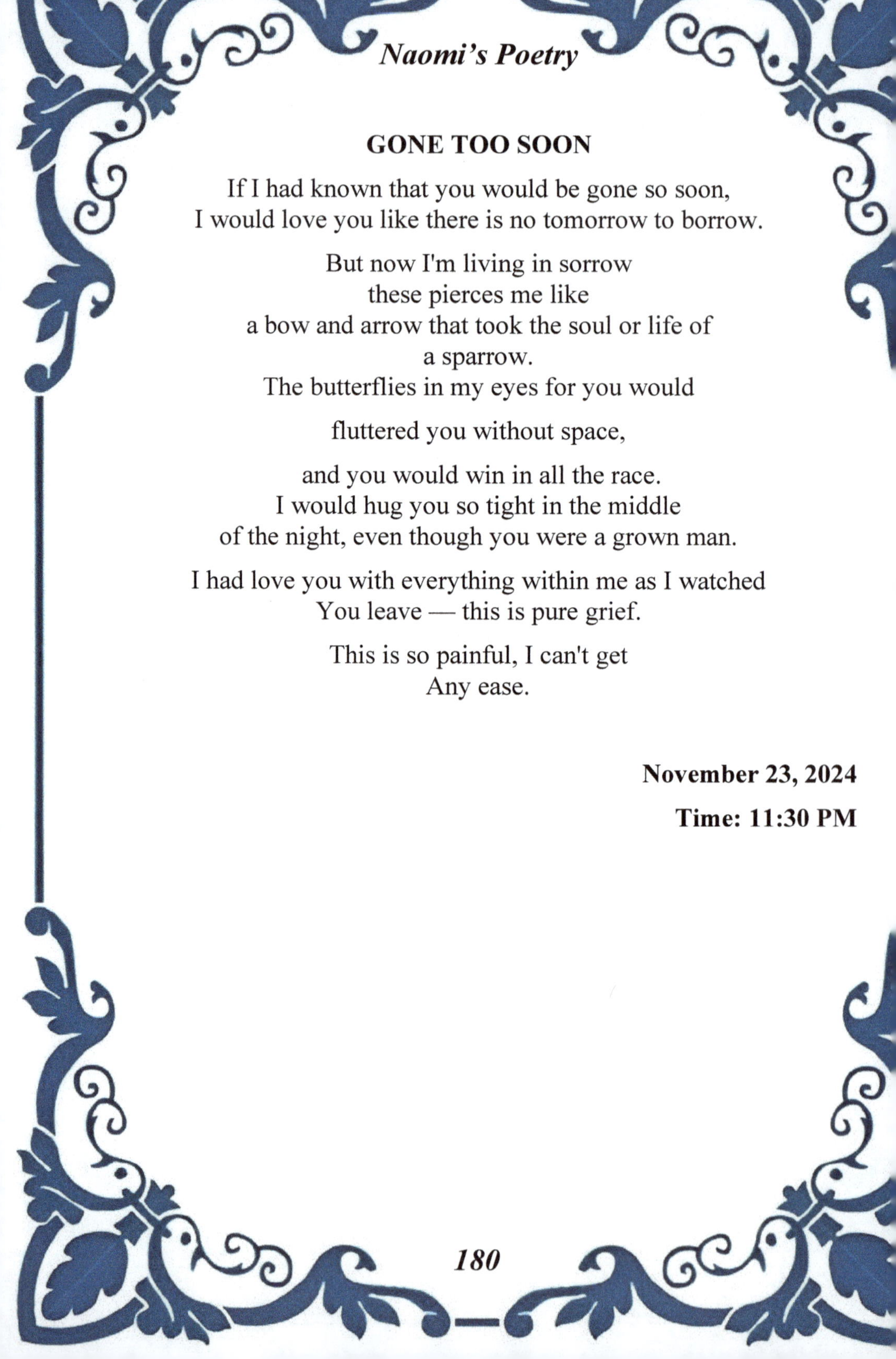

GONE TOO SOON

If I had known that you would be gone so soon,
I would love you like there is no tomorrow to borrow.

But now I'm living in sorrow
these pierces me like
a bow and arrow that took the soul or life of
a sparrow.
The butterflies in my eyes for you would

fluttered you without space,

and you would win in all the race.
I would hug you so tight in the middle
of the night, even though you were a grown man.

I had love you with everything within me as I watched
You leave — this is pure grief.

This is so painful, I can't get
Any ease.

November 23, 2024

Time: 11:30 PM

If, I had known
you'd be gone so soon,
I would love you like
there is no tomorrow

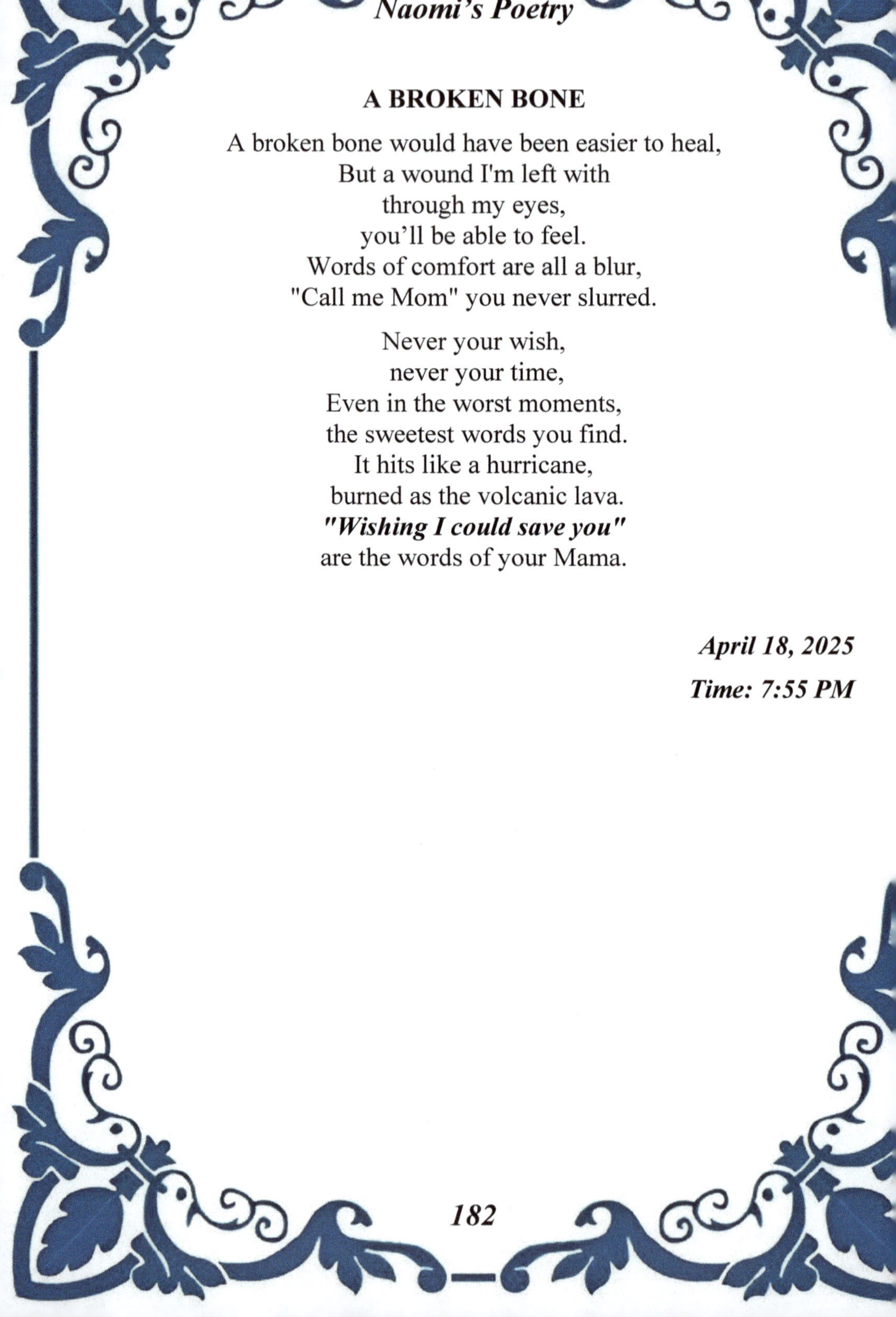

A BROKEN BONE

A broken bone would have been easier to heal,
But a wound I'm left with
through my eyes,
you'll be able to feel.
Words of comfort are all a blur,
"Call me Mom" you never slurred.

Never your wish,
never your time,
Even in the worst moments,
the sweetest words you find.
It hits like a hurricane,
burned as the volcanic lava.
"Wishing I could save you"
are the words of your Mama.

April 18, 2025
Time: 7:55 PM

Wishing
I could
save
you
— Mama

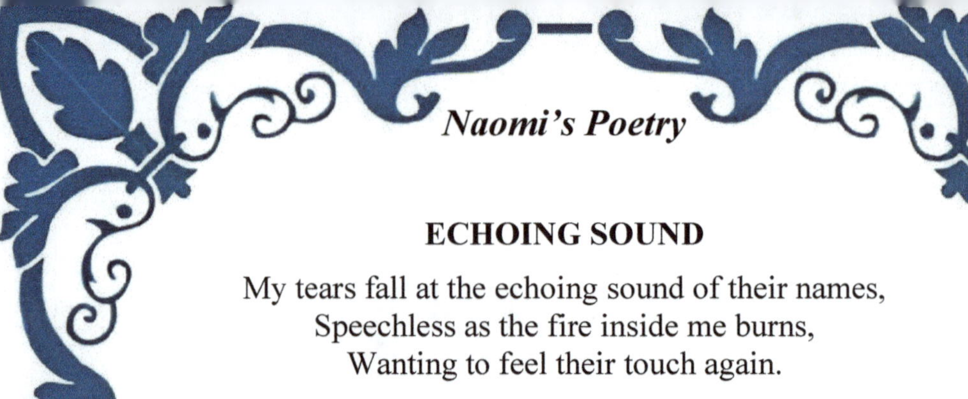

ECHOING SOUND

My tears fall at the echoing sound of their names,
Speechless as the fire inside me burns,
Wanting to feel their touch again.

The shift in my stomach and unforgiveness
I bear holds me like a hostage throughout the day and night.
A lump in my throat
finding it hard to swallow,
The pain in my heart that won't go tomorrow.

As the chills in my spine
I'm still fighting in my mind,
Asking the Father to let me see them one last time.
Will I ever forget,
or will this keep chasing me?

I ask you, Father,
keep vengeance away from me,
As my spirit yearns for payback
But never will it be,
so I'm trying to set my mind free.

April 3, 2025

Time: 12:30 AM

My tears fall
at the echoing sound
of their names

THIRST

The thirst in me that cannot be quenched

with water or a drink.
It's a thirst for peace of mind,
happiness,
joy, trust.
The scars are here as living proof-
of all that I'm longing for.

Even though I'm carrying my own water,
which is heavy,
If you need help,
I will help you carry yours.
I'm already broken
There's no need for someone-
else to be struggling-

with the load of brokenness.

I will give you my shoulder, if needs be.

April 4, 2025
Time: 6:00 PM

Naomi

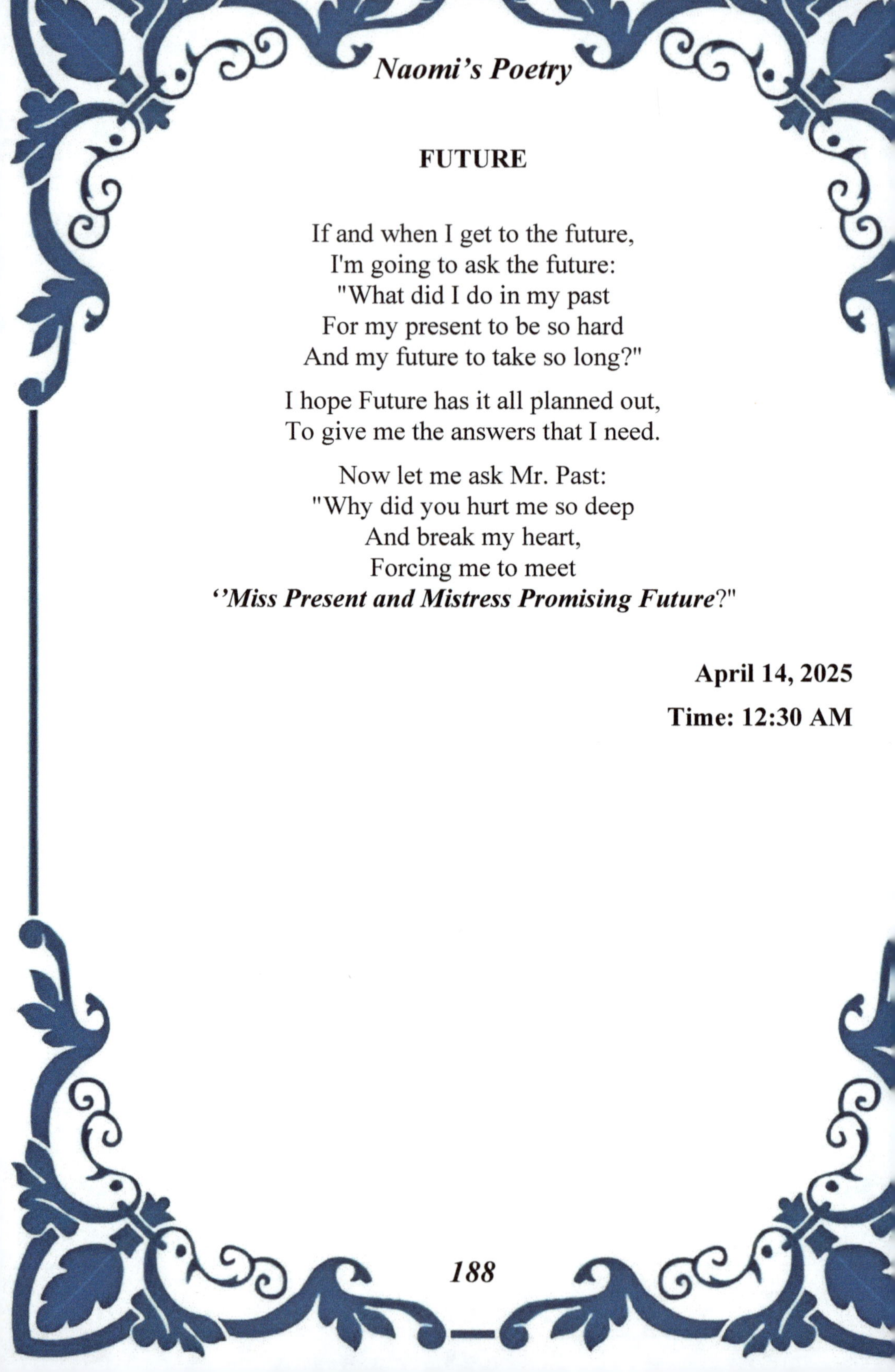

FUTURE

If and when I get to the future,
I'm going to ask the future:
"What did I do in my past
For my present to be so hard
And my future to take so long?"

I hope Future has it all planned out,
To give me the answers that I need.

Now let me ask Mr. Past:
"Why did you hurt me so deep
And break my heart,
Forcing me to meet
''Miss Present and Mistress Promising Future?"

April 14, 2025

Time: 12:30 AM

Future, why do you hide from me?

Past broke me... present confuses me...
future, please answer me?

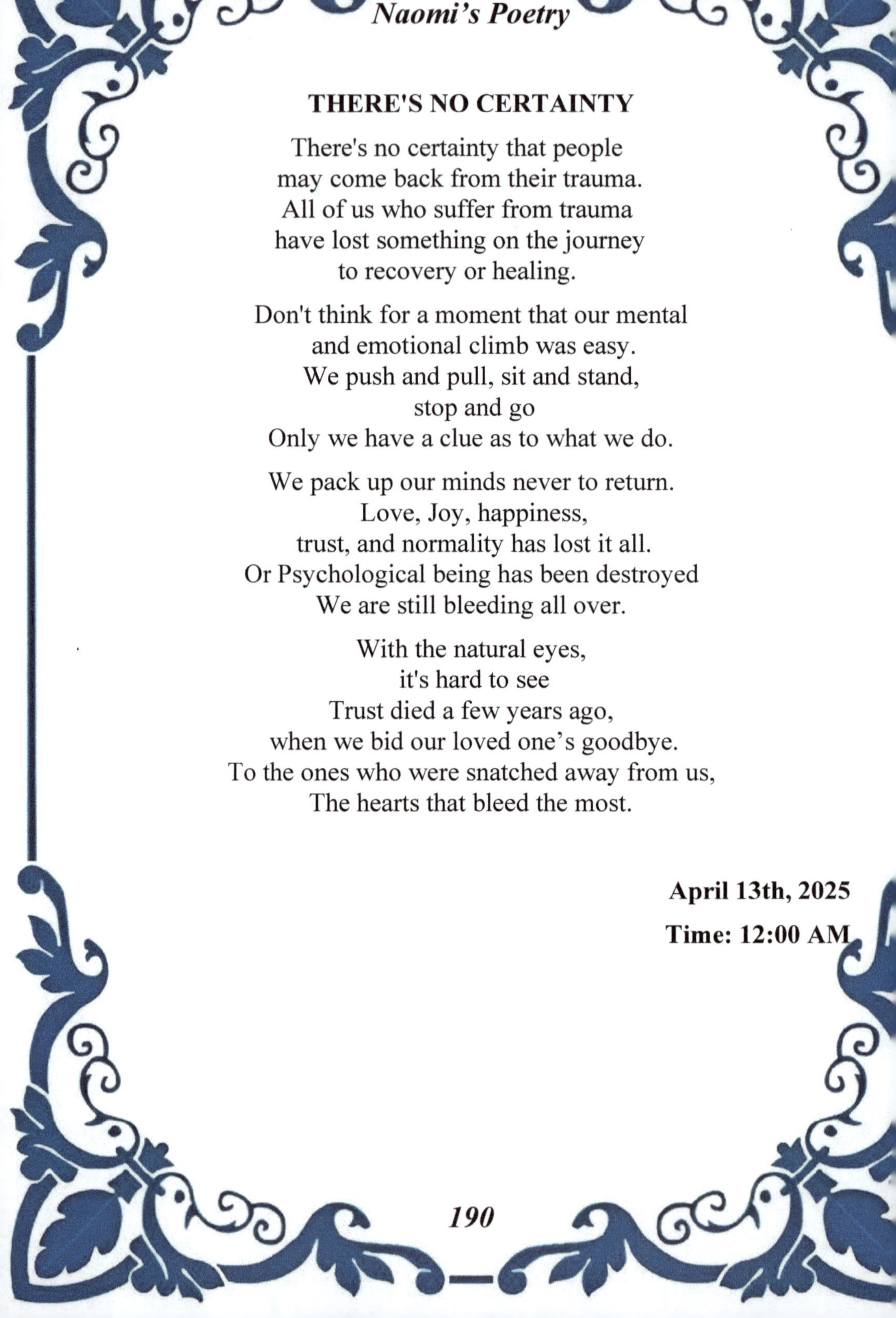

THERE'S NO CERTAINTY

There's no certainty that people
may come back from their trauma.
All of us who suffer from trauma
have lost something on the journey
to recovery or healing.

Don't think for a moment that our mental
and emotional climb was easy.
We push and pull, sit and stand,
stop and go
Only we have a clue as to what we do.

We pack up our minds never to return.
Love, Joy, happiness,
trust, and normality has lost it all.
Or Psychological being has been destroyed
We are still bleeding all over.

With the natural eyes,
it's hard to see
Trust died a few years ago,
when we bid our loved one's goodbye.
To the ones who were snatched away from us,
The hearts that bleed the most.

April 13th, 2025

Time: 12:00 AM

HURT
LOSS
TRAUMA
PAIN
SUFFERED

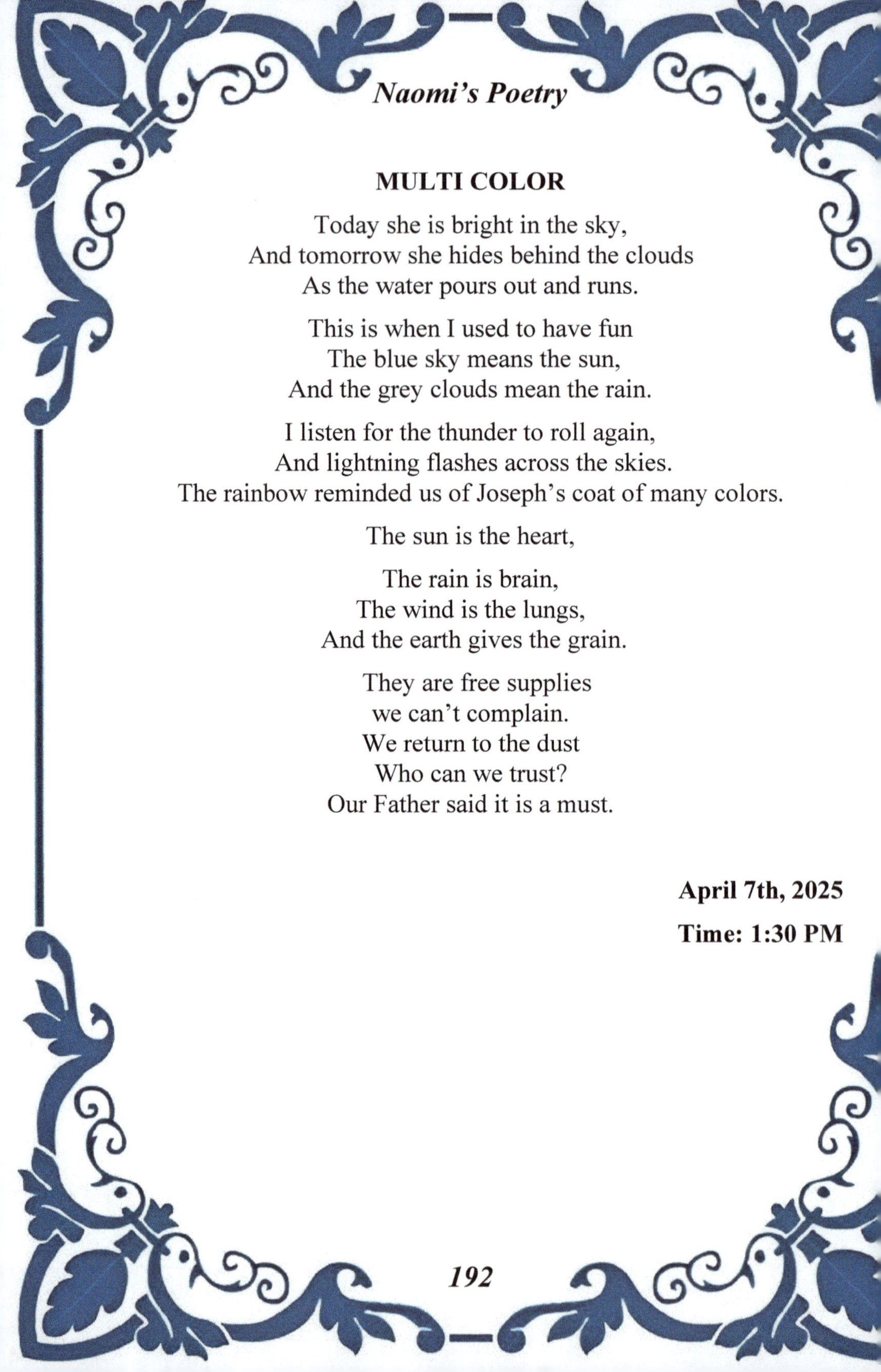

MULTI COLOR

Today she is bright in the sky,
And tomorrow she hides behind the clouds
As the water pours out and runs.

This is when I used to have fun
The blue sky means the sun,
And the grey clouds mean the rain.

I listen for the thunder to roll again,
And lightning flashes across the skies.
The rainbow reminded us of Joseph's coat of many colors.

The sun is the heart,

The rain is brain,
The wind is the lungs,
And the earth gives the grain.

They are free supplies
we can't complain.
We return to the dust
Who can we trust?
Our Father said it is a must.

April 7th, 2025

Time: 1:30 PM

Naomi

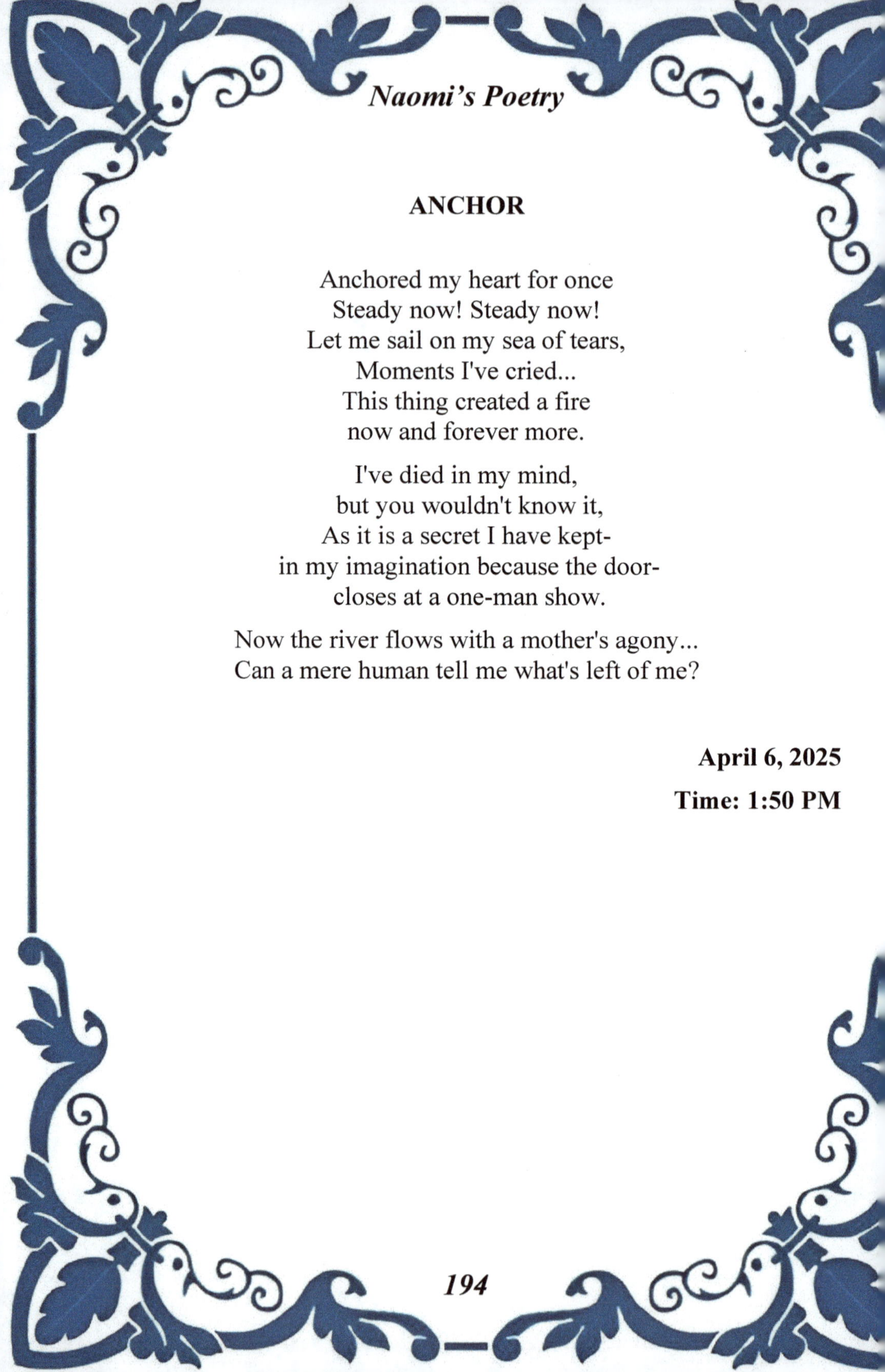

ANCHOR

Anchored my heart for once
Steady now! Steady now!
Let me sail on my sea of tears,
Moments I've cried...
This thing created a fire
now and forever more.

I've died in my mind,
but you wouldn't know it,
As it is a secret I have kept-
in my imagination because the door-
closes at a one-man show.

Now the river flows with a mother's agony...
Can a mere human tell me what's left of me?

April 6, 2025

Time: 1:50 PM

Anchored my heart for once–steady now!.!

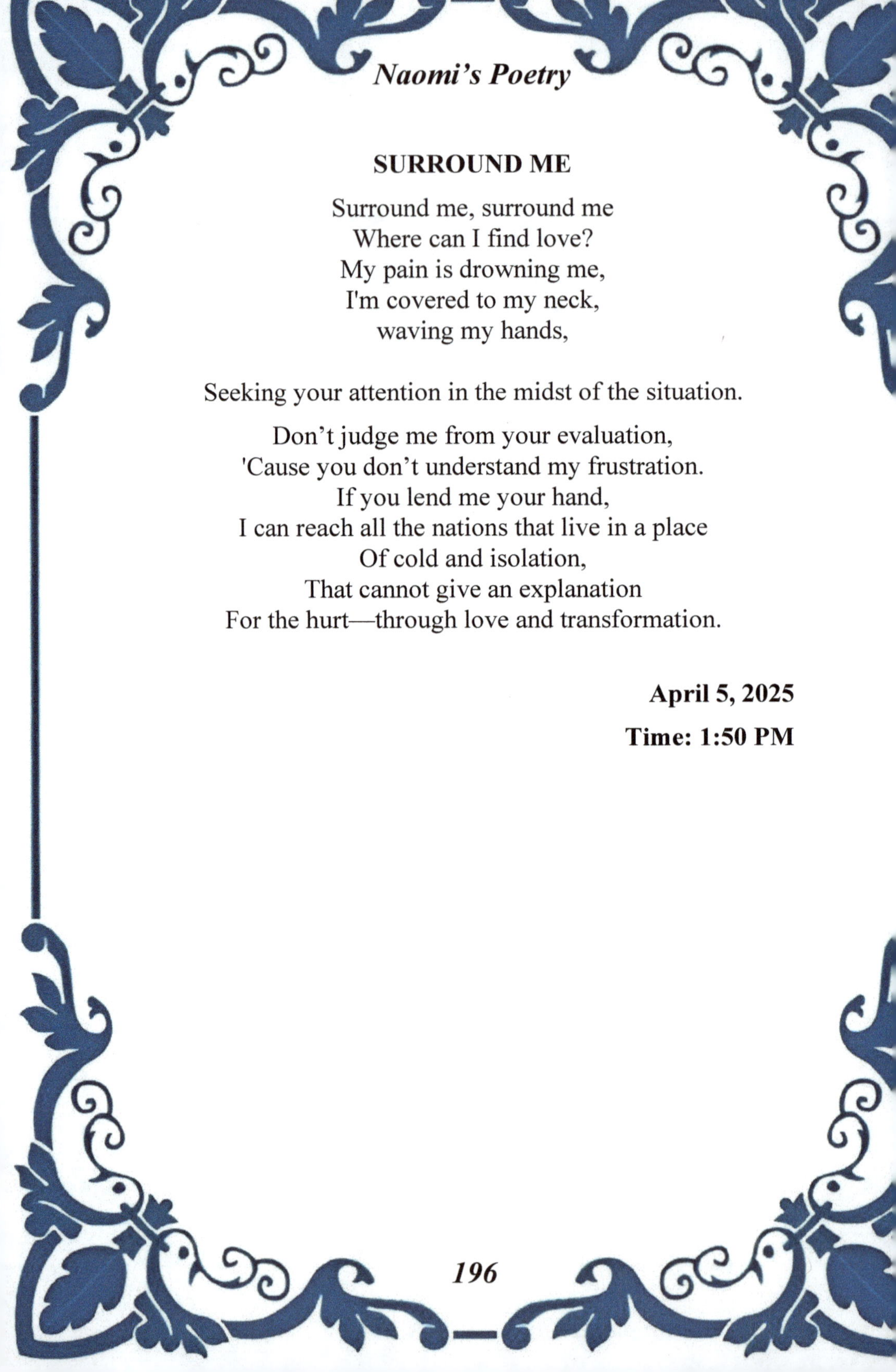

SURROUND ME

Surround me, surround me
Where can I find love?
My pain is drowning me,
I'm covered to my neck,
waving my hands,

Seeking your attention in the midst of the situation.

Don't judge me from your evaluation,
'Cause you don't understand my frustration.
If you lend me your hand,
I can reach all the nations that live in a place
Of cold and isolation,
That cannot give an explanation
For the hurt—through love and transformation.

April 5, 2025

Time: 1:50 PM

"Surround me, Surround me—
"Where can I find my innocents?"

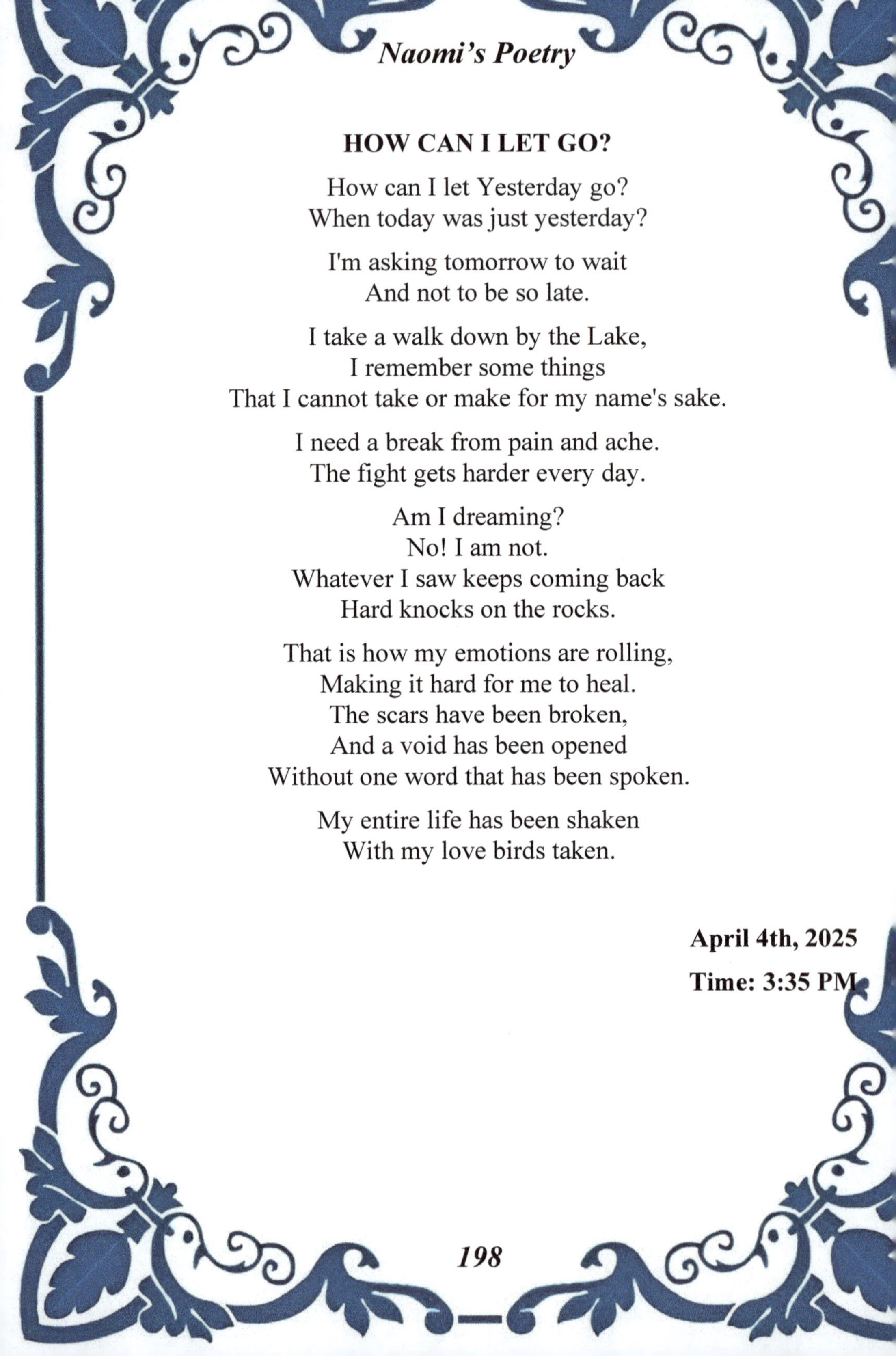

HOW CAN I LET GO?

How can I let Yesterday go?
When today was just yesterday?

I'm asking tomorrow to wait
And not to be so late.

I take a walk down by the Lake,
I remember some things
That I cannot take or make for my name's sake.

I need a break from pain and ache.
The fight gets harder every day.

Am I dreaming?
No! I am not.
Whatever I saw keeps coming back
Hard knocks on the rocks.

That is how my emotions are rolling,
Making it hard for me to heal.
The scars have been broken,
And a void has been opened
Without one word that has been spoken.

My entire life has been shaken
With my love birds taken.

April 4th, 2025

Time: 3:35 PM

POLICE
POLICE DO NOT CROSS
POLICE

MY PRAYER

I pray that my life may change,
And that I may find joy in my life
just pure joy.

A season where peace, love,
and happiness...
Happiness is knocking on my door,
But for some reason,
I can't open it.

The spirit of gladness lingers
As my heart rejects the feeling—
Feeling, not knowing when there will be healing.

I stayed up at nights, staring at the ceiling,
Wondering what was the point of stealing
My love bugs' hugs and kisses.

I need you both—my love.
Sigh!
Where do I go from here?

April 3, 2025

Time: 3:59 PM

I pray
that my life
may change,
and that
I may find
joy again,